ASMODEUS:

The Legend of
Margrét and the Dragon

Brooks Hansen

STAR PINE

STAR PINE BOOKS
5359 Star Pine Road
Carpinteria, CA 93013

Cover photo, design, and interior design by the author.
Printed and bound in the United States of America
First edition
978-0-9973979-0-1

*In lasting gratitude
to my early collaborator on this one,
Theodore Sergius Hansen.*

I charge you, O ye daughters of Jerusalem, by the roes and by the hinds of the field, do not arouse or awaken my love till he please.

– Song of Solomon

Margaret is the name of a precious gem, or ouche, that is white, little and virtuous. So the blessed Margaret was white by virginity, little by humility, and virtuous by the performance of miracles. The virtue of the stone is said to be against the excessive spilling of blood, against passion of the heart, and for the strengthening of the spirit.

–Jacobus de Voragine,
The Golden Legend

This is not the story of that Margaret...

CONTENTS

Prologue: The Lair..............................1

PART ONE:
The Uplands

I. Olybrius 11

II. Margrét............................14

III. Seeds 18

IV. Orabas 23

V. The Truth (I) 37

VI. The Invitation 42

VII. The Trading Post.....................49

VIII. The Truth (II) 54

IX. The Messenger 57

X. The Carriage. 62

XI. The Choice 68

PART TWO:
The Capitol

XII. Old Yinny 75

XIII. The Cave and the Cathedral......... 80

XIV. The Ministry and *The Minarik*....... 86

XV. The Gift............................ 91

XVI. The Mob 95

XVII. The Reception..................... 98

XVIII. The Starets..................... 107

XIX, Night (I) – Olybrius 111
XX, Night (II) – Margrét. 117
XXI, Night (III) – Orabas 121
XXII, The Pond 125
XXIII, Morning 130
XXIV, Myrrh 137
XXV, Blood 143
XXVI, Antonia Pecca. 148
XXVII, Forgiveness 153
XXVIII, "Good News" 156
XXIX, Ymir 161
XXX, The Flood. 165
XXXI, Failure. 172
XXXII, The Long Pier 175

PART THREE,

The Northern Castle

XXXIII, Flowers 183
XXXIV, The Northern Castle. 185
XXXV, Hope. 191
XXXVI, Goats 198
XXXVII, Seven Rooms 202
XXXVIII, Fruits 207
XXXIX, The Door 211
XL, Crows... 216
XLI, The Key... 224
XLII, The Sanctum 229
XLIII, Finale. 235
Glossary

ASMODEUS:

The Legend of
Margrét and the Dragon

Prologue:
The lair

Modo slept.

Deeply.

Even while the sky shuddered outside and rumbled and cracked and the rain came down in sheets, while the walls flickered and flashed and wind played his tunnels like a flute, the great wyrm did not so much as budge.

Which was a good thing. All part of the plan, though the question did occur – and still does – what could he possibly have been dreaming of? After fifteen hundred years of stalking the earth, of soaring over, tunneling under, plundering, shape-shifting, laying waste and taking whatever he liked, what was there left to occupy the mind of a slumbering dragon? Sea adventures in the Indian Ocean? Desert piracy? Aerial battles in the Himalayas? He had lived them all. And dreams aren't really for *remembering* anyway.

So what yearning can there have been? What wish could he possibly have wished to see fulfilled? Of a cool dark lair, set high in the blissful solitude of the innermost peak of the northernmost fjord? He had that – with pools and hearths, and a cataract spilling just outside, over the cliff and down a thousand feet to smash and mist and fling a rainbow every morning there was sun.

Did he dream of a vast kingdom splayed beneath him, blanketing the northern wilderness and all the beasts and creatures who made home there – the elks, the wolves, the adders, the foxes and deer, all fearing and revering him, from the largest to the small, from the sea swallows to the great orca whales bowing down at the sight of him? But they already did.

Did he dream of treasures, then? Of heaps of jewels piled high throughout his private catacomb – rubies and diamonds, emeralds,

1

lapis lazuli, pearls and mother-of-pearl and silver and gold, of course, gold coins and chalices, crowns and goblets. He had all that. And he had the purest and most powerful gem of all, the wyrm-stone. He kept it in the den where he slept. He curled around it like a kitten on a pillow, only with a more guttural and therefore more deeply sated purr.

It wasn't until the rains had passed and the sun beat through the clouds and drank in all the flavors of the cowering, pliant earth, that he finally roused, but even then it wasn't the light or a sound that finally awakened him, but a scent – or not a scent exactly – but something in the air that set off that familiar tremor high up in his snout:

Gifts nearby.

His golden eyes flicked open, blinked, and narrowed to a squint as he finally lifted up his great, horned head. He shrugged the veil of wings. He uncoiled from his most precious gem and lumbered upward, following the airborne trail up through the high tunnel to the opening just beside the cataract.

Only his muzzle appeared at first, shining like tar in the slanting sunlight, but even that merest of appearances stirred notice among the hovering hawks and vultures: Look. Be warned and wary. The master had awakened.

His head slid further out, taking in the day. The clouds had lifted. The sky was polished glass, but the familiar whisper was still there, coming from below. Down on the near shore of the inlet was a scuttled boat. Again his eyes narrowed, trying to figure from the tides just how long ago the wreck had occurred, and whether its victims were still on premise. He hoped not. Men had their place, but it wasn't here.

He had actually used to like them quite a bit when he was younger. He'd thought they had a nice crunch, until the one – a monk with plague. Asmodeus had been sick for days, and ached for months afterwards, and it was still the case that whenever he saw or sniffed a man, something in him turned with the memory, the deep-seated knowledge that of all the creatures that roamed the earth, none was more impure than man – the "Georges," as his cousin called them – the way they turned and spoiled and rotted from the inside out.

Blech.

He crawled further out onto the ledge and extended his neck toward the curtain of water, which was fuller today than usual, gushing down from the mountains after all that rain. He helped himself to several gulps. He let the bracing cold beat on his head a while, then shook free with a glistening, majestic explosion, lifted his wings and leapt. He glided most of the way down, turning three wide circles in the crux of the fjord, his great spanned shadow dashing along the cliff-side, flicking across the cataract, then across the blue surface below, around and up and around again three times before finally re-meeting him, claw to claw, on the strand beside the boat.

It was a longship with a split keel and several gaping holes smashed into the hull. Propped on the sand, it groaned with each lap of the rising tide.

Did they never learn?

This was hardly the first time he'd seen this sort of thing, after all, pirates returning from the emerald isle, looking for a place to sneak in and hide, only to be dashed on the skerries. The boats rarely made it as far as this one, but clearly the men had ditched it here and run, and if his nose was correct (which it invariably was), they'd buried their loot nearby for later pick-up. They didn't want to be mugged on the highway.

He tried ducking his head inside the galley, but there wasn't enough room, so he turned and with a swipe of his great tail smashed the hull to splinters, the more easily to pick through the remains: cutlery, tin and pewter, a few trunks of clothes and blankets.

Then a breeze stirred. He turned. There was a pig down the way, alive but limping on a broken hoof. Apparently it had been too much trouble for the Georges to bring with, or to slaughter before they fled. Perhaps they'd meant it as an offering of some kind, but if that had been their purpose – to distract him – they'd failed. Not much further along was a large boulder which had obviously been moved, having no business where it was. The great wyrm clambered past the pig, which simply stood there, too hobbled and petrified to move.

The stone was the size of a shed. The men must have used planks to wedge it over here; the dragon merely nudged it aside. The sand and dirt was a soft mulch underneath. He dug in with his claws and it only took a few scoops. There in the sandy muck was a chest, half the size of a coffin but certainly worth a look, if it had been worth the burying.

He hooked it to his claw and turned back around. The pig was still looking at him with one eye, scrambling on its mangled leg. Modo put it out of its misery, setting it aflame with a good long blast, then in a single bound snatching it firmly and with a twist. A quick snap and the squealing stopped. He jumped up onto the limb of a dogwood growing from the cliff-face, then leapt, dipping at first, his wingtips tapping the water simultaneously and just once, setting off a pair of concentric circles, and then again further on as the drops fell. Up and up the side of the fjord he rose, through the morning rainbow, and further up – an ascent of eight or nine strums, the chest still jangling in one claw, the swine still sizzling in the other, leaving a faint trail of smoke curling in his wake.

He brought his take into the largest of the caverns where the light was best. A single tap on one of the stalagmite posts cracked the lock like crystal. He flipped the chest open to find a gunny sack inside, holding all the keep. Another flick of his talon and out they spilled: Coins mostly, but some jewelry as well, and goblets, golden plates, and brass rings and strung pearls.

He took a healthy gnash of the blackened pig while he sorted through. Not a bad take for no work. As always, he was annoyed by the sheer amount of ornation the Georges had chosen to carve into of the brass and gold, all those pointless curlycues, garlands and words and hideous portraits of their own snarly faces. Could they not simply leave well enough alone?

Still, one had to give credit where it was due. As foul and lily-gilding as the Georges were, they had a remarkable streak of ingenuity, and they were tireless miners. That's what made it so strange, how they seemed to have no idea the value of what they worked so hard to chisel from the hills.

He began dividing his keep, then – coins among coins, gems with gems, trinkets among trinkets – when out of nowhere his stomach turned. There was an awful, croaking, moaning sound, as if a wildcat were mewling in his belly, then came the first violent twist. Something was not right. There was something foul about that pig, but worse than rancid, worse than turned, worse even than that disgusting monk. Something had been planted *inside* the swine, like a sack of poison.

He could feel it spilling all throughout him now, rushing through, a peristaltic ebb and flow of shooting, searing pains like spears inside him, followed by numbness, followed by the spears again. He staggered. He fell. He began dragging himself, thrashing back to his sleeping den, back towards the wyrmstone, but he couldn't stay upright. He fell against the walls and pillars, scattering fortunes with his tail. The world swirled, but he needed to get back – to hide the one, to bury it, swallow it – and he could see it, too, gleaming there, but he couldn't quite reach it, collapsing in such a sudden heap his left wing bent beneath him.

He was powerless to move, but he could sense them as they entered – four, maybe five of them. They had been waiting, hiding somewhere downwind, but he could smell them now as well, even as the brown blackness smothered in around him. He could hear them, stuffing their sacks, laughing, whistling in admiration.

And the one coming into where he lay. That was the last thing he heard before going completely cold and stiff, was the tell-tale two-beat tread creeping up to him.

This was Barbatos, and he was proceeding cautiously – understandably. Even a Great Wyrm was not above playing possum, and one dirty trick deserves another. Yet he couldn't help himself, the body of the beast was so magnificent, even in its fallen state.

Barbatos stood above it a moment, gazing. He studied the sculptured mosaic of its enormous head, the black and dark-reddish scales, the massive horns, thorns, and teeth.

He knelt down. He removed his glove and set his hand directly on the softer plates that covered its breast. He felt the body cooling. He set the back of his wrist against the jagged opening of its mouth. Nothing. He thought about taking the heart right then. It was said that whoever smeared the blood of a dragon into his skin could never be wounded; whoever ate a dragon's tongue could persuade the world of anything; whoever ate a dragon's heart would understand the language of birds.

But first things first. The beast had nearly made it back to its prize. His great body was like an arrow pointing, the thorned tip of his chin just inches away, though Barbatos would have known in any case. Just as he had been told, just as he had read, the gem was the size and shape of a barleycorn, but set upon a black slate stone its color was perfectly offset – an iridescent white that seemed to drink in every thread of light within the den and then return it. It was what seemed impossible, to be both clear and glowing.

He took it in hand. He held it there a moment and remarked the weight, which was much greater than one would expect from its size. There was even a kind of buzz, it was true – a reverberation in his arm – but he didn't want the others to come and see, so he quickly wrapped it in lamb's wool and set it in the special lead box he'd brought, filled with grain.

But now there was a rustling behind. He turned. Out of nowhere it seemed, the ceiling was suddenly thick with bats, thousands upon thousands of them hanging there, all turned and looking at him. He peered through the entrance and could see the black outline of vultures as well. Even a curious wolf, ears perked, snout high.

As gently as he was able, he closed the box, but just that muted *click* was enough: all at once the ceiling seemed to drop and swoop as ten thousand bats and twenty thousand wings came thrushing in on him. The sound was deafening. He ducked beneath his cape and a moment later they were upon him, thumping and flapping and shredding at him in a mad frenzy of wings and claws and little sharp teeth.

He could hear the others yelling as well, and grunting, also besieged. He began beating his way back out, blind and staggering, the box tucked tight beneath his arm. There was light up ahead, but the weight of the bats was overwhelming him. Finally he let them have the cloak and thrashed his way out into the sunlight again, but there were snakes at his feet now, stabbing at him. He leapt and fell forward out onto the ledge. The box came loose, skittering toward the very edge, opening and coughing up a handful of grain, which was instantly swept up by the breeze.

But only grain. The gem remained. As he crawled toward the box, he could see it still resting in its bed, exposed. He reached out and clamped the lid shut, allowing a smile; how close he had come to losing it. Again.

Then he heard the growl. He turned his head. Two wolves now, standing at the entrance of the cave, poised and snarling. Slowly he curled the box beneath his arm. They saw. They charged. The first wolf grabbed his leg. He struck at it. The second came for his arm, and the momentum of his strike sent all three bodies tumbling over the ledge, adjoined by teeth and clenched fists, falling, falling, falling like three seeds, spinning through the mist and down into the thundering white...

PART ONE

The Uplands

I

Olybrius

Several hundred years later, and about as many miles to the Southeast, a little motorcade made its way along a narrow, lonely lane that wended through the rolling meadows, between the craggy ridges, over the heath and between the random farms and hamlets that counted for towns up in these parts, known generally as the Uplands.

Led by a bright yellow (though now fairly muddy) Speedster, the caravan had been having a rough go of it all morning. Even the trailing Jeeps had been sputtering, spinning, and skidding along the road, which was no road at all really, but an old goat path long ago commandeered by ox-driven carts. It had never been paved or rolled other than by the wagon wheel, so the little caravan of cars had been tilting and swerving, lurching their passengers this way and that, or sometimes nearly catapulting them from their seats, as had just happened.

This was up in the high back of the Speedster, the passengers at question being the two ranking members of the junket: the handsome young Provost, Olybrius Korda (the recent royal appointee as governor of the whole Ileyan state), and beside him the less young but still robust and barrel-chested General Zitri, veteran commander of His Majesty's Royal Guard, otherwise known as the 'RG'.

"The rain is to blame," said Olybrius, frustrated by all of this, the mud on his goggles and the indignity of once again having to push himself back into his seat. "These roads are actually fine when they're dry."

This was at least the third time he had said this. For at least the third time General Zitri simply grinned, though it was hard to be

11

sure. The breadth and bulk of his mustache made it so he always seemed to be grinning, but only for show, and only to show that he was usually feeling something very different – contempt, impatience, discomfort, or, as seemed to be the case right now, all three at once.

"Is that another?" He pointed across the heath. There was a large stone standing upright, as tall as a man and maybe twice as wide. At this distance, Olybrius couldn't see the chiseling, or even if there was chiseling, but why else would it be there?

"Most likely."

Zitri glanced back to the officer in the Jeep behind and gave a nod.

"I really don't think anyone reads them anymore," said Olybrius.

"Then no one will mind," said the General, now tapping the driver Vassago with his crop. "Keep going. I'm sure he'll catch up."

As the officer behind hopped out of his car and started across the field with his little brush, his boots gumming and chomping through the muck, Olybrius barely hid his annoyance. This was hardly the reason he brought them up here, to mark the legend stones. The annexation had taken place a full seven months ago, peacefully and by decree. Of course there'd been the predictable stirrings of protest down in the capitol, in the taverns and at the University – some brawls and public scrawls – but for the most part the people had been accepting; the children quite liked the flag.

Still, no one from the new regime had yet to venture beyond the Southern Ridge – or no one besides His Majesty's geologists – up into the more rural territories like Tuvin and Tami or here in Antayak, where the sheep grazed, the women smoked white clay pipes, and the children sang songs about the giants buried in the hills. Olybrius had wanted the new ministers to see this, and to appreciate it. There was more up here than coal.

Out ahead, a trail of smoke could be seen drifting from the hilltop. "That's the Killiki."

"Are they the ones who sacrifice the goats?" asked Zitri.

"No, that's the Welka. We may see them on our return if they haven't started north already."

Zitri only sniffed, both at the names and at the idea that there should still be nomads in the world – goat-sacrificing nomads no less. Smugly he asked, "Do you know why the first Barbarians were called 'Barbarians'?"

Olybrius didn't, and was on the point reluctantly shaking his head when his driver Vassago jammed on the brakes so suddenly they were all nearly thrown from their seats again. Just down the slope and seeming to have appeared out of nowhere, three dozen sheep stood in a pack, grazing on the road. The Speedster skied straight for them, and looked like it might plough right through until Vassago turned the wheel and managed a stop just inches away from the wooly rump of the nearest ewe, who merely turned her head to look at them, as dumb as she was stubborn.

II

Margrét

The shepherd – or shepherdess, in this case – was unaware the flock had wandered. Her name was Margrét, and she was a maiden, though her maidenhood was largely hidden by the drape of her thick wool tunic. Only her face showed beneath her hood, fair and faintly freckled with hazel eyes that at this moment were peering down at a hand-sized seashell.

She was kneeling in the hollow of a diverted creek bed, having climbed down to get a closer look, for this wasn't just a cockle shell or a scallop shell – she had dozens of those. This was an actual conch, swirled and nubby on the outside, polished and pink and caverned within, and all the way up here on the bluff.

"You know what this means." She held it up to Cassandra to show.

The old fat sheep looked down at her, a blank.

It meant the books and the legends were right: All of this had been under water at one time, long ago, after Odin slew the ice giant, Ymir.

"'His body became the earth,'" she said, reciting. "'His *blood* became the sea.'" And this would happen again someday, according to the legends – the water part anyway.

"Ah, but you don't care," she looked back up at Cassandra. "You care for one thing. *Baaaah.* Grass."

Baah, Cassandra replied, still trying to get her attention, as now her two little lambs, Yosi and Nella, appeared alongside, hopping and bleating more plaintively. Something was the matter.

Margrét would not be rushed. She squinted back around at the mountains. She liked to think of it: all those distant peaks as islands, the only dry land cresting an ocean that otherwise would swallow all of this, all these grasses and wildflower drifting and lolling in the unseen current.

Up on the ridge was the old oak tree, as dead as dead could be, but still her favorite tree in all the pastures, it looked like so many different things depending upon the angle you were looking from. From the Five Homes, a bear. From the heath, a rabbit. From here it couldn't have been more clear, with the two high branches rising up behind like wings, and the broken limb like a long neck bowing down. She imagined it nuzzling, serpent-like, among a bed of coral, feasting on crab and abalone, only pausing now at something. A sound.

HONNNNK!

The great head lifted and for a moment their eyes even seemed to meet. His were a simmering golden-orange like fire, and something flared in her as well in that brief instant. Had the two of them not been swimming together again last night? Or flying?

But there was that strange sound again and off he went, departing her imagination, scattering the silvery sand and shells around its feet, spreading his wings and lifting up, gliding up towards the surface and the sun.

But what was that honking? It sounded like a goose almost, and there it was again, coming from the direction of the flock.

HONNNNK!

Margrét slipped the conch into the pocket of her tunic and clambered up the bank.

The sheep were down a ways from where she'd left them, and blocking the path of the strangest row of carriages she had ever seen. Two of them were still up at the top of the slope, but the one among the sheep was the most extraordinary. It was shaped like the skull of an enormous deer almost, but smooth and shiny and painted bright yellow, with headlamps like large flaring nostrils, and it seemed to be humming and puttering. There was one man sitting in the high backseat with goggles on his head, while another in a visored cap was down in the lane, trying in vain to shoo the flock away, waving his hands and tugging at their coats.

She simply stood there watching until he returned to the carriage again and took hold of coiled horn on the door.

HONK-HOOONNNNK!

"Stop that," she finally said. "They won't move if they're frightened."

The driver stood back and Margrét proceeded to usher the sheep along, tapping her staff and gathering them into a huddle, keeping to the outside, turning them toward the sun. She spoke to them in her most soothing voice as well, and in the old tongue. A moment later, the way was clear.

The man in the back seat of the carriage looked at her as if he'd just witnessed some form of sorcery. "Thank you." His cheeks were slightly windburnt, a stark contrast to the pale white surrounding his eyes; the goggles he'd been wearing were up on top of his head.

"Where is your horse?" she asked, looking down the far side of the lane as now a third officer, with a great mustache and a barrel chest climbed from the other side. He was buttoning the top of his pants.

"We have no horse," said the goggled man.

Just then all muttering carriages started grumbling much louder and growling and smoke started puffing out of their tails. The driver was back in the front seat of the bright yellow one, and the barrel-chested man had taken his place beside the fair one in the goggles. The carriage rattled and shook and then the wheels began to turn all on their own, but so jerkily that the goggled man's grateful nod was lost in all the bumps and joggles.

§

As soon as the way was smooth enough, Zitri asked, "So was that the language?" The girl was still in view, but barely, looking back at them through the roll of the meadow. "The one she was using with the sheep?"

Olybrius nodded.

"I thought you said they didn't speak it anymore."

16

"Maybe to the animals."

"And what was she saying, do we know?"

Olybrius wasn't sure; he leaned forward to Vassago. "Did you make out what she was saying back there? To the sheep?"

Vassago did, but had to swerve around a boulder first. "'Don't fear the barking dog,'" he said

Olybrius sat back and looked over at the General to see if he found this at all amusing. He appeared to be smiling, but again, who knew?

III

Seeds

The early thaw and all the recent sun made for so much fresh clover and heather along the pastures, the sheep had gorged themselves all day and took an especially long time getting back to Five Homes,

The fires all were burning. Night was falling. The lamps and lanterns were lit. Margrét's nursemaid, Inger, had taken down the meat already. The birch bowls were set out beside the wooden spoons, and she was feeding onions into the pot, and carrots and rutabaga, the fire lighting her plump and always slightly consternated face from below, exaggerating its scowl. The wisps of her russet-colored hair were drifting and dancing about the tight braided buns in which she always *always* bound it; otherwise it reached below her knee. How often Margrét wished she'd simply let it.

Tasha was out to greet her — a grey ermine, she curled against Margrét's ankle and followed her back inside the cabin, which like all the homes at Five Homes was really more of a hut, first cobbled together by Inger's great grandparents from stones and boulders, mud and sod, just sturdy enough to survive the summers without them and still be standing when they returned from the north; then they'd rebuild and shore up.

Theirs was actually smaller inside than the tents they took to the coast. But there were three chairs and the stove, and over in Margrét's corner was the dowry chest that had been her mother's. That's where Margrét kept her shells, alongside her mother's gloves and scarves and linens, which she never let anyone see.

She was just tucking away the new conch when Inger entered, Margrét closed the trunk directly.

"They opened the kirkhas, by the way," said Inger, nodding at the trunk. "We can take that down tomorrow, if you like, with the sledges."

"No, we won't! And why so soon?"

This was an annual fight. The kirkhas was a storage house – a boarded hole in the ground – where everyone at Five Homes kept their winter store while they traveled north. Inger always insisted they leave the trunk behind, it was so heavy. Margrét always insisted on taking it with them.

"It's at least a month before we go," she said.

"It's early," Inger conceded, "but there won't be space if Onni-miika gets in there first. And don't make faces. You've still time to choose."

This was the compromise they usually struck: Margrét got to choose five things from the trunk to bring. *Five things!* She sighed, though it was really more a huff, as Tasha hopped up onto her lap and started pawing the sill of the hut's one window. Torvald was coming in from the field where he'd been helping build a wall.

He looked weary; he always looked a little weary. Margrét went straight to get the book, but Inger clucked. "Come come." She tapped the bucket with the side of her foot. "By the time you come back and wash there'll be supper."

"*Aiy,*" said Margrét, but out she went, with pail in hand and Tasha following – again and as ever – because Tasha liked to tease the sheep this time of day, to run between their legs and steal sips while Margrét milked.

"A pest, you are," Margrét was saying. "Why must I scold you every night?"

She didn't see until she looked back up. Parked up against the long fence of the paddock was the bright yellow carriage again, mud splattered and hanging like weeds from the bottom. They'd lost one of the passengers. The barrel-chested one with the shoe-brush mustache was nowhere to be seen, but the driver was lurking around the side of the barn with an apple in his hand, and the younger man was still in his seat, not wearing his goggles now. His hair was blond, and shone in waves, and he was looking back at her with an oddly familiar smile, as if they had planned to meet, as if she were late.

"Your way is clear," she said.

"It is," he replied, taking pleasure at her nature, which she'd long been told was aggressive.

"Are you lost then?"

"We are not." He held out a small envelope. "We forgot to give you this."

She took the envelope and heard a rattle inside.

"Seeds," said the man, "from the King's own garden."

"What for?"

"It's a gift," he said, "to everyone. Plant them now, they'll be your height by the time you return. Are you headed north?"

"Not yet."

As she peered inside the envelope, he noticed the amulets she wore, a black stone on catgut. The truth was, Olybrius had always felt there was something otherworldly about the Welan, eerie almost. An inward breed – as one would have to be, living in such a high and unforgiving climate, in the rugged world of mountain, cave and scrub. They kept to themselves for the most part, turning grim hard-featured faces to the world while nursing inner candles that only flared when they were bothered – something their former occupiers, the Sud, had needed several ugly incidents to learn. Still it seemed to Olybrius that for every dozen scowls one encountered, and secret keepers, there would be the one who met your eye, the one who glowed from the inside out, and who, it always seemed to him, made up for all the rest.

"Tell me your name."

"Margrét."

"A lovely name, as suits. Is that your father?" He gestured back in the direction of the homes. Torvald was sitting out front, beside Inger. They both were looking back.

"No," she said. "My uncle. My nursemaid's brother actually."

"Who is your father, then?"

"Why do you want to know?"

"So that I might commend him."

"Then you would have to commend Theodosius," she frankly replied.

"And where is he?"

"Kyiv."

The man stood back, as she knew very well he would.

"You mean the *Bishop* Theodosius?"

She nodded, not hiding her pride in the least, though in fact she had never met her father, and would probably not have recognized him now if he were standing right next to this man.

The Provost was nonetheless impressed, Theodosius being counselor to His Majesty for many years now and, as such, one of the highest ranking men in the empire to which he, the Provost, had just negotiated entry.

"Worthy again," he said, only wondering now: why was Theodosius's daughter being raised in the Ileyan Uplands by a nursemaid and her brother? He supposed the answer was clear enough in the blush of her cheek, the blemishlessness of her brow, the motelessness of her hazel green eyes.

The nursemaid and the brother, meanwhile, were still sitting at the fire, confused as to why this conversation was taking so long.

"Is he lost?" asked Inger. "I'll show him the way."

Torvald shook his head – the man wasn't lost.

"I'll still show him the way." She stood up and called out in the old tongue. "*Come along now Manga.*"

"*Aiy. I'm talking to the man!*"

"*Who is he? What does he want?*"

"*He's a messenger.*"

"*And what's his message?*"

"*He wants to give us seeds.*" She held up the envelope with a scowl. "*From Henryk the King.*"

"*Well, milk the sheep and bring them in, and tell the man to thank the King.*"

Again, Olybrius was lost. He used to know the language a bit when he was younger, but he couldn't follow when they spoke so quickly. And now the young maiden was taking up her pail and setting it on her head. Margrét. He bid her good day. She replied with a quick tilt and a curtsey, and off she went, the ermine curling back and forth between her strides.

As soon as they'd started off again and the engine had settled down, Olybrius leaned forward to Vassago. "She will be my wife."

Vassago had heard the Provost's boasts before, especially when it came to women. "And if she's spoken for?" he asked.

"Then she will be my mistress."

IV

Orabas

Olybrius had a brother named Orabas. Bizja and Bazja, they were called by the family, and they were twins. Bazja – that is, Orabas – was born eleven minutes after his brother. He lived in a log cabin he'd built himself out by the bank of a river that ran through a forest deep inside the Uplands, deeper even than Five Homes, though Orabas was not a nomad. He called his home 'The Bend', and he lived there all year with his wife, Maren, and their daughter Anna, who was three. Their nearest neighbor was ten miles away. The nearest dry goods, ten more miles than that, but they did not want. They grew their own food, and hunted and fished, canned and trapped, as they had to do. The woods were filled with prowlers. Every other day Orabas went to make the rounds.

This day's yield was turning out to be especially good. Orabas's dog, a four-year-old Spitz named Noli, was first to notice there was something thrashing in the big pit beneath the alder. He sprinted out ahead and scrambled around the hole three times, barking, before steeling into a crouch.

"Easy, Noli. Let's see what we have."

Most of the sticks he'd set were still in place. Orabas peered through the lattice and found the pale yellow eye of a hobbled lynx, its right foreleg clamped in the teeth of Orabas's best spring trap.

"We meet," he said. He'd seen this one before, a stalking shadow in his wood. The lynx only hissed in return, first at him and then at Noli, who was still poised and growling. A good catch. Lynx were usually too clever to be caught, and their pelts fetched well, in part because they were so rare. This one seemed a bit shamed. Already he'd begun gnawing at his knee in hopes of making a three-legged escape.

"Good spirit." Orabas cleared aside the sticks and leaned down into the hole. He used the handle of his staff to pin the cat by the neck, then clubbed it with the blunt end of his axe.

§

A while later Orabas emerged from the same wood with the bodies of two more badgers and a fox clipped to his belt. He was headed round behind the smokehouse to the little nook where he did his tanning when Anna came running up.

"Look!" She was holding up a doll for him to see. A fine expensive doll, with a porcelain face, marble eyes and real red hair. Orabas didn't dare take it in hand.

"Now watch," she said. She tilted it back as if to put it to bed. The eyelids closed. They had real lashes as well.

Orabas looked back to the main house, already suspecting. He could only see the very front of the car, which he had never seen before, but he knew whose it was, and here he was now, rounding the corner in his vermillion officer's coat.

"Bazja."

"Governor."

They clasped hands. They hugged.

"You said thank you, Anna?"

"I did," she said, but she said it again. "Thank you, uncle Bizja."

"You're very welcome." Olybrius gave a deep bow. "I have something for your father as well."

He showed him back at the car. There was a trunk behind the high seat, which he let Orabas open. Inside was a hat, a trooper hat made of dark, thick fur. Orabas recognized it at once.

"Is it from Dobrovo?"

"I found it the last time I was there."

Their grandmother had said it was her grandfather's, who claimed to have received it from Barbatos himself, though it was hard to know if she was telling the truth. Still, the hat had been like a crown to the two boys. To think it had rested on the head of the great Barbatos, the one who finally vanquished Modo.

Orabas tried it on now. Warm.

"And a perfect fit," his brother said. "At last."

Orabas nodded. He picked up Anna to let her feel the fur, how deep and soft. "Thank you, Bizja. Thank you."

They ate the badger that night, adding its meat to the stew that Maren had been preparing. They drank wine that Olybrius had brought. A very generous visit, and it may simply have been that – all the gifts – that gave Orabas pause, but his brother seemed different somehow. Softer. He took an extra interest in Anna, and in Maren, whom he had never paid much attention to before. He'd brought her a chair from Paris, which they set up at the table to let Anna's new doll sit in, and Olybrius asked after it throughout the meal. He pretended to feed it. Orabas couldn't help looking at his brother's fingers as they handled the little spoon, how slender and clean they seemed, compared to his own.

The doctor had always said that he and Bizja were identical, which he supposed was true, though to a trained eye they'd never been hard to tell apart. Olybrius's features had always been the finer. His nose, the slightly longer and more slender. His mouth, more narrow and more bowed. Orabas's face was broader, the bridge of his nose more flat. As their uncle Gower put it, Bazja looked "like Bizja ran into a wall."

Their hands, however, had been nearly indistinguishable. Orabas remembered laying them out on the white cloth of their grand-mother's dining table, all four in a row, so that others could see as well. From the bump of each knuckle to the taper of the fingers, no jeweler could have told the pairs apart. Even Orabas could get confused looking at them.

Once when they were nine, his brother had sliced his finger on a fence – a deep gash to the bone. After they'd cleaned and dressed it, Orabas went out alone, found the fence, and sliced his own finger so that it would bear the same scar. It was still there, yet as he closed his fist now, he might as well have been wearing gloves. He could hardly feel his own fingers for all the calluses, and how thick they'd grown, how rough from the life they led and the dirt that never seemed to wash away.

He and Olybrius had been nineteen when their paths parted. They were in their second year at the military academy at Boryuti when news came that their father had fallen from his horse and died. They were summoned at once to their grandmother's estate, Dobrovo, which was only a half-day's ride from the city, but which felt like a different world: a great white manor with gables and onion-domes, crowning an emerald green hill in the summers, snow white in the winters, surrounded by a thick birch forest. He remembered how the cherry blossoms along the entrance road had been in outrageous blossom that spring, as if to mock their grief, only there wasn't much grief to mock. The brothers had not known either of their parents well. Their mother had died of pneumonia when they were two, and their father had always been distant. When Orabas first heard of his death, he felt as if a hole had been blasted in him, only he didn't know quite what was missing now.

Following the funeral, which took place there on the family grounds, their grandmother, Iso-aitti, received them in her library, just the two of them. The family lawyer – the Dutchman Vanderoo – was there as well, hidden behind a stack of ledgers two feet high, while Iso-aitti sat rod-straight in her wingback chair, her chin propped so high upon her starched collar, Orabas often wondered if her head might simply topple off. In her lap was a small dark box the size of a brick.

Vanderoo had spoken first, without introduction or preamble, laying out a concise summary of the family estate, here represented by the stack in front of them. He detailed all the known accounts, the monies and properties, the deeds and titles – and hearing it all at once, it was an impressive testimony to their father's stewardship of the family fortune, which had been impressive before he got his hands on it.

Still, Orabas's attention had drifted, in part because he'd never had a mind for such things, in part because of that box in his grandmother's lap. He knew what that was. He had been hearing about it for as long as he could remember, though he had never actually seen the thing in person, or even been certain it really existed.

It was only the gentle clearing of Vanderoo's throat that alerted him: the financial inventory was complete. Presently and without expression, Iso-aitti took the box from her lap and set it on the table in front of them. Just hearing the weight of it clicking down on silver tray was all Orabas needed. The box was made of lead, just as they had always said. He had heard the story countless times, the one that Iso-aitti was about to tell again. Orabas did not mind. It was his favorite story.

Of course she didn't tell the whole thing. She couldn't, there. The saga was too long and involved. Like a tapestry, it had too many different parts and tangents and stories-within-stories, each of which admitted to any level of detail and elaboration depending upon who was telling it and who was listening. That day, their grandmother had offered a more Spartan digest, intended mostly to convey the scope of the history of the object at question, which everyone in the room understood to be sitting inside the dark lead box on the table.

Here, then, a passably faithful rendering of her account – submitted for much the same reason, though with the clear assurance that the reader need not trouble *too* much keeping track of all the names. They are many, and for our purposes, of more historical than strictly narrative relevance:

Iso-aitti's Brief History of the Shamir

Though certain versions, including their Uncle Gower's, trace the gem's origins all the way back to the six days of creation, it is generally agreed that the first actual *mentions* of the name "shamir" are contained in the ancient rabbinical texts, the Midrashim, which spoke of a strange and powerful blade used to engrave the breastplate of the High Priest's frontlet. This same blade – also called the "worm-stone" because of the apparently shimmering, wriggling, quality of its light – passed down to King Solomon, who used it to cut the stones for his Temple, and who believed it to be the most wondrous of his possessions, which is saying something considering all the wondrous things that Solomon possessed. Such was his respect for the holy shamir, in fact, that as with the Ark, and as with the Key and the Lesser Key, he sealed it away in secret vaults beneath the Temple so that it would never fall into the wrong hands.

There it remained for three-hundred years until the invasion of Nebuchadnezzar, who found all the hidden secrets and treasures of the Kingdom of the Jews, and who, likewise recognizing the beauty and power of the stone (which he called *uzha*), took it back to Babylon and made a gift of it to his beloved Amytis, the same for whom he built the hanging gardens.

When Amytis's daughter Cyaxis was buried, they placed this same jewel around her neck so that its light might guide her across the bridge of Chinvat to the world beyond. Later, when the pallbearers of Cyaxis's daughter, whose name is not known, brought her body into the family tomb, they all saw the *uzha* still set against the breast of Cyaxis.

However, when one of those pallbearer's thieving cousins returned a month later to steal the stone, he discovered that someone had come in the mean time, tunneled in through the wall and taken it before him. The cousin followed this tunnel out to a cedar forest but could find no further trace of the bandit – no trail, nor footprint. The shamir was lost.

Six centuries later came the twins' great great great grandfather Naberius, a former knight of tremendous appetite but questionable judgment, and about whom a whole book of his own could well have been written (and was, by his faithful, though nameless, Squire). According to the Squire's account, Naberius had won a map while gambling at a bazaar in Tunis. According to its former owner, the map showed the way to a secret lair located high up in the innermost peak of the northernmost fjord of Norway, a lair said to contain riches and treasure from all the world over and dating back to the dawn of time, but which could not be got, as it was protected by a winged, fire-breathing leviathan.

Naberius was not a man inclined to believe what he could not see. He set the map aside, but fate, curiosity, and a trail of increasingly angry creditors conspired to push him further and further north until, by an extraordinary sequence of unlikely events, he found himself hiding out in a cave not far from the innermost peak of the northernmost fjord. Remembering the map, and seeing as it was high summer, he set out to find the peak at question, and probably would not have, but for the happy accident of actually witnessing the legendary beast bathing in the shower of the adjacent cataract.

Reasoning that if this one element of the story were true, then the rest might be true as well, Naberius remained in the fjord, hiding his scent by smearing juniper on his skin and clothes. Purple and pungent, he waited seven months in a nearby cave – through the winter – observing the creature's habits as best he could. When the dragon emerged the first day of spring and embarked upon a constitutional flight, Naberius snuck inside the lair, found the mounds and mounds of treasure and stole as much as his pockets and satchels could carry.

Being something of a knave, he soon lost almost all the treasure, save for one gem, the shamir, and a good thing too, as his further flights and wanderings led him into the hidden valleys of Abyssinia, where he fell madly in love with a Temple maiden and was subsequently arrested for stealing horses from the stable of the local Priest-King, John. Facing the gallows, Naberius wormed his way free either by bribing or by mesmerizing the King himself (this depending upon the version one heard) with a gem he said reflected "all things" in its face, including the past and the future. When two of the King's most trusted seers confirmed the claim, the King accepted the gem as payment for Naberius' crime and, heedless of the very specific and forbidding prophecies his holy men had glimpsed, gave it to the fairest and most favored of his concubines, Ondina. She was happy to wear it, of course, in both public and in private, not out of obedience or devotion to the King – to whom she was in fact indifferent – but as emblem of her true love for another in the kingdom, none other than the horse-thief Naberius.

Ondina passed the gem onto Thomas, or "the bastard Thomas," her son by Naberius, who took after his father in many ways, but apparently didn't inherit his luck. In his twenty-seventh year, he went missing during a hunt. Days later his body turned up in the woods, hideously burnt and dismembered. The assumption at the time was that he had been killed by His Majesty's guard upon discovery of his true parentage and his mother's betrayal.

Thomas's grandson Ulder, however, believed otherwise. After consulting with a hermit named Ilyukh, he made the journey alone to the innermost peak of the northernmost fjord. Alas, no one knew for certain what happened to Ulder. He never returned.

A generation later, and motivated by similar suspicions, Ulder's son Barbatos undertook the same mission but with more forethought. He gathered together a band of criminals to come and help him with his scheme, which was to lure the dragon from his cave with the scent of buried treasure, plant a poisoned boar nearby (having stuffed a twice-encased bladder down its throat, filled with the venom of three hundred pythons) – then sweep into the cave as soon as the dragon fell.

The plan worked. Scavengers drove Barbatos from the cave before he could claim the dragon's heart. He fell a thousand feet into the water, but somehow survived, and somehow managed to hold onto the one thing he'd come for: the wormstone, or the shamir, or the Uzha, depending upon one's preferences. By any name, the gem had remained in the family ever since, its one most secret and precious heirloom, passing (though not without event) from Barbatos to his son Foras to his son Modur to his son Amdusias.

Amdusias, or "Duzja," was the twins' father, the man they had buried that morning, and so that more or less is where their grandmother Iso-aitti's account ended.

She was not through, however. Pausing only for a sip of water, she went on – with characteristic calm and not a tremor of grief – to inform the boys that though their father's passing had come unexpectedly, and prematurely, she knew it was his wish that the estate be divided evenly between them. He had said as much. Given the size and nature of the various assets, this was no easy task, but it had been decided (and by this the boys both understood she meant that *she* had decided) that the simplest solution would be for one of them to assume all the known holdings of the family estate – and here she gestured mildly in the direction of all the ledgers and papers – while the other would inherit the shamir – and here with an equally subtle tilt of her head she indicated the lead box. That was the proposed split.

Olybrius was immediately concerned. "But do we know who gets which?"

No, Iso-aitti shook her head. "But as you, Olybrius, were first-born, the decision has been left to you."

Olybrius settled back, greatly relieved. Orabas was as well. He was used to his brother's privilege, and he did not mind that the decision had been taken from his hands, not that he really felt it had been. Olybrius sat a moment, glancing back and forth between the two choices like pieces on a chess board. Orabas could hear the deliberation as if it were taking place inside his own head, or as if he were crouched inside his brother's, listening in...*Best at least to have a look at.*

"May I?"

Iso-aitti nodded gently, of course.

Olybrius reached out and took up the box, and again Orabas felt as if the weight of it were in his own hand, and the small brass latch as Olybrius opened the lid. They both looked in:

The box was filled with grain, just as the stories had always said. That's all either of them could see at first, but Olybrius dug his finger in and came upon a small swatch of wool, folded over once like a book. Gently he removed it. He held it in his palm, then opened it finally and gazed at what was there. They all did, even Iso-aitti.

It was not so large – the size of a barleycorn, as the stories also said, with an arrowhead tip – translucent, but with a milk-white haze that was difficult to make out against the wool bed. Olybrius took it between his thumb and forefinger and held it up to the light, and it did seem to glow – to Orabas anyway – not just catching and reflecting the light in the room, but somehow radiating it as well.

Did Olybrius see? He peered. He squinted. He blew gently, to clear away any stray fiber of grain that might be marring the surface, then set the jewel back on the lamb's wool, replaced the wool on the bed of grain, and slid the box over in front of Orabas.

Orabas hadn't been sure at first what his brother intended by this. He might just have been giving Orabas his turn, but as he lifted his finger from the lid – again like a chess player completing his move – Olybrius let very gently, but very clearly, with the word "Yours."

So the decision was made.

Iso-aitti offered no sign of pleasure or displeasure, but accepted Olybrius's verdict the same as she would a morning's rain: as the unprejudiced expression of Fate itself. For his part, Orabas was tremendously relieved, not so much because he had wanted the shamir. In many ways, he still feared it, as anyone would fear such a thing – a legend suddenly set in hand, come to life – but he feared that stack of ledgers even more. He knew he wasn't suited to assume such responsibility, and that his brother was, so it was only right that he, Orabas, should be the one to protect the family jewel.

In fact, the shamir remained there at Dobrovo for another six months. The twins returned to the Academy to finish their training, both served briefly but ably as officers in the eastern theater against the Sud, received several decorations, then went their separate ways. Olybrius took the titles and deeds back to Kreisenig, the capitol, and wasted no time justifying his choice, assuming most of his father's old alliances, continuing to serve the interest of the Sulka against the Sud, and rising rank by rank within the prevailing empire – from lieutenant to senator to lieutenant governor, and then following the victory, to Provost over the entire province of Ileya; and all this before the age of twenty-seven. He enjoyed the world of privilege that attended, as attested by the manicure of his slender hands, and the confusion of medals, ribbons, chevrons, and stars that bedecked the breast and epaulets of the starched crimson coat that now hung on the back of Orabas's homemade dining chair.

Orabas, on the other hand, had taken the shamir up to the northern Territory. He had already met Maren and her father, Per-Malfi, who lived up there and who had offered to help them make a start. Together he and Maren set off for the remotest frontier, it never once having occurred to him that his inheritance was to be gifted or displayed or really used in any way. In his mind, the line of those who'd known custody of the shamir divided into two clear categories: those who'd lost it, such as Colais the crypt keeper and Hamad – and they were the weak, the villains and scoundrels; and those who had protected it – and they were the heroes, the strong and the brave. And the strongest and bravest of all were Naberius and Barbatos, notwithstanding everything else that was said of them, for having actually *recovered* the gem from its other most fearsome claimant. It was to their column, the column of the keepers and protectors, that Orabas aspired; so the woods, so the cabin, so the life that followed. All of it was built and joinered to keep the wormstone safe, and though he rarely took it out of its hiding place to look at, though he rarely even mentioned it, Orabas had no doubt that every blessing in his life – his wife, their home, the roof, the garden, his child Anna, and the unborn child who was growing in Maren's womb – all were provided, preserved, and protected by the presence of that same little stone, tucked away in the secret little hiding place he never told anyone about.

§

After supper, Anna asked that her uncle read to her. She sat in his lap and was asleep before he'd finished. Then the brothers went out to the barn behind the house, to the nook where Orabas tanned his leathers. Olybrius had brought a bottle as well, and while Orabas stripped the lynx he'd caught that morning, the two of them spoke:

"Roof needs fixing."

"Before the next snow," Orabas agreed. The same as the main house, the barn had a turf roof, but the brackets on this side had a tendency to rot because of the shade and all the smoke. Orabas hung the lynx above the tub. "So what's happened?"

"Did you hear something?"

"I see it," said Orabas.

Olybrius smiled. He was not surprised if he had given himself away. "I remember you after you met Maren. I laughed at you. Now I laugh at myself. I have never felt anything like what struck me upon seeing her. The first time, it was thunder in my chest. This was a month ago. I have thought of nothing else. My mind is useless."

"Who is she?"

"That's the mystery. She is the daughter of Theodosius, but for some reason she has been raised in the Uplands."

"What reason?"

"I assume to keep her away from the filth. Preserve her in her maidenhood."

"And he succeeded?"

"Oh, what he has done. He has ruined me, I tell you."

With a swift swipe of his blade, Orabas made a clean slice down the front of the lynx, from the neck to the tail. The blood was like a long black thread streaming into the bucket. "And is there something I can do?"

"I want to give her something. A gift, to show her, but it has to be a worthy gift."

Orabas kicked the stove for smoke to cover the scent of blood. "You have many gifts to give, I'd think."

"But she is an extraordinary creature, Bazja. She is not like the other women I have seen. She's . . . powerful. Not big, but her brow. Her eye, it's fierce. What I'm telling you is that I have had a kind of vision."

Orabas said nothing. He just kept tugging at the cat's skin, pulling it off like pajamas from a child.

"It doesn't sound like me, I know, but I'm quite sure."

Orabas cleaved a leg and tossed it over to the corner where Noli had been waiting patiently. As the dog dug in, Orabas finally answered. "If you're asking what I think, you know I can't."

"Why not? I'd compensate you. We're men."

"It isn't a matter of compensation, Bizja. I am avowed."

"'Avowed'."

"I gave my word."

"To what?"

"To protect it. Never to bargain, never to trade –"

"Not even with you brother?"

"Not anyone."

Here Olybrius took hold of his brother's arm. "Look at me, Bazja. You said yourself there was a change in me. There is. Until I saw this girl, that gem was a bauble in my eyes. It was beach glass. Now it is the only thing worthy. I have to prove myself."

"Then do."

Olybrius stood back. He downed a shot and watched his brother, so dull and stubborn, sharpening his blade against the strap again, preparing to remove the head of his catch. He downed another shot. "I'd like to think this isn't small of you."

Orabas said nothing. He tapped the stove again with his boot.

"I would give Dobrovo."

"Don't."

"Or the dacha. Take your pick."

"I cannot do it. And you shouldn't need what's mine if it's true the way you feel."

"But what good has it done you, gathering dust? If you had seen her, Bazja, you would agree. Where is it?"

Orabas shook his head. "I can't."

"Even to show me."

"No. And if that's why you're here, Bizja, then you can go."

Orabas sat on his three-legged stool and began sorting through the bowl of bones he used to rub the hides. Again Olybrius watched him and his thick fingers barely able to feel their way. He downed another shot and it seemed to calm him.

"I don't want you to think that's why I came. I thought I would ask and you would say yes. That's all. I forgot."

"Forgot what?"

"That my brother is a man of his word." He reached out and touched Orabas's shoulder, and was surprised again by its bulk

§

That night, Orabas and Maren slept on the floor beside Anna. Olybrius took their bed. Vassago, his aide, slept in the back seat of the Speedster, declining the loft in the barn. The following morning after a breakfast of bread, jam and brown goat cheese, Olybrius set off. All seemed forgiven. Anna thanked him once again for the doll, Miss Marta. Maren thanked him for the chair; Orabas for the bearskin hat.

"We will be thinking of you," he said, smiling, "and we will hope."

Olybrius let Vassago drive the first two miles, then just beyond the ridge that protected his brother's little vale, he had him stop. He told Vassago to go back through the woods. "Watch out for traps. He sets them everywhere." He told him to find a blind and observe his brother's every move, as he would lead him to the hiding place. "He'll want to check. He'll need to make sure it's there."

Vassago didn't seem all that surprised. He turned to the Provost with lazy eyes and the typically slacked jaw that gave expression to what was his finest attribute by far: beyond his loyalty, dependability, and aversion to complaint, it was the sense that he had seen everything before, and many times. Nothing under the sun was new to Vassago. "And if he doesn't?" he asked dryly. "How long should I wait?"

"You won't have to wait," said Olybrius. "He'll go tonight, if I know him."

And he was right, of course.

V

The Truth (I)

It should at this point in our story be mentioned that there was one crucial error in Iso-aitti's account of the history of the shamir. The chain of custody she'd described was more or less accurate, and it was also true, as the reader knows, that for two large swaths of its history the jewel had resided in the lair of the most fearsome dragon of the north, Modo (or Modor, or Azimo, or any of a number of different variations depending upon the clan at question); was his most prized possession, in fact, up until the twins' great great great great grandfather had come and stolen it by such devious and ingenious means, with the buried treasure and the venom-filled pig.

The plan had worked to perfection, inasmuch as the purpose had been to recapture the gem. That, at the cost of a hopelessly shattered femur – the lone result of Barbatos's miraculous fall down the length of the cataract – had been a bargain of historic proportion.

The mistake was in thinking that the Great Wyrm's death had also resulted. This was an assumption based upon appearances and further assumptions: First, that no creature on earth could possibly have survived the amount of poison Barbatos had planted in that pig (certain accounts had the venom coming from as many as three *thousand* pythons, not three hundred); second, that the silence of the great beast's breast was absolute and that the chill of its softer plates was as such the chill of death; and third, that the interest of all those bats and vultures descending on the cave in the wake of Modo's collapse had been self evident. What other purpose could they possibly have had than to come and feast on the fresh carcass of the terrible king?

Opinions differ. There are many who will agree that the scavengers had indeed come to scavenge, that the bats were there to drink the dragon dry while the blood was still warm and reasonably tasty, but that by acting as quickly and as concertedly as they did, what they actually succeeded in doing was sucking the poison out of him before it could do any lethal harm. They leeched him, in effect, saving his life at the expense of thousands of their own.

And this might be so.

There are others, however, who, with somewhat more vigorous defense, will claim that it was the clear *intention* of the bats to suck the poison from the Great Wyrm's body – to succor him – and that their efforts went well beyond leeching. In fact, while several thousand bats attended to getting the poison *out of* their lord and master, just as many went out in search of pure blood to feed back *into* him, draining lambs and returning at once to the lair. Likewise, adders slithered down the dragon's throat and removed the bilious refuse from his stomach, morsel by morsel. Vultures brought him water. Crows brought him carrion. They fed him as they fed their young, with the digested flesh of those same sacrificial lambs.

Most important, all the swallows and swiftlets, the spiders and snails and blind mice who also called the lair their home took all the treasures in the catacomb, every coin and crust of diamond, and piece by piece transported them back into the chamber where the great wyrm lay. They made a kind of glittering nest surrounding him, to cleanse him, that being the real value of such gems and metals: not their beauty or rarity, but their purity, and the literally healing, replenishing quality that such purity bestows. It was the enveloping presence of the treasure hoard – far more than the leeching or the feeding – that finally revived the great dragon, providing the only real antidote to the toxic cocktail of poison and treachery that the Georges had introduced into their master's home and body.

But before the reader rolls his or her eyes at this, the very idea that mere animals would ever behave in so charitable or unin-stinctive a fashion, be reminded that there really is only one instinct – to survive – and that the domain of an ancient dragon turns out to be not a bad place for doing just that. Dragons are loners in the first place, and not particularly gluttonous. They understand that death is more often a function of rot than hunger. Once they've established a territory and amassed a sufficient hoard, their need for meat falls off precipitously to the point that they can go months without a good meal, generally making do with gifts and poachers. They have no tolerance for challengers, that is to say, and enjoy loyalty of their subjects accordingly, not only for generally leaving them alone, but for keeping away all the other fiercest threats and predators. It only stands to reason, then, that the beasts and creatures of the northern fjord, posed with the prospect of actually losing their master – he who had overseen an economy by which they all had been thriving literally for centuries – were very likely stunned, rightly feared a world without him, and responded *instinctively* by doing everything within their power to see that he keep living.

Fortunately, it is not so crucial for now which of these two versions the reader is inclined to believe – whether the wyrm was saved because his minions wanted to preserve him, or because they wanted to devour him. What matters is that he did manage to survive his poisoning, and was eventually able to recover his full strength and powers, including flight, including fire, and including his intelligence, which is to say he knew very well what had taken place. He knew from the moment the venom entered his veins, in fact, that the Georges had once again come to take his most precious stone from him. He even knew which ones – or the line anyway. They'd been vying for the stone for several centuries now; the scent of the cape the bats had torn from the intruder's back only confirmed it was they, which only stoked Modo's fury all the more. Once again he had forgotten their persistence. Once again he'd paid.

But they would pay in turn. No sooner was he able to open his eyes again than he sent out his minions in every direction, to search out every hidden path and corner. The bats went out. The wolves went out. The snakes and the vultures and falcons, too, (the peregrines had good noses) to see if they could track the thieves. Of course, by then the men were gone, and they knew enough to cover their tracks. But they were still fools, for Modo was not about to forget, or forgive. As soon as he could spread his wings again, he set off himself, enlisting the bats to guard his hoard while he scoured the land, high and low, searching all the same places he'd gone before, tunneling into crypts and tombs, laying waste to castle towers and deep dark dungeon, routing hidden caves and smelting heaps and heaps of treasure in search of that one irreducible stone. He did not find it, which was no great surprise. The world was large, the stone was small. It might be a pebble at the bottom of a thousand different rivers.

But if a Great Wyrm's blood is slow to heat, it's slow to cool as well, and Modo's simmered and seethed inside him. He did not waver, he did not rest or ever resign himself to having lost his most prized possession. In fact, in all the years and generations that were to follow, there was not a moment that its absence did not burn inside him like a poisonous seed, or a cancer. He could feel with every breath the deadly fungus creeping though him. But here again to understand just how the beacon burned and lured him on, certain basic features of the dragon's nature must be borne in mind, principally the fact that this one, as we have noted, was over fifteen hundred years old.

This was exceptional, but not without precedent, dragons being uniquely well adapted to longevity. Their only natural enemies are other dragons, to whom they are admittedly hostile, and man, to whom they are vastly superior. If a dragon can manage to survive the various battles of his youth (which tends to last a hundred years or so), there is nothing to stop him from living five hundred more, and if in that time he manages to acquire a sufficient hoard of treasure – sufficient, that is, to stave the rot of age – there's nothing to stop him from living another seven hundred, or eight, or even, as was the case with Modo, a thousand.

In that time, he had acquired all the usual and most useful attributes of age: a certain implacability, the wisdom to know what he needed and what he didn't, when to conserve and when to exert, and in general a far more relaxed perception of fate and of duration than we could ever know, contingent as such perceptions are upon the span of the life that measures them. Think of the common housefly, for which the descent of the deadly swatter is like the fall of a sequoia. Think of the dragonfly, which must cram the whole of its adolescence into a fortnight. Or think of one's own experience (assuming the reader is of sufficient age), and how a week in the life of an average schoolboy, or girl, can seem like an eternity, while in the experience of even the most hapless adult, those same seven days will pass in the blow of a nose. It is a cruel trick of the cosmos, that the more time one is given, the faster it seems to slide by.

But now take this rule and apply it to the life of a fifteen hundred year old dragon and you can begin to understand the peculiar combination of urgency and calm, fury and forbearance with which our hero (or villain, that choice belongs to the reader really) undertook to have back what had been so cleverly, and so under-handedly, stolen from him.

He brought the cape into his sleeping den. He hung it on a stalagmite near to where the gem had been. He let it permeate the air, so that all who entered would know the scent. It haunted the space like a ghost, its human stench a vivid reminder of what was missing now, and what would someday return. He never for a moment doubted that the turn of the earth would eventually bring the gem around to him again, and restore it to its place, to light the darkness which had been creeping in around him ever since its disappearance, to breath fresh and fragrant air into this putrid space, and purify the rot that was slowly taking hold. Deep down in his slow, timpanic heart, he knew the glow would be his again.

Why else would he still be alive?

VI

The invitation

Looking back, Margrét would consider it a good thing – another sign that fortune was finally smiling on her – that there was no one else home, or in any of the Five Homes, when she and the flock returned that day. Inger was still over in Uhlo caring for the twins, one of whom had developed croup. Torvald was still helping build the wall.

The only person in view was a messenger out in front of their hut – a large and burly man with a great dark beard. He looked like a bear. Margrét felt sorry for his horse.

"Lady of the house?" His voice was gruff. He had been waiting there for a while apparently.

Margrét told him she was the Lady, which he didn't believe, but she insisted because she could tell this was an important message. It was written on sheepskin, and sealed with wax.

"Yes, but *that's* me," she said, pointing at the name. "Mistress Margrét of Antayak. The lady of the house would only give it to me."

The man finally relented. The girl was stubborn, he had places he would rather be and not much light to get there.

He did not simply hand it over, though. He let her break the seal – red wax, bearing the imprint of a crown and a serpent, meaning Henryk – but then as a matter of form, but also assuming her to be illiterate, he took the parchment back from her, held it up and read aloud – or announced really, as if a crowd had gathered to hear:

"The Lord Chamberlain is happily commanded to invite Lady Margrét of Antayak to the reception of His Majesty Henryk, aboard the SS Minarik, at the first pier in Kreisenig, 24 September, the year of our Lord, 19–"

"Let me." Margrét practically snatched the sheepskin from the man's hands so she could see for herself.

She was not one for tears. She never cried, in fact, but she could feel her eyes welling and the thickness in her throat even before she finished reading the words to herself. She had to turn away from the man, not because she was sad. Not really because she was overjoyed either. The feeling was more one of relief, tremendous and unspeakable relief, that the thing she had been waiting for all this time – quietly insisting to the sheep and to Inger and to Torvald and the clover, that it was definitely going to happen – had finally happened. Today.

He had summoned her. He wanted to see her.

As soon as the messenger and his horse were gone from view, she entered the hut and went straight to the dowry chest, which she had *not* yet moved to the kirkhas. She already knew what she wanted for the dress. She wanted it to be white with a green sash at the waist, made from her mother's silk and perhaps the lace as well, for the collar and cuffs. She took the fabrics out. She took out the pearls, too, to see if there was a way to weave them in.

There was one more thing as well, down beneath all the scarves and the gloves, beneath the pouches of shells and special stones – a little wooden case, the size of her hand but slimmer; it closed on hinges the size of two pins. She held it to her cheek just to feel how flat and cool it was, and she was murmuring thank you to it – "thank you, thank you, thank you" – when she heard the cough outside.

Inger.

Quickly she stuffed the frame back in its place, the silks and the lace and the invitation as well. She closed the dowry and went to get the pail just in time to meet Inger as she came to the door.

"Not yet?"

"*Naiy*," said Margrét, and out she went. But just hearing Inger's voice she knew – she would not be telling Inger. She knew too well what Inger would say.

§

Of course, if she was really going to try to do this thing alone, it wasn't going to be easy. Three weeks wasn't nearly enough time, and Margrét was no seamstress. All she'd ever made were tents and tunics, and now she would have to work in secret. The following morning, she had to wait until Inger left for Uhlo before running back to the hut and fetching the material, taking the needles from Inger's chest and smuggling them out to the meadows, to the great rock where she could finally sit and focus.

"But I have done my part," she spoke aloud, taking the thread between her teeth and snapping it. Yosi's ears flicked at that. "I have not complained – not really, not when you consider. I have done as they've asked." She glanced around again, just to make sure that no one was coming, no one would see. "And I will miss all this. I will miss you very much Yosi, and you Nella. I will miss the ridge-which-looks-like-a-sleeping-woman; I will miss the dead oak tree, and even you, Karla, who are so blind and stupid." She found herself growing very nostalgic all of a sudden, but her time here was done. She had known this even before the messenger had come. In her bones, in her blood, she had felt it. "I am no good here anymore."

And he had felt that, too; her father had.

Now, just how she was going to get to the capitol was another question. It was probably just as well that Inger and Torvald didn't know, their cart was so rickety and filthy and not something you would ever want to be seen in – in the city, at least. Over the heath was another little village – Tami – where the charcoal burner Jurgen lived, and he had a fine carriage, according to Torvald. He took it to the city, too. The only problem there was that Jurgen wasn't very friendly. Maybe it was because his face was always smeared with soot, but he seemed taciturn, and tall and bony. Not the sort of man one liked asking favors of. So she decided not to pose this as a favor.

With exactly eighteen days to go before the night of the reception, she awoke at dawn. The sheep were all still huddled together near the crook of the fold where the slanted roof met the ground.

"Come on, then." She tapped the stick, and as usual, Yosi and Nella were first to trot up, always the most game.

Tami was a morning's walk, three hills from Five Homes and not much bigger, though the houses were more sturdy, being built of millwood. Jurgen's was the first in the row, with ornately carved casings around the windows that gave Margrét hope about his cart, even though there was no sign of it out front. She rapped on the door three times before hearing a pair of little feet pit-pat up and yank it open.

It was Jurgen's wife, Til, who was shaped like a stove, her head a kettle. She bore a very startled expression, as if it were a kind of impertinence for Margrét to have come calling.

"I was wondering if your husband was in."

"Jurgen?" Til's eyes darted from Margrét to the flock, confused. "But he's not here."

"Where is he?"

"He left two days ago, for Ossa." She said this as if Margrét somehow should have known.

"When will he be back?"

She thought. "Today."

"When?"

She thought again. "Today," she said impatiently. "Depends on the roads."

"Do you mind if I wait?"

Til looked back at the flock, which was dispersing now in search of weeds and grass. She did mind clearly, but shrugged. "As you please." She showed her where and closed the door.

Margrét walked the flock just down the lane to wait. The sheep spread out, all but Nela and Yosi, who stayed beside her.

She had already made up her mind that Karla was the price she'd pay. Not only was Karla old, she had also taken to biting the other sheep ever since she'd lost her sight. If Jurgen wanted more, then maybe Luka too; his coat was getting patchy.

Yet as she looked over at Karla now, not really looking back at her through those milky, clouded eyes, it didn't seem right sending her off just because of the way she was. It wasn't Karla's fault, after all. Perhaps it would be more fair to leave the question to fate.

But how did one do that? All she could think of was the fairs they used to go to down in Tuvin, where they would blindfold the children, spin them around and point them at the billboard posters of the strongmen and the donkeys and Little Bo Peeps. So right there Margrét shut her eyes. She pulled the hood down over her face to make sure she couldn't cheat, then she started spinning round and round right in the middle of the road, in the middle of the flock. The lambs began bleating. She could tell which ones, so she started bleating too, singing nonsense just to drown out the loud ones – *Yala-yala-yayaya*. She stretched her arms out further and further and kept singing and spinning like a top. She spun until she practically fell down, but just before she did, she opened her hands and reached and grabbed hold of the nearest wool coat. She toppled to her knees. She opened her eyes.

Lina. Another one of Cassandra's girls, about whom Margrét had never felt one way or the other. That was better, she thought. And maybe Bjul, too, who was looking straight at her now, chewing. Bjul would do.

Just then she heard the rattle and clip-clop of an approaching carriage. It was Jurgen coming up the road! He looked grim as usual, but the carriage was much larger than she remembered, high and broad, with a flatbed behind the driver's seat you could have fit three oxen on. It may not have been the handsomest thing – it was sooty, like him – but it was certainly sturdy enough to make the trip.

She dashed up the slope and met him even before Til, who had also come out at the sound. As Jurgen pulled his horse to a halt, Margrét walked alongside.

"I'm Torvald's niece," she said breathlessly. "Actually, his sister is my nursemaid, but I need to go to Kreisenig. Soon."

Jurgen looked down at her, confused.

"They haven't any carts to spare," she explained. "But Torvald said that you go sometimes – to Kreisenig."

"Who said this?"

"Torvald. He's tall. He helps with the walls." She mimicked his stance, hunched and gangly. She even mimicked his face a bit, the loose-lipped bewilderment, but Jurgen didn't seem to recognize. He climbed down, looking around at the sheep.

"I'm willing to pay," she said, though all of a sudden it didn't seem fair to Lina either, or to Bjul, just handing them over because of fate, or luck, or whatever you wanted to call it. She looked down at the two lambs, Nella and Yosi, who were right there beside her, munching on a tuft of weeds at her feet, their velvety black ears dancing gently.

"These two," she said, to her dismay. "I'd recommend, depending on what you want them for. They're young, but they're not suckling anymore."

Jurgen seemed even more confused now.

"It's still three weeks away," said Margrét, "but whenever you were going to go, if you were going to go. And even if you weren't, I could give you more."

"I don't keep sheep," said Jurgen

"Then you could sell them. That would be up to you, but they're all I have. Here." She actually picked Yosi up. "Please. I have to go." She set the lamb in Jurgen's arms, which he only accepted because he was so surprised. Margrét did the same with Nella, handing her to Til. She didn't look either of them in the eye. She didn't want to give them the chance to refuse. "Just tell me when."

Jurgen looked at his wife, baffled.

"You don't have to say right now," said Margrét. "But those are yours. You can do as you like. And I would cook for you as well." Her voice was breaking. She turned away. Without waiting for an answer, she tapped the staff and the sheep all gathered, all but Nella and Yosi. She could hear Nella bleating, but she didn't look around.

She felt strange the whole way back − hollow and slightly dizzy. Was it because she felt so guilty? Or grieved? In part she supposed, but she felt excited too, she had to admit, because this meant she was really going, didn't it? The truth was, as painful as it had been giving the lambs away, she knew that it was the right thing − because if a person really *wanted* something, then a person should have to prove it. A person should have to give up something that they cared about, because that was the only way to show – that she *must do this* – and the more a person gave up, the more they would get in return. That just made sense.

She stopped along the way, halfway home but not where she could be seen by anyone. She took the bread out of her pocket and some cheese, but she wasn't hungry. She took the slender wooden frame out of the pocket as well. That was where she kept it now, ever since the invitation had come. She clicked it open and looked at the picture of him – which was a painting actually, but all she had.

He had a long face – longer than faces really were, if truth be told. A slender nose, but very large eyes the shape of almonds. He wore a short beard that forked in the middle, and he had a golden plate behind his head, and a black book in his left hand, which was also very long. Both hands were, with tapered fingers held gently, loosely. But it was the eyes she looked at the most, they were so deep and peaceful – so gentle and patient and sorrowful. And she felt the same way whenever she looked at him – sorrowful – but grateful, too, because she knew she hadn't earned his kindness really. Her thoughts were mean. They were contemptuous and selfish, and bored, and resentful, and they were often worse than that – at night. They were impure. And he knew that, too, because he listened. There was nothing he did not see or hear.

"Thank you," she said, again. "And I promise I will try to be better. I will show you, and I will make you proud."

With that she kissed the image and closed it away, and promised one more time, just as she had been promising every day and night, because she broke the promise every day and night.

VII

The Trading Post

Orabas tried to go to Per-Malfi's trading post at least once a season, to shore up rations and hear the latest. Often he brought Maren with him – Maren was the youngest of Per-Malfi's six daughters; Anna the youngest of his eighteen grandchildren – but Maren had been feeling tired. She was showing now, so Orabas decided to make a quick trip of it and go alone. The weather was obliging – sun on snow, but still cold. He left Noli behind as guard, taking Gerti the plough horse with him instead, and the sled and his new hat.

It was a two-day trek, the last part of which he and Gerti were joined by a lone white wolf. It was with them for a mile or so, trailing behind at a steady five paces, which Orabas might have found more disconcerting except that Per-Malfi was almost as popular among animals as he was among the 'steaders in the area. All sorts of dogs and foxes gathered at the Post for scraps, as did birds for seeds; Per-Malfi used them as messengers as well. Even the bears counted him a friend. They fished nearby in the same river.

The last part of the trail was marked by posts and stumped trees that Per-Malfi had carved into various elves and goblins and woodland creatures. Two wide-eyed wooden owls welcomed them into a brief clearing. At the center stood the Post, a well-built, hatched and joinered home not unlike the Bend, but larger and 'L'-shaped, the shorter leg of which gave rise to loft space.

It was mid-morning, the sun was high. The shadows all were hiding underneath the half dozen carts parked out front. Hitching posts divided the little lot – more carved owls, a bear and several trolls. Anna liked to play among them whenever she came to visit, though at the moment they'd been claimed by perched squirrels and blackbirds and one peregrine falcon. Unpacking his sled, Orabas did not take much notice of the falcon, assuming it was one of the couriers. The falcon noticed him, though, and the white wolf slinking up behind.

Inside, the conversation was in full swing. The usual customers were there – the Trinko brothers, the quarrymen, Koos and Ole and Gaino, the postman Yoonas Sloot, and a few others, propped variously on stools, benches and shelves, puffing away at long-stem pipes, contributing a chocolate-scented smoke to all the other smells that drifted about the shop from the shelves and walls and rafters: leather from the saddles on the rails and wall hooks; cedar from the chests; coffee and tea, from slumping sacks in the middle of the room; birch tar, pelts, and all the herbs and medicines that Per-Malfi kept in the pantry behind the long counter from which he did his business. Along the outer shelves were spirits as well, and cider and preserves – pickled eggs, beef, onion, berries of every imaginable vine, even peaches – and any other sundry one might need to make a home on the northern frontier. Nails, traps, and hunting knives. It was something of a regional joke, the boundlessness of Per-Malfi's store, but this included gossip as well, which could just as well have been about the Bergen sisters, or the Trinkos' dogs, or – as this day – the true intentions of their new protectors, the valiant vermillion Sylka.

This morning's item, courtesy of Yoonas the postman, concerned the latest and most telling gaffe. Apparently the Sylka had just, as a gesture of goodwill, issued a new coin bearing an inscription in the old Welan tongue – a phrase from an ancient aphorism that roughly translated "our song (or voice) unto the heavens." Unfortunately, the brain-trust responsible hadn't bothered to check the translation, so instead of reading "Our song (or voice) unto the heavens," the coin ended up reading "Our song unto a soup spoon," meaning that all the coins would have to be recalled, pulled from the pockets and cash registers.

Koos chuckled. "And how much is that?"

"Oh, who knows?" said Yoonas. "More than we can count, that's for sure."

They all grinned, it served 'em right. Only Andjes the Younger (now quite old) didn't join in. To him, the story just went to show what he'd been saying all along, which was that Sylka were no better than the Sud. They didn't care a stick about the Ileyans or their history, and they aimed to kill the old tongue as soon as they could, just like the Sud. He was sure of it.

"You heard about the legend stones in Sami?" he said. "Someone went and busted them. Nothing left but rubble."

"That could just be the Salo," said Koos, "taking a piss."

Others agreed, it wouldn't have been the first time, but Andjes was having none of it. "Oh, it's the Sylka," he said. "They didn't come up here to smell the flowers."

It was at this moment that the front door clanged opened and in stepped Orabas with his dozen fresh pelts. All the traders knew him, and respected him. He was Per-Malfi's son-in-law, after all. But he was also the Provost's brother – and twin – and about this there was more misgiving, the Provost being thought an opportunist and even a collaborator by some. As Orabas made straight across to Per-Malfi's long counter, the traders all offered suitable nods and grunts of greeting, which he returned in kind, now laying down the string of pelts, lynx on top.

Yoonas the Postman was on the verge of calling out – "a customer" – when Per-Malfi emerged from the pantry.

"Bazja, Bazja" Of a sage's years and posture, Per-Malfi wore a clever grin that never quite faded, and gentle eyes that resided in the shade of ample white and wiry brows. "No girls today?"

"Protecting the fort," said Orabas, with regrets. "Is that raspberry leaf?"

It was, in a pouch all ready for his arrival. Per-Malfi slid it across the counter alongside a jar of birch tar. "The hat is new," he squinted, "to you."

"My grandfather's," Orabas smiled and took it off to show, "who said he got it from Barbatos himself."

"Did he now?" Per-Malfi admired it. "Well, well. Weary lies the head . . ."

"I'll need some brackets too. Birch, if you have any."

With a nod, Per-Malfi returned to the pantry to see what he could find, leaving Orabas with the others, who kept puffing their pipes, thickening the air and pretending to mull.

Finally it was Andjes who broke the silence. "So how is your brother, then?"

Orabas could tell already that Andjes' purpose was to provoke. "He's well."

"I'll bet he is. Clever one, that Bizja."

Orabas said nothing.

"Knows how to choose his horses, doesn't he?"

Orabas turned. "Did you have a message you wanted me to deliver him?"

"Just a question's all," said Andjes, briefly emboldened by the challenge. "Just wondering – you speak the old tongue, Bazja? 'Cause I've heard the Sylka mean to do away with it."

"I wouldn't know about that," said Orabas.

"True, though. Just like the Sud, they mean to kill the tongue."

"'Kill the tongue'," Per-Malfi clanged back in from the pantry. He had the brackets under his arm, and he was grinning. "Tongue would've died long ago if someone didn't keep trying to kill it."

Most of the traders grinned at this, as it was true, but Andjes ignored them. "Not true," he said. "I speak it as my father spoke it. I speak it as *your* father spoke it, Per-Malfi. But what about you, Bazja?" He actually stood up from his stool.

"Easy now, Andjes," Sami Trinko quietly tried to keep the peace. "Bazja's not his brother."

"I know he's not. I'm just asking, does he speak the old tongue?'

"*I do,*" said Bazja, turning to prove it, and in an accent more than fair. "*Well enough to tell you now: Remember your friends.*"

'*Remember your friends*' was another old phrase, said to have been spoken by Hamar just before he plunged the knife in Hurka's back. Bazja was facing Andjes square when he said it, reminding the room that he was a good deal younger than Andjes, a good deal taller and broader, and that his gentle temperament was a harbor for legendary fire. They said that Bazja slew ten Sud in Denben with nothing but a bayonet; skewered two at once – in a single thrust, they said – and good for him.

Andjes, remembering this with the rest, resumed his stool. "All right then."

The room was silent for a moment, though whether the threat had passed no one knew until Orabas turned back to Per-Malfi. "A bottle of vita for Andjes," he said, "to share."

"Good lad," Per-Malfi replied. He had a store of the local spirit right behind the counter there.

Orabas spent the next few hours at the Post. They finished the bottle of vita and then another, and all the 'steaders were reminded again that Orabas was not his brother. He showed the hat around, and they took turns remembering the man who'd worn it once, tales of him anyway. They drank to him seven times, but even after all of that, Orabas didn't stay the night. He had resolved to get a quick start back. If he got to the fork by nightfall, he could be at the Bend by late afternoon the following day.

Long shadowed, Per-Malfi walked him out with his provisions: In addition to the brackets and the tea leaves, he had tar and coffee, nails, three sacks of flour, and enough dried fruits to get them through to berry season.

Oddly, the falcon and the white wolf were both still there waiting: the falcon, as before, perched on the cap of the little wooden goblin; the wolf engaged in a quiet standoff with the plough horse.

"You know this one?" Orabas pointed to it. "He walked us from the creak."

Per-Malfi shook his head, he didn't, but looked to make amends. He fumbled in his pouch for a scrap of dried meat. The wolf took no notice, his nose still trained on the man bent over the sled, the one in the thick brown hat. He glanced up at the peregrine, and the peregrine confirmed, lifting her wings and quitting her goblin-perch, strumming up and up and tracing one circle around the edge of the clearing before disappearing over top of the shivering pines.

VIII

The Truth (II)

Inger was no fool. She knew the girl was up to something. She suspected the answer was in the dowry chest, but she would never have opened it to see. It wasn't her place.

She knew Margrét was working on a dress, though, and that she had been stealing needles and thread, or borrowing them. She was also milking the sheep without being asked, folding them every night. She was coming home with cloudberries and mushrooms, and mending and beating the skins they used for tents up north. She was definitely hiding something.

However it wasn't until Torvald returned from his visit to Tami – with the two lambs trailing, Yosi and Nella – that she finally confronted the girl. It was after supper, a stew that Margrét had made of reindeer meat with potatoes and carrots and mushrooms; also cabbage, bread, cheese and coffee. Inger agreed with Torvald, "I will sleep tonight." Margrét made her some fennel tea for her throat; she hoped she hadn't picked up the babies' croup. Torvald took his chair, he lit his pipe. Inger took hers and her mug and Margrét read to them from the Saga Book, the story about how Odin, Vili and Ve turned the Ash and the Elm trees into Ask and Embla, the first man and woman.

Torvald was drifting in his pipesmoke when Inger finally asked her.

"What's your business in Kreisenig?"

Margrét simply turned her head. "Who told you?"

"Not you."

She looked at Torvald, knowing it was him. "I have been invited to a ball, if you must know."

"A' ball'?" said Inger. "What, the King again?"

"Yes, in fact."

Torvald had roused, and watched with heavy lids as Margrét went to her dowry and came back with the sheepskin and a lantern.

Inger didn't read well, but recognized a royal seal. Her brow knit. "When did this come?"

"Last month. Two weeks ago."

Inger rocked in her chair, seeming to examine them. "And when does it say?"

"Three weeks."

"Three weeks?" She gestured at the sky. "We'll be gone already."

"*You'll* be," said Margrét firmly, leaning in and pointing to the invitation. "I am going. I'm not *not* going."

Inger sat back again. She understood this would be a difficult invitation to refuse. Perhaps impossible. Torvald's hand was out, he wanted to see, even though he couldn't read a thing. Inger passed him the parchment. He looked at the seal with a bit of suspicion. He sniffed it.

"Why did you not show this before?" asked Inger.

Margrét replied, "Because I knew what you would say."

"What would I say?"

"What you are thinking right now."

"I am thinking questions," said Inger. "How did they find you? Who is it from?"

"Give it back." Margrét took the letter from Torvald. She practically snatched it. "You know very well who. Who else?"

Inger could not help her expression, which Margrét saw.

"I can tell you don't believe it."

"I don't believe or disbelieve. I do not know."

"Well, I do. I know." Margrét gave a daring look. Her chin was high and jutting, her eyes glowering – very proud she was, and very sure for someone who was almost surely wrong.

Inger did not say this, of course. There was a great deal she didn't say, seeing as she actually *had* known Margrét's father, having served in the retinue of Margrét's mother, Irina. She knew the kind of man he was, the kind of things he did and did not do, but she could see just as well that Margrét had made up her mind. Her eyes were beaming with certainty. And purpose. *And don't even try to stop me,* they said. *If you try to stop me, I will run. If you try to catch me, I will eat your arm. I will.*

Inger didn't doubt it. Just look at her...

She looked like him.

"And you have been making yourself a dress?" Inger finally asked.

"Yes," said Margrét, though the tilt of the head conceded, not a very good dress.

"Show it to me."

IX

The Messenger

B eing a peregrine, her territory was wide. Come winter, she had been known to travel as far south as the Great Sea, but she was born up north, far north. Her mother had made nest in the cliffs of the high fjords, and she had spent her fledgling years there before discovering the warmer climes and waters.

She knew of the Great Wyrm, therefore. All the hawks and falcons of the region were aware that the entrance of his lair was a reliable hunting ground. If ever a day failed to yield, any bird of prey could rest assured that, come dusk, the easterly mouth of the dragon's cave would explode with a churning black cloud of bats, swarming out for their evening run. An acquired taste, to be sure, but easy pickings. No raptor ever went hungry in the realm of the great wyrm.

It was during these same twi-lit feasts of her youth that she had come to know the peculiar scent of the cave he called home, peculiar not because of the musk of the ancient dragon, nor bat-droppings, nor even the countless treasures (for some of them had a scent as well, the ones that tarnished). There was the faintest trace of something else in there, something which stood out for its dissonance from the rest. She had never been sure what it was, in fact, until encountering the man, or the hat of the man, who entered Per-Malfi's trading post that day.

Now why that recognition should have sent her immediately north one can never be sure. Again, some might simply say instinct, and they might be right – because scents are all clues, because clues are to be connected, because in addition to being a hunter and a wanderer, the peregrine is also by nature a messenger.

Whatever the reason, the fearsome bird did with an unwavering sense of direction fly straight – three days north and to the west, across the Fences and up onto the great plateaus, until the morning of the third day she came upon the jagged narrow canyon like a crevice, or like an axe had cleaved into the coast.

She couldn't be sure the dragon was there, yet as she glided into the great canyon and once again saw the pockmarked cliffs, the lone white cataract plunging down so slowly and softly into the white capped water below, she could sense from the quiet of the landscape that its deepest heartbeat still resided in the cliff, keeping time for all the other creatures thereabouts.

Likewise, she had only to land upon the highest jutting ledge to know that her nose was right. That scent, the one she had detected on the man, was the very same as she had remembered. She smelled it now, drifting ever so faintly from the mouth of the cave. By the same instinct which had brought her here, she followed the scent inside, down a brief and narrow passage to a darker and more open space where a thousand ears turned at her entrance, the prey of her youth, all hanging from the ceiling like globs of tar; she did not pause. The mannish scent, growing stronger the further in she crept, kept drawing her deeper and deeper into the cave tunnels, guiding her turns past a strange assortment of odds and ends – furniture and furnishing, fraying drapes. She didn't pause to look, heading to the right and then left and then further down until she came into an even larger cavern than the first, lit – if dimly – by a small beam spilling down through a hole in the ceiling, glancing off the heaps of goblets, pearls and jewels. She did not see them either. The milky water dripped down from the tips of the stalactites, spearing and splashing on the equally fine tips of the stalagmite posts, leaving their residue but over time extending their height until the two yearning tips would meet. In other parts of the cave they already had, appearing now as natural columns.

Near the middle of the room, a ragged cape was draped on a planted scepter, and this of course – the cape – was the source of the scent that permeated the cave. Even after all those years, the air retained that same tincture she had detected back at the trading post.

the uplands

She was alone with it only a moment before she became aware of something else, something shifting in one of the lower passages and much much larger than any bat. A deep guttural groan followed, then a black shape emerged from the tunnel on the far side of the chamber. The head appeared first, though it was only recognizable as such by the two golden-orange orbs mounted on the muzzle, peering directly at her and growing as the creature drew closer. The long dark body followed, climbing smoothly, panther-like up from the ante-chamber where he had been resting.

The falcon stood her ground, even as the beast circled and encircled her. The bats continued to stir, but their master calmed them. No sound came from his throat, but still the thought was delivered:

Easy, m'dears. She isn't here for you.

Finally the great shadow stopped and propped itself before her, though the long tail continued, curling around behind her, teasing her, testing her, while the eyes remained locked.

She understood his suspicion. Her kind were known to do the bidding of the Georges, for scraps. So in he leaned, those fiery globes glowering down upon her two black pellets and managing, despite their size, to climb in through and enter her mind as if it were another hidden catacomb. The Great Wyrm snaked and sniffed about the caves and chambers of the peregrine's past – her youth, her kin and her ancestors. From season to season and roost to roost and hunt to hunt, he searched for some unclean purpose, some ulterior motive or foreign loyalty. Finding none, he withdrew – back and back like two retreating snakes to where their eyes had met, back into the sky-lit chamber and the tattered cape. Pupil to pupil they stood, and from his mind he spoke to her.

Where?

From her mind, she replied, *Come, and I will show you.*

§

59

ASMODEUS

He led her now, back out onto the ledge, the highest on the cliff. The sun was low and to the west, slathering all the facing stone in glaring golds and reds, sending jagged blue shadows across the rest. They waited until the edges faded and all was bathed in a cooler blue. Even then the falcon remained, perfectly still and quiet until the high crown of the sun had disappeared beneath the horizon.

Only then did the great beast lift its wings and disembark. The falcon followed, up and up and further up, finding winds and thermals strong enough to carry them both to a magisterial height; the falcon could only assume it was for the same reason as he had waited until dusk to leave: stealth. The known presence of a dragon had a way of changing a landscape, alerting all its creatures to lay low. From up here, however, and with darkness descending, he could easily be mistaken for a much nearer hawk.

He also seemed determined to head east. Again, the peregrine didn't know why, but understood that she was here as guide, not leader, and the brief detour gave her a chance to gauge his speed, never having flown so near the wing or the mind of a dragon. Considering their differences, they made good partners. The dragon was bigger obviously, but the strokes of his wings were more languorous, while the falcon was skilled and fast and able to keep pace.

The longer she did, the clearer his purpose became. He was looking for something, someone to watch his keep. The same as a hawk might train her eye upon a pasture or a stretch of river, searching for that shift in the tall grass or that shadow beneath the surface, he, by means of an organ far beyond her ken, was scouring the vast expanse below, searching for some glow but not finding it. He seemed confused almost, until finally, just beyond a great flat lake, down he turned and down they flew.

They came upon a bracken-shrouded bog, surrounding a mound formed from the roots of a dying ash tree. They landed at the base. The great wyrm briefly sniffed about, then descended to the water's edge and slid into the black. A few bubbles gurgled up, then nothing.

A moment later, the falcon heard a rumbling sound below, coming from within the mound. Then came a light, dim but discernible, scissoring up through the holes and tunnels that twisted around the roots. The falcon hopped up onto the splintered trunk and looked down through. There was an opening in the base just large enough for her to stick her head through, down into the space below.

The wyrm was there and dripping, having entered by an underwater passage, having lit the chamber at the expense of an old pile of rocks, or coal. The stones glowed just enough to reveal what looked like an abandoned lair. The peregrine could see several other entrances leading down into deeper pools, and although the roots of the ash had been allowed to grow down to the floor, here and there they could be seen to drape what were clearly heaps of treasure very like the ones that Modo kept. The dragon nosed about one of the larger piles, but seemed more concerned by who else was − or was not − there. Kin. He sniffed down corridors as if some remnant or clue might point him, blew plumes of fire to light the way but it was clear: whoever once had lived here was gone.

Resigned, he chose the darkest corridor and entered, long tail trailing, leaving behind the smoldering stones. The falcon withdrew her head and scanned the black surface of the pond. A moment later he emerged, head first, then the quills on his back. He climbed up onto the bank and crouched there for a moment while the water drained off him in the moonlight, running down his plates and scales in countless stream and rivulets that gathered again beneath him and slid further down, back into their source like scurrying beetles or snakes. The Great Wyrm's mind was elsewhere, still preoccupied by the question he'd descended with. *Where had they all gone?*

But was it possible, wondered the peregrine, he hadn't known until now he was the last?

X

The Carriage

"Oh, I can't stand it. It's terrible." Margrét flung the necklace down into Inger's lap, which was already draped in the white silk of Margrét's dress-to-be. Inger was sewing the pearls into the lace around the collar.

"Just look at it," Margrét moaned. She had decided the day before that the black amulet was much too dreary to wear to a ball, so she'd been trying to make a whole new necklace out of the smaller shells she'd collected, but they refused to cooperate. "And I don't even think it goes."

"It 'goes'. Listen to her." Inger set aside the dress and held the necklace up to look at. It *was* a mess. The shells were pointing this way and that like shark's teeth "...Well, you don't *have* to have a necklace. There is no rule."

"There is too. And how would you know?" Margrét looked out at the clouds, which were low and dark again this morning, and the wind was blowing from the east again. It had rained three times this week already, and Tasha was sleeping under the salt pans, which meant one thing.

"We should have left already," she said.

"We can't go without wheels."

"But he hasn't been working on the wheels. He spent all week on the head board –"

"Because you said the cart was too ugly." Inger focused back on the collar. "And stop worrying about the clouds. There will be sun."

"The sun's even worse," Margrét grumbled. "If the thaw comes, we'll *never* get through. And look at these." She huffed. Her shoes. They were an old pair that Oni-miiko's wife had lent her for the ball, only they were much too big, so Oni-miiko had tried to fix them, claiming he'd been a cobbler's apprentice when he was a boy. He'd made a whole project of it, sending to Tuvin to get the nails and glue when they could just as well have gotten a brand new pair, and now the shoes were much too tight. Margrét had been wearing them for two days straight to try to get the leather to relax.

"I look like I'm wearing hooves!"

Inger couldn't stifle her laugh, which upset Margrét even more. She stomped out, then stomped back in, then back out again; there was nowhere to go. She removed her left shoe and was about to fling it across the Common when a terrible groan sounded. Margrét wasn't sure what it was at first – Torvald's voice or something bending – then a sudden clang and a snap, then definitely the sound of Torvald grunting. Inger burst out of the hut and she and Margrét ran around to where he'd been working, behind the fold.

They found him down on his rump in the mud, scratching his head. The cart looked like it was kneeling down in front of him. The wheel was over by the rain barrel.

"Are you all right?" asked Inger. "What happened?"

Torvald shook his head, dazed, but Margrét could see the axel was in two pieces.

"What do we do?" she asked. "Can you fix it? Do you have another?"

"Manga!" scolded Inger.

"Do we?" She looked to Torvald, and now she could feel the first flecks of rain falling down. "What about Jurgen?"

Torvald shook his head, Jurgen had left for Tuvin the day before. "But someone might come through."

The clouds replied, as it began raining much harder now – large, smacking drops, pelting Margrét's eyes and the mud. No one would be coming through Five Homes. Even Torvald knew that.

"You did this on purpose!" she cried, and at that moment she believed it. He *meant* to break the wheel because he didn't want her leaving, because he needed someone to read him his stories, or because Inger wanted to punish her. She howled and ran, but the rain was coming so hard now she ducked into the fold where all the sheep were huddled in the corner.

"I hate you all!" she shouted. She overturned the trough, but the sheep only looked over at her, ears splayed in confusion. Some shuffled away, though this wasn't the first time they'd seen her like this. She had a streak.

"I would give you *all* to a butcher, I would." She broke down sobbing. The only thing that had ever made this life tolerable was the thought that it would end some day, that she would be able to leave and show him, but Inger was right. What foolishness all that had been, letting herself believe that he had wanted to see her. He hated her too, and she knew why.

Her tantrum lasted until she was all worn out. In addition to the trough, she toppled the water tubs and managed to split one the overhanging beams; that would have to be fixed. She even considered throwing the lantern down. She imagined the huts all burning like torches – what would it matter? They were nothing but sticks and mud anyway.

But she didn't. She would never harm the flock really. In fact, when she was done and her rage was spent, she lay down and slept among them in their hay, pressed between the soft matte of Old Cassandra's coat and Yosi's, her tears mingled with the oil of their wool, no longer wishing she could go. She had lost all hope of that; she only wished that she were one of them, mute and dull, a wall-eyed grazer on a distant windswept pasture.

§

Even in the rain, Inger heard much of this from the hut – Margrét taking out her fury on the stable, storming, cursing the animals and the hills, then going quiet.

Inger's heart went out, but she had also resigned herself to the will of the Gods in this matter; she let this be her bedtime prayer. If they chose to open the sky, to thaw the ground, to snap Torvald's wagon in half, so be it. There was reason to go to Kreisenig – maybe – but there was reason not to go as well.

The girl knew none of this, of course – Inger having offered only the kindliest and most minimal answers over the years – but Margrét's father and mother were never married. Theodosius, who had only been a presbyter at the time, had been obsessed with Irina, it's true, but in a violent, rabid way, and despite the fact that he was engaged to another woman, the Viceroy's daughter. Irina tried rebuffing him by every means imaginable, even to the point of joining the Sisters of Hamar, but her resistance only fed his fixation. Jealous and extravagant, strict and cruel, his attentions were finally impossible for her to fend, and it came as no surprise when she was found to be with child. Accordingly, she removed herself to a little windswept island off the western coast to bear the term in secret. It was a troubled pregnancy from the start, made worse by the climate and her seclusion. Irina survived the birth by less than two days, long enough to hold the girl and name her. She was buried by shepherds on the highest hill of the island, with no one but Inger as witness.

No response followed from Margrét's father, who was by then both married and a Bishop. He never acknowledged the child. Never inquired or wrote or sent a penny in support, even after Inger and Margrét returned to the mainland. The two of them lived in hiding for almost a year. The first time they strayed into the public square, it was only so that Margrét could see the lighting of the Cathedral. One of the Sisters recognized them. "Get her away!" she cried. She practically assaulted Inger, but only to warn her. "You must never let him see." She explained, the death of Irina had driven his Holiness half-mad apparently, this according to his closest advisors. He'd been heard to curse the child, in fact, and to blame her for killing the only love he had ever known. He called her a demon.

"You must take her far away!" the Sister said. "At once!"

So that was why Inger had returned to the Uplands – not to keep Margrét pure or chaste or anything of the kind – but to protect her from her own father and what she feared he might do if he ever found her. She brought her to Five Homes. They had the Völla come and bless her, and baptize her beneath the Hammer, but even then,

Inger was still afraid. Afterwards, she went alone to the Völla to ask how she should raise the girl.

"Just see that she reads," was all the wise old woman said, "so she'll be ready when they call for her again."

§

Inger was awakened by the sound of Margrét's voice exclaiming – squealing for joy, and now she was running in and jostling her shoulder.

"Inger, wake up! Wake up!"

Her face was alight and beaming.

"Look!" She practically lifted Inger's head and turned it to the door.

Sun and blue sky and white scudding clouds, but more than just the sun. There was something in the road, large and gleaming black. Was it a carriage? She squinted.

"Is that Jurgen's?"

"Jurgen's? No!" said Margrét, pulling her over to the door. "Look!"

Inger rubbed her eyes. It was a car, shining in the morning light. And a driver too.

"He did it!" said Margrét. "He actually sent one!"

Inger sat up now and tried to clear her head just to make sure she wasn't seeing things. The driver had one foot up on the runner and he was smoking.

"We can still go, yes? Say we can!" Margrét was tugging at her. "Say it!"

"Yes," said Inger finally, not because she was swept up in the girl's delight, and not because a car was here to take her, but because the sun had come, which seemed to her to be as clear a sign as any that the Gods were in favor. The way was made ready.

"Can you believe it, Tasha?" Margrét was dancing now, her tunic twirling around her. "We can go! He did it, he did it, he did it!" Tasha was dancing, too, jumping and leaping at her feet.

the uplands

They left that same morning, as soon as they gathered up their things – the gown, the shoes, even the shell necklace. They packed them all in the dowry chest and waved good bye to Torvald and to all the neighbors who came out to watch, to see the two of them – and their chauffeur, of course – puttering off down the southern road in the highest and most gleaming style.

XI

The Choice

From her window Little Anna had seen her father get the ladder out of the barn. That was all the invitation she needed. She ran outside in her coat and her frock dress, her red hair still wild and frazzled from sleep. "I want to help."

"Where is your mother?"

"Still sleeping. I want to help."

He set the ladder against the roof. "There's more bark around back. Go see if it's flat, but stand on it first. And count to a hundred."

She stomped.

"Two hundred then. Then come and tell me. But not too loud. Don't wake your mother."

She stomped again, but off she went.

Orabas continued hacking at the eaves of the roof, pulling down the rotten boards as well as the sod, which might have fungus. He was examining a fresh clump of mushrooms, in fact, when Noli's growl turned his head. There was something stirring just behind the tree line. A wolf, it looked like, and not a bashful one. It stepped out now to show itself, the same white wolf that had followed him to Per-Malfi's. Here he was again, lifting his nose as if to point and sniff all at once.

"Easy, Noli."

A moment later, the falcon followed, likewise swooping in from the tree line. It landed on the peak of the smokehouse, not five feet from Orabas, and pointed at him with her black pellet eye.

Orabas looked back at the wolf. To whom were they communicating? There came a shudder and a gust, then an enormous black shadow leapt out from over the treetops, blotting out the sun like a giant ship sweeping overhead, with wings for sails. Orabas nearly fell from the ladder craning to see it circle the vale, cowing the trees then gliding in and setting down behind him with a thud and hop against the soft turf.

The great beast lifted its head and Orabas knew at once that it was Modo, here in all his flesh and armor. How many times had he read the descriptions in the Squire's Tales: its wings like crimson sails; the haunches of its hind legs, so powerful and spry; its long tail – the length of a barn and big enough to crush the cabin with an inadvertent swipe. Even the coloring – its underside a dark cream, while the scales and plates and thorns were a blend of black and red, just as the legend said. He was spawn of both, and for that reason the most fearsome dragon who had ever lived, possessed of his father's malice, his mother's fire.

But then I am dreaming, thought Orabas, and not because he knew the dragon was centuries dead, but because he had dreamed this dream so many times before – of the day that he and Modo would finally meet, the day he would discover that the Great Wyrm was not dead. Had he ever really believed that?

And yet if he were dreaming, then why could smell the smoki-ness in the dragon's breath? Why when he looked into the black slit pupils of its golden eyes, did he understand so clearly what the beast was communicating to him, as clear as if his Uncle Gower were reading it to him from the book.

This is no dream.

Orabas did not dare look away. Nor could he have, for like all who have ever met a dragon's eye, he felt himself instantly overpowered. The force of its mind was like the blast of a furnace, or the impact of a shell, and its meaning was equally emphatic:

Give it to me.

Orabas shook his head. "I don't have it ..." but he could not finish the thought, the hot gust returned with such a fury, swarming in through all the cracks and crevices of his mind, making words unnecessary — a clumsy, wooden substitute for everything that he was thinking and feeling. He felt himself laid bare before this creature. He did not have to speak the words, though he had rehearsed them many times.

Look around you, he replied. *Is this the home of someone who keeps —*

"Papa?"

His heart clutched. It was Anna's voice, coming from the far side of the main house.

The dragon heard as well. Its great head turned slowly like a black boat.

"Anna, stay where you are!" Orabas called, but too late. As she appeared around the corner, the dragon bounded, with a single strum lifting himself to where she was, too fast for her even to scream. He pounced upon her, swept her up in his enormous claws then drove her into the soil like a limp doll. Orabas bolted to go save her, but then stopped again, knowing that with a single flex of his talon, the beast could have snapped his daughter's neck and rent a hole in the sun.

"Bazja!" It was Maren's voice now. She was standing at the stoop of the main house now, with one hand on her belly and the other to her mouth. Her eyes were round and welling.

The dragon saw. He slid his claw up to Anna's little neck so that only her pale round face showed, terrified. The beast turned back to Orabas, its long mouth fixed in that jagged grin:

Give me the jewel.

"I will," Orabas cried out. "But leave her. Let her go."

The beast studied Orabas's face and knew that he had succeeded. He relaxed his grip.

"I have what he wants," Orabas said to Maren. His voice was hoarse. "And I will give it to him."

The wyrm shoved the little girl aside like a rag. As Maren came to gather her in her arms, the beast turned square to face Orabas and briefly spread his wings again: *Where?*

Orabas started for the main house, his legs numb, the world a sudden fog. The wolf and the falcon both watched from their places, the roof peak and the tree line. Orabas did not see. He did not look at either Maren or at Anna as he walked past them. He could hear Anna's still whimpering in her mother's arms. He touched her head, but already he was resolving in his mind, *I will kill it.* On entering, he went straight to the hearth. He swept aside the rug. *I will give him the shamir. Then I will hunt him down and kill him.* He knew how. He had studied the books. *I will not be the one to lose the gem.* He plied the board from its place. *I will be the one to kill the beast.* That was the only way, the only rationale for doing what he was doing at this moment. He reached down into the little cubby he'd built there, but already he felt something strange.

He set his hand on the lead box, but something was wrong. Not that it felt lighter; more that it felt dead. Always before he could sense a kind of hum inside, a vibration in his wrist whenever he held the box in hand. Now as he lifted it out, there was no life.

Already he knew why, and at that moment Orabas could feel an emptiness in himself as well. He opened the lid, but only to confirm. The bed of grain was there. He dug his finger down. Nothing. It was not there. Of course it was not there.

He did not waste time with curses or remonstration. Maren and Anna were still outside, within striking distance of the beast. He went and retrieved his hat from the wall, and his coat. He took his hunting knife, his dagger and his shot gun. He carried them all back out.

"What are you doing?" asked Maren.

He kissed Anna on the head. "I will be fine. I'll be safe. Listen to your mother." Her mother's eyes were wide, and swimming. He spoke quietly, though he was sure the beast could hear. "Go to your father's. Take Noli. Take Gertha. I will find you there."

He kissed them both and turned back to the dragon. The falcon was already airborne, circling above, awaiting direction.

Orabas held out his weapons to show that he was yielding them. He set them on the ground – the gun, and the two blades – and

71

knelt. He lowered his eyes, but spoke aloud so that there would be no mistaking.

"I will take you to the stone," he said. "I know who has it. I will lead you there."

An impatient groan rattled from the Wyrm's long throat, but he consented with a flick of his great tail, the contract clear:

Defy me, and I'll be picking
their bones from my teeth.

Orabas showed his hands again. He had nothing but his coat. The dragon bent its front legs and lowered its head so that Orabas could climb onto his back, just as he had seen in drawings, just as he had dreamt so many times. He swung his leg over the spine and found a kind of saddle between two spurs, which were warm, despite the hard veneer. And just as he had done so many times in his dreams, he took hold of the horn in front of him. He gripped it as tight as he could, and the dragon lifted its head again.

Orabas focused his mind. *Kreisenig*, he thought. *The city on the fork.*

The falcon knew the one; it peeled off from its circle. Modo raised his great wings. Three strides, a strum, a leap and one more strum, and it was up above the birch trees, with Orabas clinging to his back.

PART TWO:

The Capitol

XII

Old Yinny

A stiff, ruffling wind swept across the river, as happened this time of year. The crisp new flags were snapping, the water was white-capped and choppy, but the people had come out to the boardwalk anyway. They were turning up their coat collars, shielding their eyes against the low morning sun to watch the armored cars cross back and forth along Old Yinny, each next vehicle tendering hope that their wait had come to an end.

"The sooner the better," said Captain Markus, chief of all security operations in Kreisenig, including the police.

"I think that's Zitri there." Olybrius nodded, squinting. There was a Jeep headed west. Even from this distance, he thought he could see the General's mustache. "It shouldn't be much longer."

"I'm not talking about the bridge," said Markus. "I mean the whole visit. The ball. I know you've been looking forward, but some things just aren't worth the trouble…"

Olybrius didn't completely disagree at this point. The reception was this evening, finally. The parade, tomorrow. Neither His Majesty nor his barge had yet arrived, but the advance guard had been here for several days already, making their presence felt. All throughout the city there were horses, armored vehicles, the same as they'd used down in Prussia. The children liked it. The government building had been repainted, the Sud cerulean blue giving way to the Sylkan red. They had shut down Olaf's Way and renamed it 'Kristiana Way' after Henryk's Ileyan stepdaughter.

Harmless stuff for the most part, but there had also been several scuffles with the students, who were using the King's visit as an excuse to make their voices heard. Several days before, the Royal Guard had had to pummel a gathering of New Welans at the Pig&-

Whistle, and throw them all in the Block. The question ever since had been whether to set them loose before the reception, or to let them cool. Zitri, being Zitri, had wanted to keep them locked up. He believed the students were actually being paid by the Sud to make trouble, which only showed how much he knew; the only people the students hated more that the Sylka were the Sud. Olybrius had opted for clemency, but that was beginning to look like a bad decision as well. The New Welans were here in force, along with half the city, it seemed, all come to watch the last and most spectacular of the pre-reception festivities.

Henryk's visit was part of a larger tour that would be taking him up into the northern rivers and eventually on out to the sea – it was the maiden voyage of his new "barge," the *Minarik*, of which he was by all accounts extremely proud. The boat was supposed to be state-of-the-art and very large. Very very large. So large, in fact, that his advance guard had expressed concerns that its high stack might not fit under Old Yinny, the two-spired suspension bridge that had been linking Old and New Kreisenig – the commercial side and the factory side – for the last two hundred years. The decision had been made, not by Olybrius, to demolish it. Neatly, of course – Zitri had assured the planning commission that his men knew how to take out a bridge. Then the new regime had promised to start construction on a replacement, "New Yinny," as soon as the *Minarik* left the harbor.

The truth was, His Majesty was doing the city a tremendous favor. Old Yinny had been sinking for decades – about two inches a year according to certain estimates. Something was going to have to be done eventually. Henryk had commissioned his top engineers to design an actual mechanical drawbridge for the midsection. They'd posted a billboard showing what it would look like and how it would work. They were even footing the bill for the ferries that would have to run to and from the factories in the mean time.

Still, for all that, the symbolism was hard to miss, and the students were making sure no one did: The Sylka were here to crush, to destroy, literally to demolish the link between Ileya's past and present, all just so the King could see the capitol from the harbor. The core students had stationed themselves by the billboard and been handing out leaflets all morning, and shouting their favorite slogans. "No Sylka. No Sud. Ileya for Ileyans." "*They take our land. They take our language, and we are expected to dance?*" (That in the old tongue, of course.) And "We are not a dowry." Pure anti-Monarchical nonsense, which the rest of the crowd had been doing its best to ignore. Whole families had come down to enjoy the spectacle and eat. They were buying their children cups of shaved ice and syrup, listening to the songs, tilting the pickled herring down their throats. Now as the band started up a round of *Oly-Keni-kenura*, some sang along. Even the students joined in, albeit defiantly.

> *Our land, o motherland, Ileya,*
> *May her valiant name resound*

"Is that Ovechkin there?" asked Markus.
"The one in the spectacles, yes."

> *In valley and in mountain,*
> *In lake and every wave-washed shore,*
> *To bless our native Northland*
> *And our ancestor's home.*

Tall, very slender, with a longish face, a small underbitten mouth and round glasses that magnified his eyes to give him an owlish appearance, Ovechkin was the putative leader of the students, and typical of the breed – a slumming son of privilege bent on proving his manhood by squandering his father's wealth and denying the people theirs. He was the charisma behind the New Welans, dedicated to the preservation of the Welan language and Welan ways, and oh-but-oh how Olybrius despised him.

> *One day her flowers will bloom*
> *While every rock endures*

77

ASMODEUS

Her song will soar to heaven's height
For all her sons to hear.

The band and the demolitionists were apparently in sync. As the final strain of the anthem sounded and the hiss of the cymbal-crash drifted out over the river, a shrill whistle piped three times in the distance, turning all eyes back to the bridge, where an officer on the near shore was giving the signal and plugging his ears.

A moment later it began. Out of nowhere the cables flew. The joints burst into dust and the popping sounds followed, like fire-crackers at this distance. The bridge itself seemed to hover there for just a moment, as if unaware of the gravity of the situation, then down it came, crashing into the choppy waters of the Ord. By the time the sound had finished clapping through the valley, three hundred years of history had been swallowed in a single, all-things-considered casual, gulp. Just like that.

The crowd along the banks weren't sure quite how to react at first, the final image was so much more jarring than they had expected. A motor boat started across from the near shore. Several tugboats and haulers stood ready to corral the floating debris, but it was the absence that stood out – where once had been…was nothing.

One of the event organizers – Goulu, was it? – had had the inspiration to light the lamps at the top of the remaining stanchions as soon as the demolition was through. Now they did flick on, one by one. The idea had been that the two spires with the great gap in the middle would look like a welcoming gate, and it did – sort of – except that the lights looked so pale through all the hovering dust. The image was more sobering than inspiring. Belittling. Frightening.

The people stood and watched, not sure what for. The waves were coming now, the ones the fallen chunks of the bridge had set off. The band started up the Sylkan anthem, to scattered boos. A baby began to cry for reasons unknown but shared by all. His mother shushed and consoled, to no avail. The child spoke for the

78

rest, all looking out at where their beloved bridge had been: All for a boat. All for a ball.

Even the students, who might have taken vindication at the site, seemed subdued. While the band played on, the waves arrived. One after another they slapped at the pilings and the concrete holding up the boardwalk. The students spat in reply, one after another, then turned and made their way, not even glancing back to look.

Olybrius finally turned away as well. Vassago was here, with word presumably. "So?"

Impassive, Vassago's eyes were on the gap in the distance, but he nodded. "She should be arriving midday."

XIII

Kin (I): The Cave and the Cathedral

O rabas, Modo, and the peregrine spent the light hours of the day inside a cave on the hidden slope of Monpel, the ridge just to the north of the city.

Remarkably, they slept – all three. That the dragon preferred to wait until nightfall before entering the city made sense. His eyes were better at night than human eyes were in the day, and he felt no need to make a scene. He wanted the gem.

What wasn't quite so clear was how *Orabas* was able to sleep, and just a length away from the beast who had threatened to kill his child. Between them was a boulder – maybe twelve pounds, and so the perfect size. He certainly considered it: waiting for Modo to fall asleep, then striking.

Similar thoughts had dogged him the whole way there, which had been a full night's journey over the Fences and then the Southern Ridges. As thrilling as the speed and the height should have been, and as awe-inspiring as anyone would have found the view – lit by a magnificent full moon above and the shimmering lakes below, like carved mirrors scattered across the land – Orabas's thoughts had been more about revenge and turning tables. Should he wait until after he had found the shamir to make his move? Let Modo have the gem, then journey north and steal it back? Or should he take his chances now, at the soonest opportunity?

Even as he pondered his option, he had been aware that Modo was listening. Indeed, from the moment their eyes had met, Orabas felt as if a kind of silvery fog had entered his mind and was creeping through, invading and enveloping every corner and crevice. That was how they'd navigated, in fact. Orabas wasn't steering the dragon so much as thinking where they should go. The dragon understood.

By the time they came upon the Ord and followed it down to Monpel, the fog had entered him so deeply, he felt as though there was nothing he could feel or think to which the dragon was not privy, and that included any plots he might be hatching. Modo was not concerned. *Try*, was his reply (for the communication ran both ways, still). *So much as flex a single muscle in defiance of my will, and I will slough you off, let you drop from here.* Orabas had no doubt of it, and that long before Orabas even hit the ground, Modo would have turned around and be headed back to find his family – the born, the bearing, and the unborn. Modo knew about that as well.

But strangely Orabas did not resent him. On the contrary, as dawn arrived and they set down beside their cave, a kind of intimacy had been established between them. They were kin, in a way – as keepers of the jewel. They were like soldiers on opposite sides of the trench, opposed in color and purpose, but victims of the very same spell.

Sleep, came the silent lullaby, and Orabas closed his eyes. *Sleep*, said the dragon, even as he slept. The word was like a blanket covering over all of Orabas's best intentions, their two minds much too intertwined to accommodate the thought of taking up that boulder. Killing Modo would have been like carving a tumor from his own brain.

§

As evening fell again, the same blanket was lifted by the word:

Awake.

Orabas joined the dragon and the falcon out at the entrance of the cave. In the purpling, periwinkling twilight, they could all see the glow of the capitol hewing up from the valley as if the river were on fire. The dragon would need no help finding his way from here, and in truth Orabas hadn't been sure where exactly to direct them. The city itself seemed like not a good idea. He had been thinking perhaps the southern side of the bridge – the "smoke side," as it was called, on account of the factories. They could sweep in unseen, then he could cross the bridge on foot to try to find his brother. That was his hope, at any rate, until they came around the last bend and saw the bridge was gone – or the midsection.

The dragon made the decision, banking right and heading straight for the heart of the city and the tallest of its towers, which still crowned the old Cathedral where long ago the pagan temple had stood, and before that King Hamar' grave stone. Sacred spots don't change. Only their dressing.

The dragon landed deftly, if heavily, on the parapet of the eastern spire, the bell tower. Two bricks dislodged and skittered down the walls and buttresses to the street below, landing near the feet of two passersby. They looked up, though whether they saw the cause, Orabas didn't bother to notice. He knew his mission. He slid down from his saddle between the dragon's spurs and started directly for stairs that spiraled down the tower shaft. He had until dawn to find the shamir and bring it here.

§

Both Modo and the peregrine waited, eyes trained on the steps below until the man emerged from the ironclad doors and scampered down. With a glance, the dragon bid the bird to follow, which she promptly did, having by now warmed to the task of scout. She glided down and around to the right, where the man on his spindly little legs had just entered a side street.

Modo remained, scanning the chiseled, gridded, squared-off landscape of brick, concrete, steel, and glass that jutted and spanned and canyoned below. They'd passed over a number of small villages and settlements on the way here – distantly, of course. Still, from the vantage of the clouds it seemed like the men were much the same as before, sending their little trails of smoke into the sky. In fact that image of them – cold and shivering, stomping and huddling around the golden glow of their various hearths – more or less emblemized them in the Great Wyrm's mind. That was the good and the bad of them, how basically naked and ill-equipped they were, and yet, because of that, clever; the only other creature to master fire, if you could call that mastery, with sticks and flint and the coaxing and feeding and taming. But that was the point – the seed of admiration tucked away inside the husk of his contempt – that man had to work so hard, so constantly, so creatively to manage what Modo already had within him, and could summon up with mere intention, literally as easily as he could breath. That was the difference.

And here was that same difference again, splayed out beneath him in this impossibly ornate cityscape. If the villages hadn't changed much, the city was transformed. It was much better lit than he recalled. All the little globes they'd posted along the walkways appeared to be beaming a new kind of light: hollower – slightly cheap, it seemed to him – but also lovely in its way. Incandescent. It didn't flicker so much as hum. Everything hummed and strained – the carts all rumbled now, and puttered and grunted along, some of them on wheels of their own, some guided along tracks, so clumsy and awkward, with gangly arms attached to more humming wires overhead. The streets were latticed with them like cobwebs

There was almost something endearing about it, the lengths to which they'd go just to be carried along, the effort they dedicated to expending no effort, and the price they were willing to pay. The stench was everywhere – of gas, smoke, and burning air. Across the water, the stacks were much bigger and taller than he's seen before, chugging great plumes into the sky. But again, to what end such industry? Leisure?

He quieted his mind to listen, to see if he could sense a difference, for this was another of his gifts: to hear however much or however little he chose; each lap of each wave in the river; or past these, and past the humming and buzzing and chugging to the human's voices, their laughter, their shouts, their whispers and inner voices – every thought if he so desired. Had that changed at all, or was the din the same as ever? It seemed to be, only more loud perhaps, more of it, more closely packed together. He heard the squabbles and the prayers, the pleas, all the same as he remembered.

Then suddenly and out of nowhere – or not out of nowhere, as it was coming from directly underneath him – a most profound and majestic sound, a driving, driven hum which caused the stones to tremble, and that same trembling to rise up through his body, to cause his wings to quiver, his skull to purr. The charge was all throughout him, and now the sound was joined by human voice, a chorus-full, diving and cascading, rising again. He thrilled. Of course he did. He pitied them no more than they deserved. They were filthy, yes, but also capable of this, this glorious sound, borne of a knowledge they possessed that he did not – those lights, those muttering wagons, and whatever it was that had humbled the man so quickly, the father. Was that his genius as well? And was this song below the sound of that?

Only now there came another sound, a counterpoint – a lone voice, climbing up the spiral stairs, wheezing and grunting to the music, as if to remind the wyrm again of just how paltry, how sniveling, and disgusting they could be; this one griping about the gout in its knee. Modo turned round to see him appearing in the door – lumpy and white and trembling, standing on the parapet, looking back at him, his back flat against the wall. Modo lifted one wing just barely, just to see the terror in his eyes.

Away!

He jetted a hot plume of smoke from his nostrils: the tower was his now. When the smoke cleared, the man was gone, tripping back down the steps, gimpy knee or no.

Oh, they were the same, thought the Great Wyrm, the same as ever, just more so, and there were more of them, packed more tightly, more frightened, more angry, more desperate. More more more, but there again, wasn't that the point? Say what you will about the rottenness of their cores, they were thriving, living and dying in untold numbers, while his own kind had whittled down to how many now? Was it just the one?

He would have to find that stone.

XIV

Kin (II): The Ministry and The Minarik

S till sprinting, Orabas vaulted up the marble steps of the Ministry of Governance, a grey-white behemoth just two blocks east of the Cathedral, and home of Olybrius's main office. Two Sylkan guards were manning the door, but it didn't occur to Orabas until he was standing there in front of them how out of place he looked, still wearing his hunting coat and his buckskin boots.

"I need to see the provost."

"Papers."

He had no papers. Fortunately, an officer inside the building recognized him, a Corporal who'd served under him at Kroylia. Zhidnik.

"Lieutenant!" He still called Bazja by his rank. "You're here for the reception?"

Orabas shook his head. "My brother."

"The Provost," said the Corporal, by way of explanation to the guards. "Look at him." They did. They saw the resemblance now and saluted. "You don't think he's at the pier already?"

"What pier?" asked Orabas. "What reception?"

Corporal Zhidnik laughed; as alike as the brothers were, they were unalike as well. "You can check his office. He may be running late." The guards stepped aside and Zhidnik pointed the way up another flight of marble stairs. Orabas bounded them three at a time.

The corporal was correct. Olybrius was at the pier, the Long Pier. He was already aboard the *Minarik*, in fact, but he'd sent Vassago back to fetch his three-quarter coat, as apparently His Majesty was opting for tails. When Orabas appeared at Olybrius's office door, the Steward was sitting by the balcony window, repairing a button by the light of the lamp outside.

"Master Orabas." He stood directly. "How can I –"

"Is my brother here?"

"He's at the pier, Sir. I'd be happy to take you if you –"

"I have to speak to him. Now."

Vassago knew why the Provost's brother was here, of course, but didn't quite understand his sense of urgency.

"You might have trouble getting through security. If you'd be willing to wait –" He stopped again. Orabas was coming directly toward him with a deliberate speed that momentarily froze him in place. He dropped the coat to defend himself, but too late. Before it even hit the floor, Orabas's fist clubbed him square in the temple, and down he went.

§

The trolleys were still running, even though the streets seemed mostly deserted. Barricades were already set up along the sidewalks in preparation for tomorrow's military parade – but Orabas hopped aboard a moving car just to catch his breath. As it swung back onto Olaf's Way – or 'Kristiana' now – he saw the falcon gliding above, not thrown by the change of coat. He didn't need to look back in the direction of the Cathedral. He knew Modo was still there, waiting.

Down on the boardwalk, a fair sized crowd was gathered at the foot of the Long Pier, pushing and shoving to get a closer look at His Majesty's ship, *which* was as tall as any of the buildings surrounding: four stacks, a black hull, red trimmed, and the flags all whipping and waving. The pier itself was a gauntlet of check-points and guards with lists, but Orabas made use of his brother's coat and resemblance. The guards and officers all saluted as he passed. Further down the pier a line of a dozen or so cars and carriages were waiting in front of yet another official with a clipboard. As Orabas approached, at speed, a woman's voice called out. "Mr. Provost!" An old family friend, the Duchess Voss, and her escort for the evening –

perhaps it was the Duke, Orabas couldn't tell, the man was so bent by age, holding his top-hat in hand.

"Could you please tell them?" said the Duchess.

"Is there a problem?" He turned to the guard, who instantly straightened.

"We're not finding her name on the list, Sir."

"Let me see." Orabas took the list and scanned the names.

"All right then, they're with me. Mark them as my guests." He turned to the Duchess. "But I'm afraid I have to hurry."

"Of course," she curtseyed, with an oddly lascivious glance that went happily unseen by her husband. It was the Duke, after all, who blindly lifted his hat. Orabas was already headed up the gangplank.

Olybrius was in his dressing room. All the top brass had been provided private suites, as most were expected to spend the night. Still waiting for Vassago to return with his coat, he was on the point of sending another of his attendants to go check on him when a member of the Royal Guard appeared at the door. On seeing the Provost there in his shirttails, the officer was suddenly confused.

"Sir, excuse me, sir."

He stepped aside and there was Orabas, in red.

"Bazja." Olybrius barely missed a beat, though his brother's eyes beamed with fury. He knew why. He turned to the attendants. "Could you give us a moment? The hall should be fine. We won't be long."

As soon as the attendants were gone, Orabas practically lunged at his brother. "So help me, Bizja, if you don't give it back to me!"

"I don't know what you're talking about –"

Orabas collared him. "I will take your life, Bizja, right here."

"Remember where you are," Olybrius stood tall. "Where is Vassago?"

Orabas drove him back into a velvet pink wingback. "What did you do with it! I know you took it!"

"Hands off me. Hands off! Don't blame me if you've –"

"We don't have time! Do you understand me?" His eyes bore in like drills, but Olybrius continued playing innocence.

"Perhaps if you told me the last time you saw –"

"He's not dead, Bizja! He's not dead. If you have it, he will find it, and he will kill you and he will kill me and my family –"

"What are you talking about? Who…?" Olybrius squinted, for a moment not yet understanding, then not *wanting* to understand. He smiled sadly. "…You should not come here drunk, Bazja. Not when you look so much like me –"

Orabas grabbed hold of his neck and drove into him even harder now. The wingback toppled. He rolled his brother once over and onto his back again.

"I am not drunk! I am not mad! He is here. You come with me to the Cathedral and you will see –"

"I told you to get your hands off me!"

"And I told you he is going to kill Anna –"

Orabas struck at him, but Olybrius ducked and the blow glanced off. His concern was less about the pain than his face; he didn't want bruises. He was also quickly reminded of his brother's strength. It wasn't just that the life he'd chosen had broadened and thickened him, but that there had always been something more animal in Orabas. While they grappled and rolled, Olybrius purposely hooked the bass of a standing screen to topple it, to make the racket that would bring the guards, which it did. They bolted in a moment later and pulled Orabas off him, or tried to. In the end it took five men to restrain him.

"He will come for you, Bizja!" he growled. "I will come for you!" He was practically frothing at the mouth, and it was only a well-trained chokehold that finally subdued him. He went purple, his temples bulging like plums before his eyes rolled.

"Get him out of here. Please."

"Where? Sir?"

Olybrius thought. It wouldn't do to have him dragged off the ship. Too many people outside. "Do you have anywhere on board? A cell?"

The guard confirmed, and Olybrius so ordered. "See that he's fed." He looked at his brother, already coming to. "But leave the coat."

They wrestled it off him and dragged him away. Olybrius went straight to the mirror to see if a welt was forming. There didn't appear to be, but it occurred to him that someone should probably go see about Vassago.

XV

The Gift

Inger was the wide-eyed one. During the whole of the car ride, which shortened the trip by a day at least, she'd been silenced by the speed, especially as they came nearer the city and roads got smoother and more wide. She nodded quietly, knowingly at the sight of the buildings in all their twilit glory. The lamps had just been lit along the sidewalks. Her lips didn't stop moving.

Margrét's lips were still. She was serene. Her back took comfort from the leather seat, having already come to accept that this was as it should, and would, be. She didn't quite feel that all this was *her due* exactly, but the sort of thing she was going to have to get used to, so best not to look too dreamy in the face of it.

Like Inger, for instance. She was halfway out the window, craning to see as they reached the boardwalk and the great ship came into view.

"Why, it's as tall as the buildings!" she exclaimed. "And look at the bridge! What happened to the bridge?"

Margrét shrugged. Whatever had happened to the bridge was supposed to happen obviously. The guards set up along the checkpoints noted the medallion of their driver and waved them on through, while the crowd strained to catch a glimpse of who was inside – what Lord, what Duchess? Calmly, graciously Margrét took the hands of the escorts as they guided her and Inger up the gangplank, not even turning to see that the porters were being careful with their trunks. Inger hadn't wanted to yield her duffel, or the dowry, but finally she relented and up they went, while all the people below could only keep wondering who.

As guests of state, they had been provided a suite as well, with canopied beds and crimson spreads of velvet and lace and flowers in vases, who knew where they'd grown. They had a bathroom of their own, with a standing tub; a waiting room with two silk couches and a roll-top writing desk. There was even a dollhouse four feet wide with little bowls of fruit inside that matched the bowls of fruit that they'd been left – with pears and pomegranates.

"When do the presentations begin?" asked Margrét.

"Hours," said her lady-in-waiting, Madame Giustine de Villiers-Lornyay, of Budapest. (Inger had three as well.) "You can rest."

"Are you hungry?"

"Are you thirsty?"

"Did you want to bathe now?"

No, Margrét shook her head, sitting before the mirror of her vanity, looking at herself and all of this in reflection: Inger in the bathroom. The tub was white porcelain with brass clawfeet, with a shelf of soaps and salts and perfumes on the wall beside.

"You go first," said Margrét. She could see that Inger wanted to. The ladies were already unpinning her hair, unbuttoning her dress. Finally all was as it should be, and everything that had happened before could be seen in its proper perspective, those countless, endless dreary days out on the heath. Even if they hadn't made sense at the time, she was proud of herself for having persevered.

"Might I try to find something more suitable?" asked Madame de Villiers-Lornyay, holding up the shoes that Oni-miiko had tried to fix for her.

"Of course" said Margrét. She was not ashamed. She would need more shoes. In Kyiv. She hoped he'd take her there. Or maybe St. Petersburg. St. Petersburg was supposed to be beautiful.

There was a knock at the door. Margrét knew better than to rise. Another of the ladies answered, and graciously accepted the offering of an unseen porter.

"It appears we have a secret admirer." Madame de Villiers-Lornyay presented it, a velvet box the shape of a half-moon.

"Did he say who it was from?" asked Margrét.

"It wouldn't be much of a secret, then, would it?"

The water swished in the tub as Inger sat up to see, but her lady-in-waiting kindly closed the door, which Margrét was thankful for. Privacy was in order, on both sides.

She took the box and right away remarked the weight. "It's heavy."

Madame de Villiers-Lornyay agreed.

Were her hands trembling, though, or was the thing inside? Margrét steadied herself, then opened it:

A necklace. Very simple. A silver chain with an unobtrusive setting, on which was mounted a gemstone the like of which Margrét had never seen – tear-shaped and white and roughly the length of her pinky.

"Hn," intoned Madame de Villiers-Lornyay, more curious than admiring, as if she had never seen such a thing either. "Moonstone? Maybe opal."

Margrét took it out and once again the weight impressed. The stone swung until she caught it. She held it in her palm to look at more closely. There was a kind of milkiness inside, that almost seemed to move like smoke if she let her eyes glaze.

"Quite lovely," the Madame concluded.

Margrét nodded, it was. And yet there was something about it that made her uncomfortable. Disturbed wasn't quite the word. More sad.

She took up the velvet box. There was no note. No clue.

"Shall we try it on?"

Margrét hesitated. She wasn't sure she should, but Madame de Villiers-Lornyay was already taking the necklace in hand. "I'm sure whoever sent it would be greatly disappointed if you didn't try."

She joined the clasp. The jewel lay in place heavily, comfortably, yet Margrét's uneasiness remained.

The Madame was aware. "It may be a bit high," she said. She made an adjustment behind and the jewel fell a half inch or so below where it had been. "There."

The height was better. Perfect, in fact. The gem's color likewise matched the white of her dress, the hint of green lifted from the sash. Yet it still felt strangely hot against her skin. Inger was sunk deep in the bath, sleeping as if she hadn't slept in years. Margrét was glad of that. She didn't want Inger to see. Yet. It wasn't that she didn't like the necklace. She couldn't think whether she liked it or not, only that it wasn't right, and that of all the things that had happened since the limousine had come, this was the first that she wished hadn't. This was the first thing that didn't fit.

"Now let me see about those shoes," said Madame de Villier's Lornyay. "I'm sure we can find something."

Margrét nodded, but her breathing felt shallow. Her head, light. She didn't even look in the mirror. To look upon the necklace was to know:

He would not have given this to her.

XVI

The Mob

The peregrine had been circling the ship, waiting for Orabas to emerge again. When she saw the other man, the one who looked so much like Orabas (but wasn't), stepping out on deck in the very coat Orabas had worn, she was not fooled. She turned on her wing and started for the Cathedral, back up the pier and into the concrete ravine that led directly to it.

She could see the dragon still crouched beside the spire of the eastern tower, his tail extending out over the edge and sweeping gently, as if to tease the crowd of people who had gathered below.

The bellringer had practically broken his neck descending the stairs again to report what he'd seen, breathlessly and stammering. The choirmaster suspected he had been dipping into the sacramental casks again. "Rats," one of the clerics had explained. "They can get quite big." But there was a growing number of witnesses on the street prepared to back up the brother's assertion – that was no rat up there. From across the lane they were pointing. Was it a statue, though? A gift of the new king? The children shook their heads. "It moved."

"Maybe it's his pet," they said, prompting chuckles.

A dozen or so intrepid souls had even ventured up the stairs of the western tower – not the one the creature had claimed, but the one across the way – so they could at least get a closer look. Lay and clergy alike, they strained to see through with deepening twilight. They peered as best they could, but still their minds would not admit what they were seeing. Something dark, with a glinting, plated, hide. Like a gargoyle, no? But an enormous one, and come to life. They could see it shift, and how the tail was curled and twitching almost, like an agitated cat. It was impatient. It seemed to be waiting for something, and now it was lifting its head at the approach of a small black bird (or small by comparison). A falcon of some kind was gliding up Kristiana Way. It ascended slightly as it came near and curled around over their heads, seeming to take an equal interest in the creature, whatever it was. The thing returned the falcon's purposeful glare. The two were trained upon each other, and as the bird completed its loop and swooped back down the way it came, the creature lifted up and heaved itself from the spire. It spread wings of its own, giving rise to gasps across the way and down below – how broad they were, the length of two trolleys at least. All watched the slight descent and recovery of the swooping black sails and the long lean body they carried. A length behind the falcon, it flew directly down the main avenue of the city, toward the Long Pier and the great ship docked in the harbor.

("See?" the children said. "He is the King's pet.")

And though the night had fallen completely by now, still the figure it cut was dark enough, large enough, that even the unsuspecting pedestrians turned up their heads to see – what was that passing over? Some flinched, and winced, even in that fleeting glimpse, aware that this was not like anything they had ever seen before. They ducked inside doorways and down little alleys, while others merely stood agape. A horse reared. Its carriage collided with a car. The drivers of both were looking skyward, pointing as well, joining in with the crowd from the Cathedral, the bold ones running in pursuit.

"Did you see?"

"What?"

No one knew. They ran after it as fast as they could, but the sweeping shadow was well ahead of them by now. It had reached the end of boulevard, where Kristiana ran into the boardwalk, but rather than follow its line out onto the pier, the winged thing took a sudden turn left along the bank.

The people raced to see, and they were large enough in number now, with the bicyclists and drivers joining, cabs and carriages and all the runners pointing frantically, that their approach caught the attention of the Royal Guard. Two watchmen were stationed at the starboard rail of the *Minarik*. The first passed his binoculars to the second.

"Look there, at the main way. What is that?"

The second peered through. They both could hear the yelling now.

"....Bring the men starboard and send word to the first checkpoint."

A moment later the field phone rang down at the first checkpoint, where the posted guards had just removed the barriers, as scheduled, to allow the people a closer look at His Majesty's ship – though the gathered crowd was also now aware of some turmoil headed this way. They turned too late to see the beast, but well in time to witness what appeared to be a running mob closing in.

The leaders had reached the boardwalk by now and were looking left – north, that is – to see if the creature was still in view. It was, if barely. It had kept to the shoreline right up to the foot of the bridge, then veered right to follow its line across the water. The people could see the flicker of the stanchion lights as its great wings strummed past, disappearing at the gap, then once again blotting the lamps one after another.

Like filings to a magnet, the people started across the street, despite the fact that the Royal Guards mid-pier were now taking up their arms, convinced that the approaching crowd was the very mob they'd been brought to fend. The people did not see. They were charging now, arms raised, running for the pier as if the barricades were not there. Look, they gestured. They pleaded. The beast had reached the far side of the river and was turning again, headed back this way along the far strand. It was rounding the bay, like a shark circling its prey.

"Look," they found their voices now, but the guards were unmoved, squinting down the barrels of their bolt action rifles.

XVII

The Reception

The main venue of the evening festivity, the "ballroom," sat right on top of *The Minarik* like a crown. The only thing separating it from the night itself was a line of doors, half of which had been opened to let in the evening breeze, the heaters having turned the hall into a hothouse. As such, the murmur of the crowds outside had been drifting in all day like the steady hush of waves, but this sudden surge of shouts and warnings did turn heads.

"Oh, shush," said the Duchess Voss, who (confusingly) had been thanking Olybrius again for his help out on the pier. She turned upon the open doors as if they were a child interrupting. "Really. Everybody is on. We need to finish this up and get off the dock."

Olybrius nodded, though the question remained, *was* everyone on board? He glanced over the Duchess's shoulder, but there was still no sign of Margrét, and now, in addition to the Duchess, there was a growing confusion of guests in the way. The ship's officers were shooing them away from the windows. General Zitri had signaled that the starboard doors be closed, while another of the event organizers – Monsieur Goulu – was instructing the orchestra to play a little louder. They did, just as another guest was being announced. Olybrius couldn't hear the name. It was the Duchess who remarked, "Did he just say Antayak?" She turned. "Who could be coming from the Uplands?"

Olybrius shifted and now he did see: it was Margrét. At last.

This was, in fact, his first glimpse of her since his visit to Five Homes. He had been trying to conjure her image ever since, with varying success. There were times the picture was vague, based only upon listed facts. The hair had been a reddish brown, yes? The face, heart shaped. That was the best he could do, while other times the image appeared to him in every detail, the precise shape of her eyes, the lift at the edges, the pattern of freckles, the way the veil had framed her face, the turn of the chin and the little scar upon it.

He had been imagining this moment as well, but right away he realized how pale his imagination had been. Had her hair been quite *that* copper color? Had the flush of her cheek been quite so violent? Or the green in her eye so simmering? Here the gown was white – he'd imagined that as well, but not so simple – with a satin empire waist, no train. No need.

Likewise, he realized he hadn't really looked at the jewel until now. On purpose. He'd glanced at it in the box to see that the setting sufficed, but he had wanted it to be a surprise to him as well as her. Could he have imagined such an effect? Pearls take their luster from skin, but this. It wasn't so much that the gem glowed. Rather, it imbued her entire figure with a kind of clarity that others in the room lacked. And that image, of them together – the jewel and the maiden – was instant vindication. Even his poor brother Bazja, crammed away below deck, imprisoned by his manic fears and delusions, would have seen: The gem had found its proper place, and use.

But he didn't want to think of that now. (He would go to his brother in the morning.) For now he would simply enjoy the fruit of his labor, this stunning image before him, and the happy inference it permitted, that in accepting his gift, and in presenting herself to the world with it around her neck, Margrét had accepted him as well.

He could see, in fact, that though she tried to keep her eye in a kind of mid-distance, pausing here and there to return the welcoming nods of the kingdom's court and society, she was searching the room. For him, no doubt, her mysterious benefactor. And so he did not move. He stayed right where he was and waited for her eye to find his.

§

Margrét did not see him – not at first, at least – because she was not looking for him. She was looking for someone older, in purple robes perhaps, someone wiser, with a longer face and a forked beard and large eyes the shape of almonds, but it wasn't easy amidst the profusion of opulence, of light and color, of pinks and creams and warm ambers, and cool royal blues shivering in through the windows. The room was glorious, ablaze with seven chandeliers as large as fishing boats, all reflected and shattered in a broad section of the ceiling, a skylight of paned glass that must have covered half its length.

In addition to the chandeliers, there were lamps and candelabra, thousands of flowers, and what felt like just as many faces looking back at her, all with the same question: Who? And her expression replied to each, which one of you? Where? She knew he would look different, of course. Older. Still she assumed she would recognize him.

Yet all she saw were the others. There was the General from the car, the one with the bushy mustache, and the ladies-in-waiting as well, Madame de Villiers-Lornyay and her cousin, to whom she curtsied and received a very approving nod of welcome. And over there by the bar, she knew him too, the man with the seeds, the messenger, and he was looking back at her so intently –

Her heart began to sink when –

THUNK!

Something struck the ship. From above.

Inger took her hand, but Margrét reflexively whisked it away. Not now.

But what was that? There were some in the hall who would later claim to have heard a kind of swooping sound just before impact, like the flap of giant flag, or a waffling sail. Maybe they did, but none – none but the most inebriated guests – could fail to have felt the initial jolt, and the great ship swaying a bit.

"What on earth?" asked the Duchess Voss.

The Duke tried calming her with a vague wave. "A whale."

"With wings?" She looked up at the roof, the glass half and then the beams.

"A flock of something?" someone else tried. "Heron? They are a pest this time of year."

Olybrius was not persuaded. But did they have men up there? He looked to Zitri, who'd felt the hit as well, and was headed for the exit. Monsieur Goulu was once again consulting with the conductor, who agreed. Three taps of the baton and up started the *purpuri* – a local version of the Schottische well known to most of the guests, and just the thing to calm the nerves. Within a bar most of them were nodding, setting aside their fans and their concerns, laughing at themselves. The ladies all headed to the near side of the hall, and the men to the far. Madame de Villiers-Lornyay was signaling to Margrét from across the room. *Come. Come join.* She was saving her place.

Margrét turned to Inger, was she joining as well?

But Inger, who looked pale all of a sudden, shook her head. "You go." She went to find a seat.

Up until the last few minutes, Inger had been doing not so badly, in fact. The bath had been bliss, and that mood had lingered through much of the dressing. Her hair was more or less as she'd planned, which was saying something, given its length. Really, she had been fine right up until their escort knocked on the door, at which point precisely a sickly feeling set in the pit of her stomach, born of a sudden realization that the assumption under which she had come here – that Theodosius would most certainly *not* be in attendance this evening – might be wrong. She'd had no idea until now the size of the affair, but now that she did, and now that the moment was at hand, it struck her as very likely that he *would* be here – indeed, that it would be inappropriate for him *not* to be – and if he were, then their having come had been a terrible, and perhaps even tragic, idea.

In the approximately two minutes it took her and Margrét to make their way from their suite up to the ballroom, Inger went from being merely deeply troubled, to being dreadful, until by the time they were actually ascending the carpeted stairs to the Main Reception Hall, she was in a stone cold panic, convinced that this all was a trap, and that she was leading Margrét right into it.

The atmosphere in the Main Hall certainly didn't help. All the shouting outside was strange and alarming. She could sense the nervousness among the guests, and now this sudden jolt. Far from snapping her out of her anxiety, it infected her all at once with a vivid sense that she and Margrét were being watched, that there was indeed a malevolent presence on board from which there was no hiding. Even as the music began and the others went off to dance, she felt distinctly as if her mind had been invaded, were being read and raided by that same dark thief.

§

Outside, the music drifted down, an off-hand mockery of what was now taking place on the pier. The crowd was teeming against the second barricade, so heedlessly that several more guards had turned their guns on them, and were commanding them to stay back, to halt, to go no further. Another turned the klieg on them directly, blasting them with a light that both shattered and emblazoned their expressions which, had the guards bothered to notice, conveyed no anger or defiance, but something more like fear and wonder − awe really, and all directed behind them, at the top of the ship.

Most of the guards were too clever to turn. Only one was duped. He saw there did appear to be something strange up there on the roof, a hulking shadow. And it moved.

He nudged the guard beside him. "What is that?"

"Just some old song."

"No, that. Look."

The second guard finally turned. He saw it too, leaning over the skylight.

"Is it a tarp?"

§

Margrét knew the steps. She had danced it many times at the fair in Tuvin, and therefore understood that the waltz-rhythm weave was bringing her ever closer to the hand of the man with the seeds. And he was looking back at her, returning a gaze of great appreciation and satisfaction. She didn't realize until she saw him there, wending his way toward her, taking and discarding the hands of various other ladies, how hard she had been trying *not* to think of him; trying not to think that of course, of course the invitation had come from *him*. And of course the necklace had come from him as well. She remembered his looking at her amulet, how his brow had knit.

But then why did she feel it so distinctly, that there was someone else? Another even keener pair of eyes upon her, burning the back of her neck? She continued to search the room, but there were only the weaving guests – the tulle and flowers and dinner jackets, officers' coats with medals and medallions, and here he was coming even closer now, the man with the seeds, the man she'd just assumed was the messenger, drawing nearer, his eyes fixed on her with a glazed, dreamy smile. She looked away, and there came a strange yelp, and the sound of broken glass.

A woman in the circle right next to her was falling back in a faint, but her last exertion was to point at the ceiling, at the sky-light windows. Margrét followed with her eye and saw: there was something up there, a shadow peering in, impossible to discern with the hall so bright and the night so dark, but it seemed too large to be real. The band kept playing, but now a beam of light struck this thing from the right side, and below. For just a moment, then, the figure was revealed, or half-revealed. The head alone must have been as large as the car they'd come in, and the shape wasn't so different – long snouted and rising, but more ornate, plated and horned. It was the face of a monster, grotesque and exquisite. Its eyes were like two great bulbs with flames inside, and they were peering down at her directly.

But she was not frightened, for did she not know these eyes already? She felt drawn by them, truly as if she were being lifted up by their sheer intensity, and the only thing that stopped her from leaving the floor was a sudden popping sound, also coming from the pier. The music stopped. There were shots ringing out. The creature turned. It drew up what look like an enormous black veil, there was that swooping sound again, and it was gone.

The popping continued, crackling against the night, a volley of automatic rifles, causing the guests within to swoon and to shout, "What now?" "What's going on down there?"

"Everyone please be calm." That was Zitri's second, Vilnius.

And now the ship was moving. That quickly, Admiral Kostitsin, *The Minarik's* captain, had made the decision to pull them out of dock. This was probably wise, but the momentous shift and the sudden blast of the horn only caused more guests to swoon and tumble. More yelps and screams went up.

Olybrius dodged his way to the window and looked down at the pier, which was bedlam now. The Royal Guard was entering the crowd with clubs. Some of the civilians were running, some fighting back, some were crumpled on the ground like blankets amidst the tugging and the beating and the staccato flash of gunfire.

He turned and began moving guests away so they wouldn't see. Already the officers and attendants were ushering the lords and ladies toward one of three doors, the largest of which led down to the main dining room, where presumably they could wait in safety until the disturbance had passed.

Inger was caught in the tide. She pushed and strained, frantically trying to get back to Margrét.

"Manga!" she called out. "Manga!"

But the girl was nowhere to be seen, and the crush of people was carrying Inger back and further back toward the door.

Margrét was caught up as well – surrounded, looking for Inger, and finding her, and losing sight of her again. She tried worming her way through, but a tremendous woman collapsed in front of her and the attendants came and she couldn't get round, and now there was a hand on her elbow. She turned.

It was the seed man. "Come with me."

She looked back at Inger, but one of the officers was already directing her out the main door.

"She'll be fine," said the man. "Come with me."

He quickly drew her out through another, smaller door, and down a flight of narrow stairs. She did not know where they were headed, except that it was the opposite side of the ship from where she and Inger were staying, which she didn't like. She did not like not knowing where she was, and her mind was still reeling from the image she had glimpsed in the skylight – had no one else seen? – and this, the realization that this man here, the one holding her hand, was clearly the only reason she was here.

He ushered her through another white door with a porthole window, down a hall and into a suite much larger than hers, though clearly decorated by the same eye. The same flowers were in the vases: Sea holly, Christmas rose.

But was he a prince? she wondered.

"We'll be safe here" he said. "I'm sorry about all this." He checked the window. The Long Pier was now a good ways off, teetering through the round frame. "Are you all right?"

"What was that thing?"

"What thing?"

"What they were shooting at. Did you not see? There was something on the roof."

He smiled. "The moon playing tricks. You needn't worry. We're safe. Here." He handed her a small glass of something dark amber, and clear. "It will calm your nerves."

She had never tasted wine, or any ferment. Just the whiff seemed to burn.

"It occurs to me I never properly introduced myself. I'm Lord Olybrius Korda of Dobrovo. The Provost."

"I don't know what that means," she said.

"The governor."

Still. "Of?"

"Well…of Ileya," he said, charmed.

She blushed at her own foolishness. The governor.

"I'm glad you were able to come," he said. "I hope the trip here wasn't too wearing. That's a long way."

"You sent the car?"

"I wanted to make sure, yes."

He looked down at the necklace, which confirmed it: the necklace was from him as well.

He smiled again. An attractive man – a handsome man, with handsome ways and postures, yet there was something about him that repelled her. Perhaps it was only that her heart was breaking.

"What's wrong?" he asked.

She surprised herself with what she did. She lifted the necklace over her head. "This is yours?" She held it out, but he didn't take it at first.

"But it's a gift." He smiled awkwardly. He looked like a boy almost. "I'm giving it to you."

As she shook her head, the gem did a kind of pirouette on its chain. He still would not take it.

"Is it that you fear you would be beholden?" he asked. "Then be beholden. That is what I want." He was bold. He had no desire in her presence other than to be frank, to tell her, to secure her. He reached out to take her hand when a knock came at the door. It was Vassago.

"What?"

"I beg your pardon, Sir. M'm'selle. There's a meeting in the Map Room."

"Who?"

"All the officers," Vassago replied.

"May I go?" asked Margrét, taking away her hand. "Back to my room?"

"Of course," said Olybrius. He turned to the steward. "Would you see Lady Margrét back to her suite?"

Before he had the chance to refuse it again, she quickly set the necklace in his hand. It nearly dropped, but he caught it, by which time she had swept out of the suite.

He looked down at the gemstone, and her refusal. Strangely his mind turned to Bazja, as though his brother were somehow to blame.

XVIII

The Starets

B y the time Olybrius got himself back up to the Map Room, most of the other ship's officers and city officials were already there. Chief of Police Markus, and General Zitri, of course; his lieutenant, Vilnius; the ship's captain, Admiral Kostitsin was standing in back, elegant as always, hands behind his back, and sporting a luxurious white mustache that flowed into his sideburns.

There were a handful of others, but it was Zitri who appeared to be running the meeting. He was interrogating one of the officers from the pier, a Royal Guard, who was saying that the mob had initially come down Kristiana Way.

"From the Cathedral?"

"We think so, Sir."

Olybrius slid up beside Markus and whispered: "His Majesty?"

Markus shook his head, but indicated His Majesty's apparent proxy, the evening's organizer Goulu, who was looking oddly content over by the arched window, plump-cheeked and with that tight black curl in the middle of his forehead. Silly looking man.

"Were they armed?" asked another, not so silly looking at all, though Olybrius couldn't place him at first, the light in that part of the room was so dim. He wore a long black tunic with a high collar and golden rope at the waist that gave him the look of a religious pilgrim.

"Were they?" he asked again.

Zitri sniffed, "It certainly sounded like it –"

"Who fired the first shots?" the man followed.

(Olybrius leaned into Markus ear again: "And who is that?

Markus shook his head, "Ship's pastor?"

No, it wasn't the ship's pastor. The Ship's Pastor was Mueller, the German.)

"...We're not sure," replied the Royal Guard.

"But why is this even a question?" Zitri put in gruffly. "We all know what happened. You set up a bulls-eye in the middle of a crowd, someone is going to take a shot at it." He turned to Markus. "What can you tell us about the street?"

"We've sent out three brigades, around the Cathedral and the University."

Zitri approved. "And obviously we can provide reinforcement tomorrow." Tomorrow was to have been the parade and the air show, in preparation for which three brigades were due to arrive by mid-morning.

"And what of the parade?" asked Olybrius. "Has that been called off?"

"That would be up to you," said Zitri.

The room turned expectantly. Olybrius pondered.

"Casualties?"

"None," said Zitri, "among the guard. Among the protestors, three."

"Dead?"

Zitri nodded.

"And how many arrested?"

Zitri looked to Markus again. "Thirteen?"

Thirteen was correct.

The room waited for his verdict, though Olybrius was most aware of the man in the black robe, who'd stepped further out into the light, and who seemed to be almost amused by the calculation taking place.

"I think we should postpone," said Olybrius finally.

The room agreed, the holy man included, though now he seemed to be wanting Olybrius's attention for some reason – a more private one. Olybrius turned to Kostitsin first. "And how soon do we return to port?"

"Not until morning."

"Morning?"

"We have room to accommodate," said Kostitsin calmly. "We also have His Majesty on board. And right now, this is the safest place in Kreisenig."

Olybrius wasn't so sure of that, but they *were* on the Admiral's ship.

Zitri crossed to Markus at this point, which seemed to adjourn the meeting for the time being, or to relax it. Olybrius turned back to the man in the black robe, who he was now fairly sure was a Starets of some kind. There used to be one who showed up at Debrovo from time to time, back when his grandmother was still alive – a kind of seer and spiritual advisor whom he had always found unnerving; probably because the groundsman used to say he could read minds.

This one here seemed at least partially aware of the Provost's concern, and with a quick tilt of his head, suggested a neutral corner. They met beside his Majesty's nautical globe, and by the lamp that sunned its northern hemisphere, Olybrius got a better look at his face: a high, proud forehead, pronounced by the tight pull of his jet-black hair. His eyes were deep set beneath a slightly prehensile brow. His mouth was broad, firm, and content.

Olybrius spoke first. "I don't believe we've officially met."

"You are the Provost, Olybrius Korda." He bowed. "And I am an emissary from Kyiv, advisor to his Holiness."

Olybrius paused. "The Bishop Theodosius?"

"The same."

The man had come from Margrét father.

"How is he doing?" asked Olybrius, fumbling suddenly. "I had heard he wasn't well –"

"Well enough," said the Starets. "So am I correct in thinking it was you who invited Lady Margrét?"

"Yes," Olybrius replied, suddenly appalled at his own heedlessness. He assumed her guardians would have cleared the invitation with her father. "I hope there isn't a problem."

The tilt of the Starets's head indicated there might be.

Again Olybrius replied, "You'd do me great service if you report back to His Grace that she was never in harm's way and that every precaution has been –"

"That's hardly the point."

"As I say, we can post more guards at her door right, if that would –"

"Our concern is not that she needs guards, Provost Korda. It's that she needs to *be guarded*."

Olybrius paused. "Excuse me?"

The Starets smiled. "You didn't expect the devil to come unmasked now, did you?"

"But we are talking about Lady Margrét, his dau –"

"A demon and a succubus –" the Starets cut him off, but with an equanimity that belied the violence of his words.

"Excuse me –"

"– a cursed thing," he said, "raised in a cursed way. I shouldn't think one needs further proof than what has taken place this evening." He pointed to the window, and now looked back at Olybrius with the same unruffled expression. "You've gone and tampered with a locked box, Provost Korda. Never a good idea."

"May I ask, on whose behalf are you speaking right now?"

"Yours. Where is she?"

"In her quarters."

"And you said you'd posted a guard."

"Yes."

"Make it two. And I'll speak to her in the morning."

Olybrius was speechless.

"Until then, let's keep this between the two of us. I believe your attention is needed elsewhere."

With that, the Starets bowed – to a depth that might have been considered ridiculous – and withdrew from the room with all the stealth of a passing shadow.

Olybrius was still stunned, but it was true. The circle by the window was gesturing for him to come join. Zitri, Markus, and Kostitsin needed to discuss contingencies for the parade.

XIX
Night (I) – Olybrius

The ball was cancelled, of course – His Majesty never emerged – but the ship was still heavy with guests and food and entertainments, all of which found their way, by various natural divisions down into the smaller venues, dining rooms and pool rooms, guest suites and steam baths. The orchestra split up into smaller ensembles that played variously in His Majesty's private Salon, the Officers' dining room, and the Chess Room, while the most raucous dance of the night was said to have been had by the staff, who borrowed three players from the orchestra and convened down next to the boilers.

Olybrius returned to his suite. So many bewildering things had happened the last several hours he expected he might be exhausted. He wished he were, but he wasn't. Vassago brought him nutmeg and vodka but it didn't seem to do any good. There were too many places his mind could go – his brother's appearance, Margrét's rebuke, the incident on the pier, and now this, this last bit of madness from the High Priest's advisor, the Starets. Had he actually called her the devil?

And that was to say nothing of the gem. He felt its presence distinctly, like a glowing humming buzzing coal on the countertop. How could he possibly sleep with that in the room?

It didn't seem safe just leaving it there, however, so just before leaving again he plopped it in his pocket, chain and all, and set off, perhaps not as aware as he should have been that Vassago's potion was finally taking effect.

His purpose (at the outset) was simply to keep moving, to tire himself. He strolled the upper deck, conducting rounds. He could hear guests below, the laughter and the music. They were like ghosts, haunting the ship everywhere, but happily.

Out in the distance the city was a copse of streetlamps, but all still and quiet now, innocent. Likewise the river, bouncing up the moonlight as it did every night. The hills lurked. The gap-toothed bridge yawned, the mountains looming behind. And the moon, the real moon, an unwavering round saucer above, foiling the night. Was she the culprit? Had she cast her spell again? Was her uncommon light the alibi they'd use, the same as served for wolves and owls? Why not students? For preying on their suspicions, coaxing them to believe what they wanted to believe.

And who was to say he hadn't fallen prey as well? To it. To her. At that moment, standing out there on deck, the moon and the maiden seemed to be one and the same – reflections of each other. Of course, he lent no credence to what the Starets had said. A 'succubus'. What talk. That only confirmed the things he'd heard (but hadn't mentioned), which was that Theodosius was unhinged – a monster to work for. Just as well that the Starets would go and see her in the morning, see the truth, that she was no cursed thing. An enchantress, yes. He'd got that from the moment he first laid eyes on her. It had been a downright physical effect, as it was now – this quickening of his heart, of his blood and breath. This lightness in the head.

He could feel her – down below, in her room – and he knew in his heart that if she'd left her door open so much as a crack, he would have gone. He would have run. But the door was closed – he knew that, too – and that was puzzling, wasn't it? Her curious resistance, for it didn't seem possible, given the effect she had upon him, that she didn't share the feeling somehow. Why else would she have come? No, deep inside her was the very same passion that she had stoked in him. He knew that. The fact that she resisted only went to show that she was frightened, which he understood. Such feelings were frightening, and she was young. He would simply have to help her find it. Coax it, but more slowly. It had been madness, really, giving her the gem up front. She would have it eventually – he knew that, too – and they would laugh. But here, tonight, it had clearly been too much, too soon.

But now, of course, his mind having touched on the subject of the jewel, Olybrius could not stop the next thought from entering. It skulked inside, unnamed at first, a furrow of concern – the thing that he would rather not consider – but of course, of course, he might as well just go and admit it, give it a name, it had a name, and the name was Bazja. Poor Bazja. (Shoo, bird. A bird had landed on the rail beside him.)

But poor Bazja. Olybrius could hardly bear the thought of him down there wherever he was, wherever they'd put him. For in fact he had to admit he wasn't so surprised by what he had seen this evening. Bazja had always had those susceptibilities. He just *was* a simpler soul, and that had always been his strength, the brute force of his thinking, the way he could not be swayed. He was a mule – in all the good ways – but it was that same stubbornness, Olybrius hated to say, that had kept him from ever really growing up.

He remembered how they used to lay on the floor of Iso-Aitti's tea house, head to head, flipping through the Squire's book, the *Tales of the Questor Naberius*. Olybrius had known it was all in fun – a rainy day fancy. The book was a rank forgery. But they would still read the passages aloud to each other – or Olybrius really did most of the reading, while Orabas drew maps based upon the descriptions and fragments inside, and copied them over, and spoke of what they would do when they traveled up north together, just the two of them, to find the lair, find the dragon, slay it, smear its blood all over their bodies, eat its heart for dinner. Olybrius played along. He believed it all, in the way a child does, which is to say that he knew he was believing, choosing to believe, suspending disbelief. Bazja, on the other hand? It sounded as if he was still there, drawing his maps.

And of course that had to do with the Uplands as well, the woods, the Bend. Clearly all that isolation, the constant need to fend and defend his little wooden castle had only preyed upon his fears, that the world really was filled with creeping, predatory, salivating monsters. Olybrius wished his brother well. He'd have prayed for him if he thought prayer would do any good, but he worried. He was worried. He should go find him, in fact – now – but he didn't even know where Bazja was. He should find that out. Now, yes now, and leave the deck to this pestering immovable bird

He staggered back inside. He found a porter and asked if he knew where his brother was. The porter did not, but directed him to the nearest Royal Guard, who might. The Royal Guard offered to escort the provost, but the provost said no, he would find the way himself. He got lost on the way down; he was following his nose. He passed the dance in the boiler room, the diners in the King's Salon (the King was not there). He found a petty officer and was asking him, did he know where his brother was, when he saw a card game under way in one of the lounges.

"What's this?"

More officers, and bottles. The men saw him as well, saw his interest and that he was listing slightly. They pulled out a chair for him.

"Governor. Please." The room stood. He staggered in and fell to his seat. They set him up with a glass, a cigar, and three hundred kroner' worth of chips.

He had never been much interested in gambling. He liked to think of himself as more of a chess man. No fan of chance, but the game this evening turned out to be just the thing, a perfect distraction from the slew of questions he preferred not to think of right now.

Of course, some could not be avoided. The officers asked if the students were behind the incident on the pier. Olybrius would neither confirm or deny, but couldn't help getting in a few digs. "Bunch of silver spooners," he called them. What did they know of the 'old way'? The names of a few heathen gods, and recipes for stale bread.

"By the way," he asked, semi-belching, "does anyone here know why Barbarians were first called Barbarians?"

The other players looked around at each other, a blank. One ventured, "Wasn't it because they spent all day talking to the sheep. *'Baaa-Baaa'*. Baabaarian."

"Oh," said Olybrius. "...I hadn't heard that...that's clever...In any case, the point is they'll do fine, as long as the students don't get in the way." He raised; three sevens. "Don't they see? Someone was going to profit. Eventually even the Sud were going to find those hills, and they certainly weren't going to make any deals, give away a piece. These students, if they'd just shut up and let someone who knows what he's talking about do their bidding, they'd see. Everybody wins this way ..."

This went on, with Olybrius saying things he probably shouldn't have and the other officers not stopping him. They might have taken more pleasure at the governor's evident inebriation, except that he concluded the speech by slapping down a full house and taking his first pot of the evening.

"And does no one hear that, by the way?"

Hear what? No one was sure.

"That...That thumping...

They paused.

"...There."

They did, now. Hidden in amongst all the music, the dancing and eating and laughter, there was the slow pulse of a much louder *thunk*.

"What is that?"

"...Whatever it is," said one of the officers, "I hope she's wearing a helmet."

Olybrius wasn't a hundred percent sure why this was so funny, but the table roared with laughter and the laughter seemed to dissolve any sense of menace. What trouble could come from something that was so easily ridiculed? Helmet indeed. Olybrius laughed too.

He was in a good mood now, and why not? His early win was no fluke. He won the next hand as well, and the hand after that. In fact, over the course of the next two hours or so, the Provost proceeded to divest the rest of the table of nearly all their chips. Others came and sat and were likewise cleaned, all while he kept up a steady offering of slurred and at points inane chatter about the students. He mimicked the "old tongue," much to the delight of the Sylkan officers, who likewise considered the language akin to baby talk.

He won again. He barely noticed the slow thumping anymore; it was the steady drumbeat of his triumph. One hand after another, he was dealt right into the catbird seat, and even when he played sloppily – which he did – he managed to pull the cards he needed. Twice he drew to an inside straight. No one said anything, but the table was certainly aware – they kept filling and refilling his glass, but the more he drank, the more pronounced the effect was: three kings became four. Two pair became a full house. It got to the point that he actually began folding good hands so as not to draw attention to himself: dealt three nines, he gave one away. He didn't fear. He knew he'd be dealt another, better hand next time, and he knew why. It was obvious. The stone in his pocket – the priceless gem – the unplayed bid that none could match. Just having it there was like a charm.

Of course, he also knew that it wasn't good form, cleaning out the junior officers like that, taking advantage, so when he felt he'd had his fun and the pillow beckoned, he threw the last few hands, tipped the barman mightily, and excused himself. He didn't actually remember any of this, didn't remember finding his way back to his suite, or whether that thump was still going. He may or may not have instructed the hall guard to release his brother first thing in the morning – he certainly meant to, but it was all a blur. His last thought was that he would see the girl again in the daylight. And fix this. Nothing good comes easy. With his boots still on he collapsed onto his bed and almost instantly fell into a deep and dreamless sleep.

XX

Night (II) – Margrét

Margrét did dream.

By the time she got back to her room, not only was Inger there, but Madame de Villiers-Lornyay as well, as well as a younger cousin of hers – Margrét didn't quite get the name. Irise? Virginie? They had come to check on her, to see that she had made it back safe, and to invite her (and Inger, of course) to come to the salon of Madame Markus, who was apparently hosting a smaller gathering in her suite. Senor Assengi might even sing for them.

Margrét declined. Inger had already arranged that their meal be brought to their suite, but Madame de Villiers-Lornyay and her younger cousin kindly stayed with them, and were joined by a Madame Aarkonnen and then a Baroness of some kind, from Poland, come to see the new young woman. All lingered even after the dinner did arrive – plates of lamb, asparagus and potato, but just for the two of them, Margrét and Inger; the others would wait. Wine was offered. The ladies accepted. Margrét declined, as Inger was there and the burn of the Provost's sherry still lingered. She had tea.

Madame de Villiers-Lornyay did not mention it aloud, but her eyes inquired about the necklace, which she'd noticed Margrét was no longer wearing. Margrét replied with a glance over at the box in which it had been delivered. The Madame tilted her head, probably wise.

"So had you met the Provost?" asked the Polish woman.

"Only once," said Margrét.

"Really? You make quite an impression." She glanced over wistfully at the niece, Irise or Virginie, who merely turned away.

They continued to talk about the Provost, how quickly he had risen, how capable he was, and handsome, while Margrét gazed. She doubted she had ever seen someone quite so beautiful as the cousin.

She had the neck of a swan, and Margrét looked at *her* necklace – blue. Was that lapis lazuli, then? She had never seen it in person. She wondered who had given it to her, or how quickly the cousin would have removed it in exchange for the one that Margrét had just shoved back at the Provost, the dashing young prince.

"Well, I've known him since he was a boy," Madame de Villiers-Lornyay was saying. "His father was very handsome too."

Margrét managed a smile.

Not once did any of them mention what had happened on the pier, much less the shadow in the skylight. Margrét assumed she was the only one who saw, which seemed to settle the question. There had been no creature. The moon *had* played tricks. Here they were more interested in talking about the scandal of Lady So-and-so's coming or not coming – or exactly how old the Provost was, twenty-six or twenty-seven. Twenty-seven, said the Madame, now sending glances over at Inger as well, the point of which seemed equally clear, that Margrét wasn't the only one who stood to benefit from their entertaining the Governor's interest.

Inger was having none of it. She seemed quite agitated, and didn't utter a word until after all the ladies had bustled away to Madame Markus's, where Senor Assengi the tenor had apparently just arrived.

Inger's first concern was the necklace. "What did you do with it?" She knew very well Margrét hadn't just returned it to the box.

"I gave it back."

Inger agreed with this. "We'll go in the morning. First boat."

Margrét wasn't sure why Inger seemed so disturbed, but didn't protest. They prepared for bed in silence, undressing and folding their clothes, while the voices, the laughter and the music murmured all around them, like those same ghosts.

Their beds were in separate rooms of the suite, but Inger came in and lay down on the long divan near the foot of Margrét's. For a while they lay in silence. Margrét did not mention the creature to Inger either, or the moon.

"…I'm sorry," she said out of nowhere. She couldn't have said what for. For everything.

"Shshsh," replied Inger. "Sleep."

Margrét tried. She tried just to feel the covers, the slight sway of the ship.   She closed her eyes, and it flashed through her mind that she had been too quick with the Provost, not because she felt anything warm toward him – she still didn't – and not because he clearly wielded power – as the ladies had made clear – but because …why? Because he might at least know her father. She tried to think of him now, to picture him, when Inger began to sing:

> *Then began I to bloom,*
> *To be wise, to grow and to thrive…*

One of Odin's songs. Inger's voice was not always true, but had a pleasing, reedy tone to it, and it did well to take Margrét's mind away.

> *Word came to me*
> *From word,*
> *Deed came to me*
> *From deed…*

No face would come to her – not the Provost's, not her father's, not the shadow in the ceiling. Her thoughts turned wearily to the sheep in the stable, to Nella and to Yosi. Had she been permitted to give them away, she wondered…her thoughts made little sense, but it was of them that she was thinking, of the sheep back in the fold, when she finally drifted off.

Inger kept on with her song even after Margrét's breathing grew even and slow. She kept humming, leaving out the words, her eyes fixed on the knob of the door, fearing that any moment it might turn.

§

ASMODEUS

Margrét dreamt she was sleeping in the limbs of the oak tree, but it was not dead. It was green and full, and when she opened her eyes it pulled its roots from the ground, wrested free and began to fly. And none of this was new. As always when this happened, she remembered this happened often – this could happen whenever she liked, if she only remembered, but she kept forgetting that she and the tree would fly. Why did she always forget? Because maybe it was better that the others did not know – how often they flew, or swam together; how many times before they had come this high, and she could feel they were reaching their peak. The limbs held her closer, and she realized (again, not for the first time) the limbs were not leaves and branches but hands and arms. They were flesh, but of a different, thicker kind than her own. It did not matter. Together they began to fall, not desperately, and without panic. They fell and she did not know which limbs were hers and which belonged to him, and though they were now spiraling, plummeting, she felt no fear. She was not cold. Her heart was beating too fast, too hot, and the warmth was growing inside her, spreading out to her skin...

XXI
Night (III) – Orabas

Orabas neither dreamt nor slept.

In fact, the intermittent drumbeat, the persistent but too-slow-to-be-quite-rhythmic thumping that Olybrius had heard while playing cards was not the pipes at all, or anchor chains, or the helmeted head of some unlucky mistress. It was Orabas escaping.

The petty officer's earlier assurance to Olybrius notwithstanding, the *Minarik* had no official brig or holding pen; it was a cruise ship. The closest thing – other than the cage for his Majesty's two borzois – was a little annex behind the meat closet where the crew had taken to stashing vodka, dirty books and noobs. The royal guards had taken Orabas directly there and thrown him in, just as he was beginning to rouse.

It was more of a cranny than a room, seven by five and sloped – a steamer trunk and a small porthole, riveted all the way around, painted shut, and facing away from the pier. The two guards closed him in, double-bolted the door, chair bolted it then clomped back to the far side of the locker, bolted that door twice, and presumably assumed their post in the relative warmth of the inner corridor.

Here in his little cell he could see his breath, but it didn't matter – he was too livid to be cold. He stalked as much as the space would allow – two paces this way and back. He cursed himself. He should have killed the dragon when he had the chance. He should have strangled it. He could now, books be damned. He could have ripped its hideous head from the body. He could have done the same to Olybrius, but what good would it have done? He needed the jewel and he knew the jewel was here. He knew the woman was here. Of course she was. He could hear the music. A ball. What better setting?

Helpless, hopeless, he sat. The bass notes thumped, the tuba *oompahed*, and the guests mingled, chuckled. He buried his head in his arms, he couldn't listen. He tried to pray but he could not pray. To whom would he have prayed? Back home at the Bend it was clear, clear to him now, at least: his thoughts, his fears, his petition, his peace and gratitude all were directed at the shamir, and all were heard, or had been heard until yesterday. The jewel was both his charge and his keeper. But what was there to pray to now? To whom would he beg for mercy? Who would hear? Only the wyrm.

This had been his very thought when the beast had landed. Orabas felt the sudden jolt. He could hear that swoon among the guests all the way up in the ballroom. He went to the bolted door and spoke through the jam.

"What was that?"

There was no answer. The guards were two doors and a frigid meat locker away, but he could feel that Modo was on the ship. And now there was shouting outside. He went to the porthole but it was facing the wrong way, the factory side. All he could see was the black water and the moon between the even blacker smokestacks.

The shots rang out, and the volleys followed. He was helpless. Screams and howls, and then another lurching. Orabas even heard the wings this time; he knew the sound. The dragon was gone, but the ball room and the Long Pier were in chaos, at least to judge by the muffled cries and trampling. And now the ship was moving. The black buoy was sliding from view.

He had to get off. He thought of the dragon flying; he knew where it was headed. If it could not find satisfaction here, then it was bound for Maren and Anna.

He considered the door. Even if he did get through, that way was a gauntlet with guns. He turned to the porthole again – double plated, plastic laminated, and set in a brass ring the size of a dessert dish bolted around, inside and out. The wall looked to be at least six inches thick. Cedar, but the only way, and the only battering ram was the old steamer trunk. There were books inside. He didn't remove them. He kept them in for weight, but hoisted the trunk up onto his shoulder – sixty pounds at least – then drove it as hard as he could at the porthole.

The glass broke, but otherwise the frame didn't budge. He lifted the trunk up over his head this time, and once again smashed it into the porthole with all his might. Still nothing. Five times more he repeated the blow before stopping to assess the damage:

A hairline crack in the paint.

But now he heard a sound in the locker. Footsteps. He put down the steamer. He caught his breath. "Hello?"

"Hello."

He didn't recognize the voice. "We've left port?"

"Yes."

He assumed it was a guard, but this one seemed larger than the others.

"What was that on the ship?"

"No one knows," said the voice.

"But did anyone see it?" asked Orabas. "Because I know what it was! You have to let me out!"

The guard said nothing, but Orabas could tell he was still behind the door. He could feel him.

"Is that what they were shooting at? Did they kill it?"

"No."

"Where did it go?"

"Who knows? North."

"North? Is that what you saw?" He heard the tread of more boots. Two more guards at least.

"I have to go," said the voice.

"Wait. You have to let me out!"

But it was too late. "He's fine," the stranger's voice said to the others. "He'll be fine until morning," and with that, all three clomped away.

Orabas turned back to the porthole. He didn't think. He took up the steamer trunk and began pounding at the ring, over and over again. He did not stop. When the trunk fell to the floor, he heaved it up onto his shoulder again, and drove it even harder.

ASMODEUS

His knuckles were bleeding, shredded. He felt no pain. He felt no weariness. He closed his eyes and pictured the cedar wood, the tiny fractures spreading with each blow. A splinter flew from underneath the brass rim. He took the iron rod from the curtain and smashed the bar through the second plate, then he began hacking at brass ring, over and over. He wedged the bar under and yanked with all his might. He hammered at it from the top, from the side. He took up the steamer again and used it as a ram, and slowly, slowly, slowly but clearly the cedar and the brass did begin to yield, not so much to the power of any single blow as to the certainty of each next return, and the immutable sense of purpose behind them. Whatever this thing was, pounding away, whatever force was driving this beast with the bleeding hands, the bursting sweat and hot breath, it was not near giving up. A good hour into the beating, it was driving and hacking harder than it had been at the start, and so in fact the cedar began to soften and to splinter, and the brass, in recognition of the same, grew warm and pliant. It even began to glow.

XXII

The Pond

Since the violence of the night before had been more or less contained to the pier, Captain Markus saw no need to declare any sort of curfew or city-wide crackdown, as Zitri had advised. To be safe, more soldiers were sent out to patrol the streets. Otherwise the city woke up and went to work, and those who hadn't heard the news, heard the news. From shop to shop and stall to stall and inside the trolleys, the rumors flew and changed and flipped and flipped again.

Predictably, the University was a hub and a hotbed. There had been a number of students on the pier at the time of the shooting. More had come to collect the bodies, and they had also managed to crank out a special emergency edition of the underground broadsheet, the *Lùr* – named after the Viking Horn – just in time for the morning rush. The headline read:

MASSACRE ON THE PIER!

Admittedly, this was an overstatement, given that the *Lùr*'s numbers matched those reported the night before in the Map Room: three dead (a cabdriver, a factory man, and a schoolteacher); thirteen arrested. The point was that the new Royal Guard had opened fire on unarmed civilians for no ostensible cause. "Savagery" the lead editorial called it. "A brazen act of cowardice and violence perpetrated against innocents."

The editors were less bold in suggesting why the people had rushed the pier in the first place. Notably absent was any mention of the word "dragon," despite the fact that many witnesses had insisted that that was precisely what they had seen – a demon in the flesh, whose sudden appearance they attributed directly to the presence of

His Majesty. Either the wyrm was his pet or it was Modo himself, the ancient dragon who, according to legend, had killed more than his share of presumptuous, interloping Kings.

None of this found its way into the paper, the editors not wanting to taint their greater purpose with reference to what were, to say the least, incredible ideas. A sidebar did report that something unidentified had caught the attention of the crowd – first atop the Cathedral, then landing on His Majesty's ship – but what it was exactly no one knew. Unnamed witnesses referred to it variously as "a large bat," a "condor," and "a windblown sail or tarp," which made a certain amount of sense. It had been a blustery night.

The more pressing concern for now – to the editors, at least – was the fate of the people on the boat. As of the first printing, no one had yet been allowed off, the clear and most dreadful inference being that the passengers were being held as prisoners for some reason, or ransomed, and that the whole reception had been a ruse designed to lure the leaders of the city off to some neo-Babylonian captivity, leaving behind the workers to do the dirty work of stripping the mines up north.

Such were the suspicions expressed in the lone opinion piece, attributed to the editor in chief, U. Ovechkin. The tone was one of open defiance and no fear. "If the purpose of the act is to exact some sort of price, the new regime can be assured, a price will be paid."

A demonstration of solidarity with the victims was scheduled for noon at the waterfront.

§

To be fair, this idea that the new regime was actually holding Ileyan citizens captive was based upon more than just a close reading of the Hebrew Bible. The *Minarik* had not returned to port as promised. It remained anchored out in the middle of the harbor, and late-night reports that boats would be headed to the pier as early as 7 AM were turning out either to have been lies or unfounded. No such boats had materialized.

On the ship itself, the air of mystery was just as thick. Inger was up well before Margrét, trying to find out what she could. One of her ladies-in-waiting had received word that boats were already taking guests back to the pier, but now another was saying that all transport to the mainland had been cancelled for some reason. Certain of the guests were negotiating, bribing, doing whatever they could to get off. That was enough for Inger. If anyone was leaving the ship this morning, she and Margrét would be among them.

It was, therefore, to the sound of Inger packing up their things that Margrét awakened. She could hear the drawers and purposeful footsteps through the door, but she did not rise. She felt strangely raw. She remembered nothing of her dream. A lingering sense of shame, but that was nothing new – she felt tired and sad. She could barely lift her head.

Inger entered. "We have to go." She handed her a brioche. Her hair was back the way she always wore it, in braided buns.

"Where?"

"Back." She hoisted Margrét's dowry up onto the bed and began folding the dress. "Come. Up. The first boat is leaving."

"Stop doing that."

"These things aren't ours." She set aside the shoes. "We must get what's ours and go."

Margrét still did not rise. She couldn't. It wasn't that she wanted to stay here. She didn't, but she didn't want to go back to Five Homes either. Just the idea made her want to bury her head beneath the pillow and dive deep away, far away.

"Manga, come!"

"No."

"You speak to me this way."

"Go!" she shouted into the mattress.

Inger scoffed. "I go? And what becomes of you? You stow away on the King's boat?"

"I don't have to stow away." Margrét sat up. "I have places. Madame de Vi-"

Inger scoffed again. "You invite yourself into her home."

ASMODEUS

"I do."

"Or his, you mean. We did not bring you down her to be a toy for some prince."

"He's not a prince! And what are you saying? That I should go with you and follow sheep for the rest of my life?"

"I say that you should get off this boat! This is not a safe place, Manga. This is not a good place." But now she stopped her folding. There was a knock at the door. "That's them. Put this on."

She flung a robe at Margrét's bed and went to answer, straightening her apron and her hair before turning the knob. It wasn't whoever she had been expecting, though. It was one of the Royal Guard, and there was someone else whom Margrét couldn't see. They spoke in hushed tones for a moment – Margrét dreaded that it might be the Provost – but when they entered the suite, she was relieved to see that it was someone else, someone she had never seen before.

A holy man, he seemed to be. He was wearing a long black robe with a golden rope at the waste. In fact he wasn't so much taller than the others, but as he leaned in through the door of her chamber, he seemed somehow too large for the space.

"May I have a word?"

"Just a word," said Inger, trailing. "We have to go. And you don't go in alone." To be with Margrét unchaperoned, she meant. She tugged free from the driver, but now the holy man turned to look at her and she stopped cold. Something in his eye seemed to chill her, then just as quickly to subdue her.

"You will wait outside," he said, and Margrét had no doubt now: he was a shaman, or a 'Seidre' as they were sometimes called. She had read of them in one of Oni-miiko's books. He signaled the steward, who took Inger away, as limp as a kerchief. The door clicked shut and there was just the two of them – Margrét and the holy man. By casual strides he rounded the room, which seemed awfully small all of a sudden, and as the light touched each plain of his face, she realized there was something else about him. He seemed familiar.

"I just have a few questions," he said. His voice was calm. "You may sit."

She did. He did not. He stopped and stood before her, looking down, smiling – as if he were a diver and she the pond. That is how *she* felt.

"Who invited you?"

"I don't know."

"The Provost?"

"I think so."

"How do you know him?"

"I don't. He came to my village."

"You had never seen him before then?"

"No."

"And he gave you the necklace?"

"Yes."

"Where is the necklace now?"

"I don't know."

He looked at her to see if this was true, which it was. "Why don't you know?"

"Because I gave it back."

"You gave it back?" He squinted at her, smiling.

"Yes."

"Did he *ask* you to give it back to him?"

"No."

He let with a gentle sniff – more impressed than dismissive. He clicked open the door and spoke to the guard in the other room. "Keep her here."

"What for?" she asked. "For how long?"

"Was there somewhere you wanted to go?"

He asked as if he knew the answer, as if he had heard her thinking before. Then he bowed and left her there in the custody of the guard, though the room seemed strangely empty now.

XXIII

Morning

Vassago had brought breakfast directly to Olybrius's suite – a bowl of fruit and one whole pot of coffee to soften the various blows, the dull ones that had been pounding in the provost's head from the moment he opened his eyes, but also the two others that his trusted steward was now obliged to deliver. Olybrius could tell just from the expression on Vassago's face – the curiously droll slant of his eyes whenever there was bad news.

"What?"

"First..." He poured a cup. "...You should know there has been an attempt on His Majesty's life."

"What?"

"According to Admiral Kostitsin –"

Olybrius held up his hand to stop him. "Perhaps outside. I think I'd like some air."

Vassago agreed and they proceeded gently. The Provost's throat felt raw; his bones brittle, as if they'd been tapped dry. On fragile steps they found their way up and out onto the Admiral's Deck.

Last night's winds had died down but it was still chilly. The sun was fighting through the morning mist, behind which the city could barely be seen, wan and drifting. A buffet table lined end-to-end with square metal bins offered the last scraps of what looked to have been a full breakfast for the officers. Both Captain Markus and Admiral Kostitsin were there, among others. Olybrius chose to stay away for the moment. He found a lounge chair and gestured for his coffee again, setting his face directly above the steam.

"So how again? According to whom?"

"There isn't much question," said Vassago. "One of the tasters has fallen ill."

"His Majesty has *tasters*?"

"Not always. You met him last night." This was Markus speaking, having come over to join. "Goulu. The little one with the curl."

Olybrius remembered. "What did he eat?"

"They think it's what he drank. Wine."

"Did anyone else get ill?"

"No, and in fact he wasn't supposed to have taken the wine in the first place. It was His Majesty's reserve."

Olybrius understood. Late-night hijinks. "But you're saying the wine made him sick?"

"Violently."

Olybrius' eyes drifted beneath his lids. He felt fairly sick himself. Did that mean someone had tried to take *his* life?

"Does His Majesty know?"

"Not yet, but so you're aware, the RG will be treating this with the utmost seriousness."

"Meaning no one is leaving the ship."

"We've drawn up a list." Markus handed it over. "You should probably take a look."

"Also," said Vassago, "A demonstration has been planned in the city this morning."

"Students?"

"Yes."

"The waterfront?"

"Yes."

"When?"

"They're saying noon."

Olybrius thought. "I'll speak."

"You're sure about that?" asked Markus.

"Yes. Let them march. Let them have their grief. Then I'll talk to them."

"We'll see that there's security."

"Please."

With that, Markus excused himself. Olybrius took up the Danish warily. "I gather there was something else?"

"There was," said Vassago, more quietly. "Your brother has apparently escaped."

Olybrius set down the Danish. "How?"

"It would appear he beat his way through the side of the ship."

Olybrius laughed, not bitterly – warmly, wincingly and with a touch of pride. Of no one else would he have believed such a thing.

Vassago continued: "Admiral Kostitsin's secretary, Lieutenant Bundt, is already conducting the investigation, with the idea that he will report to you as soon as you're ready. Sausage?" A steaming tray had just been brought out and set on the buffet table.

"Thank you."

Vassago went off to get them, giving Olybrius a moment to collect his thoughts, which were now scattered like jackstraws. Had the world gone stark raving mad? The alleged attempt on His Majesty's life – he was hardly convinced of that. His brother, however – he should have known. Bazja was an ox when he really wanted something –

But then his breath caught: the shamir. Where was it? He had no idea. He didn't even know how he'd gotten back to his room last night. Had he shoved it in a drawer? Bid it in the poker game? He searched his pockets, the same he'd slept in and suddenly calmed. There it was. Trusty little nugget. Warm, too.

It was at that moment, as he was fingering the family jewel, he saw the Bishop's man, the Starets, standing over by the buffet table, helping himself to a dish of blintzes and looking to be in good humor.

Olybrius went to him directly, and was greeted by a full-mouthed grin. "Morning, Provost."

"Good morning. I was wondering if Your Grace had had the opportunity yet to speak to Lady Margrét?"

"I did, yes." He caught a glob of jam on his knuckle, then turned his eye quizzically. "How well do you know her?"

"Not well. I was in the Uplands. We met."

"And you decided to invite her to the King's reception?"

"Well, not exclusively. We sent out dozens of invitations. Hers was one."

The Starets grinned, unfooled.

"Why?" said Olybrius. "You don't still think she has anything to do with what took place last night?"

"Oh, I think she has *everything* to do with it." He took another bite.

"You must be joking."

"I couldn't be more serious. If not for her, then none of this." He cast a quick glance around, hitting on the distant pier.

"But she is a shepherdess," said Olybrius. "She's a girl."

"Doesn't seem to have stopped you now, does it?"

Olybrius was speechless – the man was as deranged as his master – but before he could think how to reply, Admiral Kostitsin and another officer approached.

"Is it time?" asked the Starets.

The Admiral nodded solemnly, and the Starets turned back to Olybrius. "Were you coming along as well? To see Goulu?"

The victim of the wine. Kostitsin had no objection. Olybrius supposed he should.

The other officer was Brazhny. He'd been put in charge of the Goulu investigation which, by the time they reached sick bay, appeared to have taken a capital turn. In the hall just outside, Dr. Verbeek was conferring with the ship's pastor, Mueller, who had presumably just administered last rites. Inside the room, the body lay flat on a high bed. The sheet had been pulled up over the head.

The Starets entered nonetheless. Olybrius followed and immediately felt that extra stillness in the room, the same as one feels in an abandoned house. The Starets went to the body. Without consulting anyone he slid the blanket from the face.

It was hard to believe this was the same young man they'd all seen last night in the Map Room. Olybrius' first thought was that he looked like he'd been gassed. The cheeks, which had been so plump and soft, were mottled and pockmarked and had taken on a sickly grey-green color. The nose had mushroomed while the chin was misshapen and goitered like the knob on a gourd. The only thing that identified him was the hairline and the hair, that silly curl he wore in the middle.

The Starets took the corpse's hand. "May I see the bottle?" he asked.

Brazhny pointed from the door. It was standing on a silver tray just to the side of the bed, draped. Before he could warn against touching it, however, the Starets lifted the handkerchief and whiffed. A fly buzzed away.

Olybrius had seen enough. He returned to the Pastor and Dr. Verbeek, who, for the benefit of Brazhny, was going over everything he'd done to try to save the victim.

"We pumped his stomach, gave him emetics, water." He shrugged. "There wasn't much more."

"And do we know of anything that creates that kind of reaction?" asked Olybrius. "Other than mustard gas?"

They all turned to look at the victim. The Starets now seemed to be performing some kind of rite, leaning over the body, laying his hand on his chest.

"What's he doing?" asked Verbeek. "Sir –"

The Starets didn't seem to hear. He was whispering into the cadaver's mouth.

"What are you doing? What is he doing?"

Olybrius had no idea, but just then Vassago arrived with yet another officer.

"Lieutenant Bundt," he whispered, by way of introduction. Bundt was the one heading the investigation into his brother's disappearance, which seemed slightly more pressing at the moment, if only because Bazja was still at large. Olybrius was on the point of excusing himself, trying to get the Admiral's attention, when the Pastor gasped, looking in at the Starets and the body. They all turned. There was something twitching beneath Goulu's blanket – his leg. It could have been a latent reflex, thought Olybrius, except that there was a kind of charge in the air: the same as had told him just a moment before that this man's life was gone, now told him it had returned, and in fact the whole of Goulu's body was now arching against the slab, stiff and spastic as he sucked in a lungful of air.

"Good heavens," said Verbeek, as astonished as the Pastor. They all were, except for the Starets, who finally turned to face them.

"He should be fine," he said casually.

"What did you do?" asked Verbeek.

He shrugged, not much. "Many poisons will mask death before they actually effect it. He'll need attending, though."

Evidently. Young Mr. Goulu seemed to have awakened to intense abdominal pains. He was writhing on the slab now and moaning, very much alive. Dr. Verbeek went straight to the patient while the Starets consulted briefly with one of the standing officers, asking directions to the chapel. The mate led him away, leaving the Pastor, Kostitsin, Brazhny and Olybrius, none of them yet certain what had just taken place.

"I'm sorry, who is he again?" asked the Pastor.

"One of the Bishop's men," said Olybrius, trying not to seem too disturbed. He turned back to Lieutenant Bundt, who was still waiting patiently to take him to Bazja's cell.

However, as they headed off, Olybrius was torn again. Obviously he had to go see about his brother. No one would have a better sense of where Bazja had gone to than he. However, given what had just witnessed, he felt a strong pull to go see Lady Margrét as well, and as soon as possible. Whoever this Starets really was, he seemed to be a man of influence, to say the least. Why he thought the girl posed a threat Olybrius still couldn't imagine, but if he did, and if he was saying so, then clearly she needed someone on her side.

As they arrived at the door of the meat locker, their apparent destination, Olybrius took Vassago aside and told him to go find her. He wanted to see her.

"Where?" asked Vassago, unsurprised.

"The Map Room, if no one else is there."

And off Vassago went. Olybrius and Lieutenant Bundt meanwhile entered the locker, wove their way through the hanging carcasses of beef to the thrice-bolted door on the far side. Bundt let Olybrius enter first:

"Good heavens."

He couldn't decide if the sight was more awesome or comical. There was indeed a hole in the side of the boat. It looked as if a small cannon ball had blasted its way through, only from the inside headed out. His brother's shirt was there on the floor; it had obviously been a tight squeeze. Olybrius poked his head through the opening and looked at the drop. A good thirty feet down into the choppy surf.

"Do we have any idea what time it was?"

"Between o-three-hundred and o-five—"

The water must have been freezing, but Bazja's blood was lava. How many times had Olybrius seen the steam rise from his head and shoulders out on the lake at Debrovo?

He looked through the hole again. The nearest coastline was the jetty and the lighthouse.

"Have we checked that?"

Bundt shook his head. "Not yet."

"Let's."

XXIV
Myrrh

The standing guard had remained just outside the suite. Margrét had no idea why, or where Inger had gone, and the guard himself was no help. He just closed the door on her and left her there alone.

It wasn't too long after, however, that the porter arrived with food. Someone had sent a whole tray full – there was grapefruit juice and cheese, blintzes with grape jelly and a whole pot of coffee. She was very hungry, as a matter of fact. She'd hardly eaten any of her dinner last night, so she sat and devoured the blintzes, which were delicious. The coffee, too. She had three cups, in addition to the cheese. Even the porter was surprised when he returned.

"Would you like more, M'm'selle?"

"Yes, please." And off he went to get her more.

She liked being here alone. Even though she wasn't allowed to leave, she still somehow felt as if she had escaped. She suspected Inger wasn't even on the ship anymore; if she were, she'd be here. They must have put her on one of the boats headed to the city, so perhaps it was simply that that made her feel so...free. So unencumbered.

She spent a while looking at the dollhouse and all the interiors. It was three stories high, with bathrooms and kitchens and servants quarters with tiny kerosene lamps. Chandeliers. Real woven rugs. Even cutlery the size of fingernails. But had it been put there for her to see? Was it foolish of her to think so? Perhaps this room was to be Kristiana's, the King's daughter.

She decided then and there, while inspecting the miniature servants' stove, that she would go – whether Inger was waiting for her or not. She would go to Lisbon and find him. Just because she was wrong about the invitation, that didn't mean she should give up. She was closer to him than she had ever been.

She found some stationery and a fountain pen in the writing desk. She sat and wrote a note, like a lady in her drawing room. She saw no need to explain.

> *Dear Inger,*
> *I have gone to find my father. Don't worry. I will*
> *be taken care of. I will take care of myself.*

She had nothing more to say than that. Still her pen tip hovered for some further word of assurance or gratitude. *Thanks to you*, she was going to write, when another knock came at the door. Oh, good, she thought. "Enter," she said, like the same fine lady.

It wasn't the blintzes. It was the Provost's driver, with the lazy lids and the lopsided mouth. "Would you come with me, please?"

"Where?"

"If you'd come with me."

"But I have food."

She pointed behind him. The porter was just now entering with her second helping.

"He can come," said the driver.

So the three of them – the steward, Margrét and the porter with the rolling table – started away. Margrét had no idea where for, except that as always the corridors of the ship all seemed like secret passages. Several turns and semi-flights of stairs brought them to another room at the very stern of the ship. At least she assumed. It was shaped like a spade, and there were desks with maps under glass and standing globes, and the walls were lined with books all the way around, all except for one arched window at the back, now framing the city in the distance.

The steward and the porter both left her there with her second helpings, though she wasn't interested in food anymore. She felt a little jumpy and she wanted to look at the books. She had never seen so many all at once. Books on botany, natural history, naval history, art, engineering, a whole shelf entitled simply *Britannica.* She thought of the person who must have read them all. It didn't seem possible, cramming all those words and ideas into a single mind. Was there even such a mind?

"Are you a reader, then?"

The voice startled her, in part because she hadn't known anyone was there; in part because she wasn't sure if the voice was in her head or in the room, it was so deep.

She turned to see it was the holy man, the Seidre. He was sitting in a great leather armchair with a book in his hand. He must have been there the whole time.

"Sometimes," she said, giving no hint that she'd been startled. "My uncle has me read to him."

The Seidre approved of this. He closed his book and stood, and she turned back to the shelves again. She seemed to have found a section on history and philosophy. He came and stood right beside her and they looked at the spines together. There was *The History of the Decline and Fall of the Roman Empire, Antiquities,* Plato, Pliny, Plotinus, Virgil. . .

". . .But do you think he has really read all of these?" she asked.

"Who?"

"The King."

The Seidre seemed to find this amusing. "I would be very surprised if he had read even one."

She looked up at him, thinking this seemed awfully impertinent, but he didn't take it back. She glanced down at the book in his hand. "And what is that, then?"

"What else?" He held it up. The cover was a soft black leather. It reminded her of the book in the picture of her father. He offered it to her. "Do you know it?"

No, she shook her head. The pages were golden-edged, too, like the plate behind her father's head. She opened it.

She had never seen such tiny words, and they were set in columns, but right off her eyes landed on a very strange pair of sentences. First this:

ASMODEUS

*Let him kiss me with the kisses of his mouth: for
thy love is better than wine*

Then this:

*My beloved is like a roe or a young hart: he stands
behind our wall, looking through the windows,
showing himself through the lattice:*

"What is this?"

He glanced over her shoulder to see. "A song," he said casually.
"Of two young lovers."

She looked back down and saw that this was so:

*His left hand should be under my head,
and his right hand should embrace me.*

"I think I have heard about books like this," she said.

"Oh, but there is no other book like this," the Seidre replied. "In
fact, one must be very brave to look inside this book."

"Why?" she asked.

"Because this is not a book at all, as it turns out," he said. "It is a
mirror."

She consulted the page again. Not that she believed him, not
that she really even understood what he meant, but these were the
words now confronting her:

*A garden enclosed is my sister, my spouse;
a spring shut up, a fountain sealed.*

Something stirred in her. She thought, if that was what this page
has seen, then it sees well. A few lines down, the voice speaking was
her own:

*By night on my bed I sought him whom my soul
loveth: I sought him, but I found him not.*

The same feeling burrowed deeper into her. The Seidre was right, this was a strange book. Of course he might just be playing a trick. Still, she felt more as if she were being read than reading, or as if just by looking at the page her eyes were somehow setting down the words.

Or his were. *'Tell me where you graze,"* they asked,

> *Tell me where you take your sheep for shade, lest*
> *I should wander among the flocks of thy*
> *neighbors.*

She blushed, which he saw. He smiled, holding out his hand now, as if to offer her a robe, as if the words had been undressing her. "As I say, one must be bold," he said. "You needn't look if you don't want to." He waited to see if she would give it back, but with such daring in his eye, she couldn't. One more time, she looked back down, searching the page for her reflection. The words jumbled in: her beloved was like an apple tree, they said. She sat beneath his shade, delighted, his fruit was sweet to her tongue, (her cheeks were burning now); for her he gathered spices; he fed among the lilies; he put his hand upon the latch and in her depths she yearned; (and in her depths she yearned); she went to let him in, (her hands were trembling); they dripped with liquid myrrh upon the handles of the lock –

At this she finally closed the book, fearing that he might have seen, though of course he had. Or he had not needed to, because if this book knew her secrets, then so did he. She could tell he did from the look in his eye, but what was strange was that she was not offended by this, or afraid, or even ashamed. Quite the opposite.

"Why have you come here?" he asked.

And this was even stranger, because if he had asked this yesterday, or if anyone else had asked, she could have answered easily. But here and now, looking up at him, she did not know anymore. In fact, for a moment she did not even know where here was.

And it was as this same moment as she stood before the Seidre, trying to find an answer, letting her answers drift, that the door on the far side of the room opened and in stepped the Provost.

XXV

Blood

H is first reaction at seeing the two of them together was far more extreme that he'd have expected. He was horrified, as if he had entered to find her in the jaws of a slobbering, fanged beast, or the clutches of the devil himself (as the Starets apparently thought *she* was). Olybrius shot a glance back at Vassago for some explanation, but the steward was just as surprised (if less expressively). He'd have sworn the room was empty.

What made the image even more stunning and painful was the fact that Margrét looked quite beautiful this morning; even more so than last night, if that were possible. She turned to him, and if he didn't know better, he'd have said she was blushing. Her hair was down and full. Her cheeks were flushed, and her whole carriage was square and strong. She was in bloom, and seemed as such to be either completely unaware of the danger posed by this man beside her, or to be – dare he say – excited by it.

Yet all Olybrius could muster in the face of this, the sheer obscenity of this picture before him – of the innocent maiden beside this insidious, delusional black magician – was "Oh," as if he'd interrupted a game of bridge. "Oh, excuse me. I didn't expect to find you not alone."

"We were just discussing literature," said the Starets brightly, somewhat coming to the rescue of her speechlessness. He took the book from her hand. He touched her back. "It seems our Margrét is a young lady of great appetite."

"I've no doubt." Olybrius tilted respectfully in her direction.

"Which bodes well, no?" the Starets posed, still looking at Olybrius. "'No draft can quench, no flood can drown. . . ' Isn't that right, Mr. Provost?"

Olybrius had no idea what this referred to, only that he was being goaded in some way. His smiled strained.

"But let me not intrude any further," the Starets said, so noting. "Clearly you two have business. Lady Margrét, I leave you in good hands."

He bowed to her and left, offering nods to Olybrius and to Vassago as well, who was stationed at the door, as quiet as an unlit lamp.

Margrét turned to face Olybrius again, and once again his breath was taken by the image of her, half bathed in the natural light entering from the window, brushing just the tips of her eyelashes, and seeming to enter her hazel-green irises from the side, imbuing them with a kind of inner glow.

"I'm sorry to have kept you waiting."

She shook her head.

"I see you ate, that's good. Please, make yourself comfortable." He gestured for her to sit, but she preferred to stand apparently, beside and even slightly behind the wingback leather chair.

"I trust your accommodations have been satisfactory?"

"Very," she said. "Is Madame de Villiers-Lornyay still on the ship?"

"I don't believe she is, no."

"Is my nursemaid?"

"I can ask. I don't like to think you were separated."

"I have a letter for her," she said. There was an envelope beside her tray.

"We can certainly see that it reaches her." He gestured for Vassago to come take it, and let that be his excuse to dismiss him.

With a gentle click, then, there was just the two of them. He stepped closer.

"I feel I should apologize, again, for what's happened here. None of this was anticipated obviously."

Her expression agreed, this was obvious.

"As you've no doubt gathered, not everyone here in the capitol is so pleased to see His Majesty. There are small pockets of resistance that seem to be using the visit to have their say." He interrupted himself. "Is this what you and the Starets were discussing?"

No, she shook her head.

"Oh. Well, in any case, that's what happened last night, I think, as result of which I'm afraid there is a fair amount of suspicion in the air."

She looked at him, still awaiting his point.

"Because you are new to the capitol, because you are not *known*, I simply wanted to make sure no part of that suspicion falls on you."

"What do you mean?"

"Only that His Majesty will be receiving audience this afternoon, in lieu of the reception. I was going to go pay my respects. I was thinking you could come with me."

Her brow knit, and he was reminded again how surprising she was. She seemed to like to wrestle when the choice was in order.

"Why?" she asked.

"Why, so that you could meet him, and to let the Crown know you're not to be feared." He smiled.

She didn't seem to see why that should even be question – understandably – but pondered the invitation in its own light and finally agreed. "Thank you," she said politely. "But then I would like to go to Kyiv."

"Kyiv?"

"If that could be arranged. I would like to see my father."

There was silence, as Olybrius wasn't sure how to reply to this. Finally he asked, "...Why?"

The wrong question apparently. She bristled. "I shouldn't think one needs a reason to see one's father. I am asking if you would help me. If you will not, I will find someone else –"

"It isn't that I don't want to help you," he said. "I want nothing more, but I must be frank." He paused, feeling himself at the edge of a cliff. Her presence had this effect on him, of first disarming him – of making him feel practically naked – and then, by that same token, bold. What else was there to do but run and jump and dive in the coldest swimming hole, and shiver and shake and yell? "I care for you, Margrét. I more than care. I think I am in love with you –"

"I don't understand why you say these things."

"I say them because they are true, and so that you know I am only trying to help you when I say…" He stopped himself again. He had resolved not to say anything to her about her father. "What were you and the Starets discussing exactly?"

"Who?"

"Your father's man –"

"I don't see that that's any of your business," she said, "and I don't think I wish to speak with you any more about this."

"Yes, but I only mean to say –" He fumbled, uncertain, but he couldn't just leave her in ignorance. "I don't think it's a good idea just yet, you seeing your father."

"I said I don't wish to discuss this with you. I will speak to the other man, the holy one."

"But he is no better."

She stopped at this and straightened, and he knew that he had misspoken, for just then something much fiercer and more dangerous entered her eye; she looked like an injured animal.

"No better than whom?" she asked, and he knew he dare not answer, but it was already too late. He was in her sights. "I think you say things that you don't know anything about," she said, "and that you are a liar. You do not know me, or my father –"

"No, and I'm sure I overstep my bounds. It's only that I wouldn't want to see any harm to come to you –"

She suddenly charged at him. She flung her fist at him, but it glanced off his shoulder. She threw another, but so hard this time he had to grab hold of her wrist. She was strong. She forced him to use his strength. He held her by both arms, which brought their faces near.

"I am not trying to hurt you," he said. "I am trying to protect you."

They were close enough that he could feel her breath and the warmth of her skin. He could see the fear in her eye, and he could smell something sweet about her mouth – berries – but it was that sudden surge of strength required to keep her still that finally drew him forward. Their lips met, and for a moment it seemed that she accepted, that she was yielding to him just as he had wished and imagined and known she would. It was another moment, therefore, before he felt the searing pain shooting through him, from his mouth down to his shuddering heart. She had clamped onto his lower lip with her teeth and she was gnashing. He howled. In a panic, he grabbed her by the hair, yanked hard and thrust her away.

"You bit me!" He looked down at his hand. "I'm bleeding!"

He looked back at her and she was transformed by her fury. She looked rabid to him; her beauty vanished and in its place, something utterly wild. Her hair was a tangle over her face. Her eyes were wide, and glaring through.

"But is he right about you, then?" The Provost said this aloud, which in retrospect he realized he probably should not have, for now she raised her hands, and from her throat their came a shriek he would not have thought a person capable of. Then she came at him again, flailing. Fortunately, her scream was loud enough to summon Vassago and a second guard, who both came rushing in and quickly pulled her off, her legs wheeling beneath her. She did not resist for too long, though. She had made her point.

"Are you all right, Sir?" asked the guard.

"I'm fine." Olybrius stood up straight, still with his hand to his mouth. "But get her out of here."

"To her room, Sir?"

"Yes, but under watch. And tell Brazhny to put her on the list." He directed this at Vassago

"Would you like me to summon Dr. Verbeek as well?" Vassago indicated his lip.

"No," he said. "Maybe. But take this." He reached into his pocket and took the out the necklace. He had brought it with him just in case.

"And do what, sir?"

"I don't care. Just get it away from me."

XXVI

Antonia Pecca

Despite her protests, Inger was on the first boat of "cleared passengers" to be taken into the pier. That list also included the Duke and Duchess Voss, and Madame de Villiers-Lornyay, who did not share Inger's concern that Margrét had been detained, thinking the reason was perfectly obvious and probably to be encouraged.

"It's not as if he bites," she said.

Inger didn't like Madame de Villiers-Lornyay. She considered nearly all the women on board to be peacocks, and better done with. She therefore kept her real fear to herself, which was that the Provost had nothing to do with Margrét's detainment. That man who had come to the room this morning, the priestly one in black, he was not what he appeared, and Inger had no doubt that he was the one who'd forced her off. The thought of Margrét trapped aboard a ship with him made her queasy. She'd sooner have handed the girl over to the Bishop himself.

And that is why, while the others on her boat were met by cars and carriages – some even inviting Inger to come along, come see their homes and wait in the shade of their beeches and poplars – she remained on the pier, determined to stay until Margrét was boated in as well.

The guards put up with her for an hour or so, then moved her along, outside the checkpoint at the foot of the pier. She was undeterred, setting herself just outside the barricade so that she could keep her eye in the ship, monitor every boat coming in, and quiz the passengers as soon as they came though. Had they seen the girl, Margrét? What was the delay? Were there more boats on the way? No one knew, but the guests kept coming in dribs and drabs, and Margrét was not among them.

Inger grew more frightened and desperate. She couldn't control her thoughts anymore. Perhaps that man in the black robe had been the one who sent the invitation. Perhaps Theodosius made him do it. Another boat arrived with no answers, and the guests were treating her like a mad woman now, understandably. She was calling after their carriages, pleading with the coachmen. The posted guards were on the point of moving her further along when the sound of the planes intruded. The departing guests looked up, the drivers and the guards as well.

Inger had never seen a plane before, but she knew they were part of the day's schedule. This was a squadron of six flying in a V formation like geese, but so much louder. The sound was awful, as if they were devouring the sky somehow. As they came near, she saw the gnashing teeth painted along the snouts and she turned away. While all the other people around her pointed and craned and ooed and aahed, Inger covered her face and wept. Where was Margrét? What had they done with her?

The squadron preened a while longer, passing over and back through the gap in the bridge three times. Parade or no parade, they gave the people a good long look before rounding off and heading for the fields just north of the city. As they did, and as the horrible drone finally drifted away to silence, a small voice spoke to her.

"What's wrong?" it asked, very clear and very smart. "Are you waiting for someone?"

Inger looked up. There was a petite young woman standing directly in front of her – no more than five feet, in a long dark coat that fell straight to her ankles, with a round pale face, large slightly Asiatic eyes and a small bowed mouth.

"I don't know where she is," Inger replied, heaving. She gestured at the ship, still anchored in the middle of the Ord and perfectly still. "I don't know what they're doing with her."

"Who?" The young woman sat beside Inger on the curb. She took her arm, and Inger told her. She wasn't sure why – because she had to tell someone, and because the young woman listened. She did not doubt. She didn't goad. She looked at Inger with her wide and caring eyes and nodded gently as Inger spoke.

Antonia Pecca was her name, and she was one of the students. That was how she described herself, though she took no classes at the University; her brother did. He had been a member of the New Welans, and through him Antonia had become a fixture at their gatherings, social and political. She modeled in the art classes. That was how she came to know Ovechkin.

"They say they're keeping some," she told Inger.

"But what for?"

Antonia shook her head. "No one knows."

"But she's a girl."

Antonia nodded, and as she put her arm around Inger, another sound intruded on her despair, this time a much more dulcet and yet doleful sound: two trumpets.

Inger wiped her eyes. Coming down Kristania Way was a large procession. Two hundred, maybe three hundred people – it was hard to see from where they were – but enough to span the width of the avenue and trail on for at least a block. There were three coffins up front, borne on the shoulders of what looked like working men in jackets and dusty leather shoes, though there were students as well, wearing University scarves.

"Are these from last night?" asked Inger.

Antonia nodded quietly.

The mourners looked more solemn than angry, the men all carrying their hats and caps. The trumpets were playing an old dirge from the Uplands, *Hugin and Munin*, about the ravens. The procession had likely started at the Cathedral, but Inger couldn't tell where they were headed. The pier itself, it looked like. Onlookers stopped to watch, to see if there was to be another confrontation. The soldiers at the check point were preparing for the same, taking up their rifles.

They needn't have. On reaching the boardwalk, the mourners all turned left, the caskets and trumpeters still out front, and proceeded in the direction of Old Yinny, broken Yinny. They passed by stationed guards and the police as well. No one moved to stop them.

"Come," said Antonia Pecca.

"I can't," said Inger. "I have to stay."

But Antonia pulled her up. "He will listen," she said. "He will help."

They followed the mourners at a slight remove at first, but when the trumpeter started up another verse of the raven's song, Inger felt herself a part, her steps in time with theirs. She took consolation in the presence of the others, as if she herself were now mourning some kind of loss.

Antonia kept pulling her along until finally they reached the front of the procession and the men carrying the caskets, which were crude and built of pine. The trumpeters were here as well, and walking just out front of them was one more man, the leader – tall, with a long chin and spectacles. Antonia came up from behind and took his hand directly; she was wearing fingerless gloves. He accepted without turning. They walked another block like this – Antonia striding twice for ever step the man took – before he finally glanced over at Inger. He saw her frock, which was typical of the Uplands. He saw that she had been crying.

"From the ship," explained Antonia.

On they walked. They were approaching Old Yinny now, and no one – not Inger, not the guards, nor any of the onlookers making their way along the boardwalk – was really sure what the mourners intended. There was a gravesite a half mile further on, but no one had used that for generations.

When they came to the roundabout at the foot of the bridge, the one surrounding the stone statue of the sleeping Ymir, the tall man and Antonia and the casket bearers all turned right. The mourners behind followed like a giant cape, one by one overstepping the rope which had been strung to block access to the bridge, or what remained of it – the ramp to nothing, to the Ord.

Along the boardwalk, the onlookers lifted their hands to their mouths. Were the mourners going to jump? To throw the caskets in? One could never be sure with the students. Were they all going to march straight off the end like lemmings?

No. They simply sat. At the signal of Antonia's friend, the trumpeters stopped. The mourners all stopped. The coffin-bearers set down their coffins and all the people followed, crossing their legs and sitting, their purpose peaceful, clear, but searing: If His Majesty wanted to leave the harbor of Kreisenig today, he would have to pass directly by the blameless victims of his gala reception.

The tall man turned to Inger now. He still had Antonia's hand in his, but he took Inger's as well. He looked at her intently, the round lenses of his spectacles magnifying the eyes behind, which were a startlingly light and inviting blue.

"Tell me."

XXVII

Forgiveness

There was no meeting with His Majesty. Olybrius went to the Royal Suite, but was told the wait would be an hour at least, and he didn't want to be seen this way in any case. His lip was still swollen. He asked for a wrap of chipped ice, and took the next boat back to the mainland to find out what he could about his brother.

He was still thinking of Margrét. He couldn't decide if she was to be more pitied or feared. Her innocence was plain – wanting to see her father, wanting the Starets to help her. She clearly had no idea who was on her side. But just as plain was that extraordinary fire inside her, and its power to entrance. He was glad to be separate from her, in fact – to be on solid ground – because even after what had happened, he still felt the sway she possessed over him. He actually didn't like the way she made him feel. Not himself, not clever or cunning. At least in that respect, the Starets may have been on to something.

"Have we checked on him yet, by the way?"

"Who?" asked Vassago, opening the door of the yellow Speedster for him.

"The Bishop's man, the Starets. I'd like to know more about where he came from."

By the time they got back to the Ministry, the lighthouse keeper had already been found and deposed. He confirmed what Olybrius suspected: Just before 5 AM a man had appeared at the lighthouse door, half naked, pale blue and bleeding. The Keeper had taken him in, gave him soup, a nightshirt and long johns. He went to get more bandages and brandy – the man had had scrapes and scars all along his shoulders and ribs – but when the Keeper returned, the man was gone. As were the Keeper's boots.

Olybrius asked to see the police blotter on everything that happened in the city from 5 AM onward. That and a fresh bag of ice.

Of course he didn't think that Margrét was *dangerous* – not the way they were saying. She was tempestuous, and it probably wasn't a bad idea letting Lieutenant Brazhny have a go at her, let her twist a bit just to remind her who her friends were – but she was no seditionist. She was simply scared, coming all the way down from the northern clans. It had been an unnerving several days for everyone.

When the police blotter arrived, he only had to glance through once. "What's this?"

At 5:25 AM a disturbance was reported at the Pig&Whistle. On an anonymous tip, two officers entered to break up a late-night meeting. They found nothing, but when they came back outside, one of their motorcycles was missing.

"Tank full?" asked Olybrius

They had to check on that. Half full was the answer, good for thirty miles or so. Olybrius had them call Boryuti, the Military Academy, which was just twenty-five miles north of the city. Sure enough, the groundskeeper there confirmed a mysterious motorcycle had been found just outside the stables, tank empty. And one of the horses was missing:

Orabas was headed home as fast as he could, presumably to see if Modo had gone to eat his family.

Olybrius shifted focus to the speech he intended to deliver to the students and the demonstrators. That was the next item on the agenda anyway. He'd been told they were all out on the bridge, sitting. He'd been brought a copy of the *Lür* as well. He read it start to finish, then prepared his remarks with typical calm. He was good at this sort of thing. Vassago arrived to let him know that Captain Markus' security detail was now ready. As they were dressing, Olybrius asked if Vassago still had Lady Margrét's letter, the one she had entrusted him back in the Map Room.

He did. Olybrius gestured for it, as he might ten kroner that he was owed. He opened it and read:

> *Dear Inger,*
> *I have gone to find my father. Don't worry. I will*
> *be taken care of. I will take care of myself.*

That hardly shed much light.

"See that she gets off the ship as soon as Brazhny is done with her," he said. "Perhaps a suite at the Imperial."

Vassago bowed, he'd see to it.

"And let me know as soon as she gets in."

XXVIII

The Good News

As usual, Margrét's anger persisted in fits and starts. She raged at the door. She flung the hairbrushes at her vanity. She toppled the dollhouse, all the little lamps and cups and saucers scattering across the Persian rug. What did it matter? She knew she was in trouble already. She just didn't know what for. Making the Provost bleed? That probably hadn't helped her case, but that wasn't the reason she was supposed to meet with this Brazhny whoever-he-was. That had something to do with all the "suspicions" the Provost kept talking about, whatever they were. She didn't care. The Provost was a liar.

"You cannot keep me!" she shouted through the door. "I will tell him! I will remember who you are!" She hurled an apple in fury, because now she did feel trapped. She tore the cases from her pillows. She flung the stationery from the writing desk, then she tired again, and weakened, and wondered why they said such things—because that was the most exhausting part, really, fending the idea they might be right.

"I hate you!" she shouted back at the door again, just for good measure

In reply, the knob at that moment turned. She held her breath and in stepped the Seidre, having heard, but taking no offense.

"Oh." She pushed herself up. "It's you. I didn't mean you."

In fact she was glad it was him. He seemed to be alone, too, which was odd. She looked behind him into the corridor. Had there been no one there this whole time?

"How are you feeling?" he asked.

"I want to see my father."

"I have some good news about that actually. Come. And put this on." He extended her a cloak with a hood.

"What about all the rest?" Her things, the dowry.

"You won't need them." He stood aside to usher her out.

They moved swiftly. The corridors were very narrow, but he walked beside her. It felt like they were escaping, but she wasn't frightened. She felt strangely comfortable, in fact.

"Does anyone know we're doing this?" she asked.

The Seidre only hurried her along. As before, she couldn't help noting there was a tremendous energy about him, a kind of magnificence to the way he moved, which may simply have had to do with the billow of his robe. They descended another set of iron stairs as steep as a ladder. There at the landing he unbolted a small iron door that opened directly to the outside – the blue sky and the water below. They were halfway down the hull of the ship. A small iron platform with a railing was all that kept them from plunging down into the river. A small boat was waiting below, swaying gently in the water, which seemed unusually calm this morning – like a lake almost. All the winds had died.

The Seidre began turning a reel crank. The ropes went taut, the pulleys turned. The boat was lifted from the surface and slowly ascended the side of the ship, turn by turn. As she watched him, it occurred to her that she couldn't really tell how old he was. He seemed to be almost ancient in some ways, or ageless – like a mountain or an old old tree – and yet he was also so full of life and brimming and new, like a spring leaf on that same tree.

"Tell me something," he said. "Did the Provost offer you his hand in there?"

The question stopped her. She didn't think so – not really, though there she supposed he would have if she'd let him.

"And why didn't you?" asked the Seidre, as if he'd heard her. He glanced in the direction of the teetering city, with all its domes and spires. "All that could be yours. And more than that, I warrant." He looked at her keenly, but teasingly too. "Is it that you've promised your heart to another? A shepherd boy? I suspect the Provost would live with that."

"No," she said, confused now; hurt almost. Was he taking the Provost's side?

"Then why?" he pressed. "Is it so repulsive to you, the idea that you might spend the rest of your life with such a man? Then don't," he smiled. "Cut his throat. Poison his soup. You'd hardly be the first." Again he looked her straight in the eye, testing.

"Who are you?" she asked. "Why do you like to tempt?"

"I'm not tempting you," he said, as just now the boat reached their level. It hung right beside them, at the ready. He locked the line. "I just want to make sure you understand the choice before you. Give them what they want, the world is yours. Refuse, and they will destroy you. Or try."

He offered his hand. She took it and climbed aboard. It was a little boat, with only two benches. They sat facing each other.

"But I have told him no," she said. "And I have told you, I want to see my father. How long it will it take to get there, to Kyiv?"

"Oh, we're not going to Kyiv." He unlatched the pulley again and gently they began to descend toward the water.

"But I thought you said —"

"I said I had good news about your father, and I do." He drew a kerchief from his sleeve. "But first you have to close your eyes."

She hesitated. This seemed an odd time to be playing games. "What for?"

"It will help. Trust me." And now he drew the rope from his waist.

Again she had no idea why she should, but she obliged. She closed her eyes, and a moment later she felt the boat touch down on the water.

"Now I want you to picture him for me. Your father. Can you do that?"

She could. There was only the one image she had of him. It came to her at once.

"I want you to see him as clearly as you can," the Seidre said. "Everything about him."

His words and his voice seemed to make the image all the more vivid – the oval face, the large eyes, the small gentle mouth and the beard; the golden plate; the book, the dark green tunic that clasped above his left shoulder. It was all as clear as if she were holding the frame in her hand right now.

"Are you picturing him?"

"Yes."

"Good. Now look as closely as you can and listen to me."

She did. She chose the eyes again, and the Seidre spoke in the same calm voice:

"So the good news is that this man you are picturing right now, whom you have been thinking of and speaking to every day and night, whose approval you seek, whose forgiveness you pray for, and who is looking back at you this very moment . . ." And so he was, so kindly, peacefully and sorrowfully – yet she knew what the Seidre was about to say:

"...He never was...He does not exist."

As he said this, the image did not dissolve exactly. In fact, it grew more clear, so clear that she could see the cracks in the blue paint, the sheen of the gold on the wood.

"He never was born," the voice continued. "He never drew breath, never drank wine or ate bread. He has only ever been in your mind."

She understood with the same clarity as she saw each chip, each crack, each missing fleck, that what the Seidre said was obviously, comically true. The picture she had been keeping of him was nothing more than that, a picture. A painting on a panel.

"But you need not grieve or be afraid." She felt the Seidre's hand. He took both of hers, and turned them upwards, and his words kept coming in the same calm tone, which was good. She felt so dizzy now, his voice was the only thing keeping her upright.

"I said that this was good news, Margrét, and it is."

And now she felt something touch her eyes and her brow – a cloth of some kind – and the image began to fade.

"Because it means you don't have to keep waiting; he will not come. You don't have to search; he is not there. He never blessed you. He never cursed you. He never was." The colors grew more and more pale until the panel was a blank piece of wood. But she was not afraid or sad, because what the Seidre said was true.

"Your path is yours," he said, and she could hear him untying the line from the cleat.

She tried to open her eyes but she couldn't. There was a blindfold around her head. She tried to move her hands, but her wrists were bound. She did not resist. She could hear him take up the oars, slide them in the locks and pull. She could feel the tug of the boat beneath her, but she did not know who was guiding it, or where they were headed.

She was free.

A moment passed.

Then the explosions began.

XXIX
Ymir

This side of the river, the bridge lane spun off four different ways from a roundabout that featured as its centerpiece the stone statue of the slumbering Ymir, father of the giants. In fact it was a point of dispute whether the giant was sleeping or examining his reflection in the water. Either way, Olybrius had chosen this – the marble bench surrounding the fountain – as his stump. From here he could be seen and heard, though to be heard well the people would have to come in off the bridge, as the soldiers had apparently been trying to get them to do all morning. Now seeing the motorcade, and him, the students appeared to be coming voluntarily.

Olybrius was surprised by the sheer number. He had been led to expect hundreds, but this was thousands. Three or four at least.

"Have there been this many all day?"

"I think they just kept coming," said Markus. "Word got out."

Olybrius didn't feel exposed or threatened. Markus had provided a half-dozen mounted police as well three jeeps. And a full complement of the Royal Guard had shown as well, on motorcycles, thanks to General Zitri, who was just now coming up to greet him.

"That from your brother?" he asked, motioning to Olybrius' lip.

With a vague nod, Olybrius let him think it was.

Zitri grinned. "And just so you're aware, as soon as you start, I'm having my men slide in and take the bridge."

"What about the caskets?" Markus asked. They all three turned to see now – the students had left the three caskets out on the bridge, as signal of their clear intention to return.

"They can have those," said Zitri. "I just don't want the students out there."

Olybrius seconded. "I'll see if we can move them along. Perhaps we can offer them escort to wherever they want to go next."

All agreed it was worth a try, and agreed the natives were getting restless. Olybrius stepped up onto the bench to find himself surrounded by a sea of faces, some open, some curious, but most defiant, in want of some explanation. Markus had a megaphone, but Olybrius refused it. The sound was too harsh and authoritarian. The purpose here was to sympathize and bestow calm. He raised his hands and the crowd fell silent with an almost eerie suddenness.

". . . Citizens of Kreisenig and all Ileya," he announced, despite the pain in his lip. He forged ahead. "Allow me to speak on my own behalf, as well as on behalf of His Majesty when I say how deeply aggrieved we are at what took place on the Long Pier last night."

He could see Zitri's men were already headed out onto bridge, walking quietly beside their motorcycles, lining themselves along the outer edges.

"Whatever the cause, what happened was a tragedy for us all, for the victims, for families of the victims, and for the regime, which wants only the best for the people – peace, progress, and prosperity. You may rest assured that a full investigation is under way to make sure that all responsible parties are held accountable, and that justice will be served –"

"Then release the prisoners!" called a voice, loud and clear but from deep within the throng. Olybrius couldn't see who said it, but now there came a second voice and a third.

"Release them. Let them go!"

Having read the *Lür*, he understood they were talking about the alleged captives on the ship, and now more voices were joining in. He heard the word "hostages" as well. He raised his hand for quiet.

"You will forgive us, we cannot be current with all the rumors swirling, but I can assure you no one is being held against his will on His Majesty's –"

"Then what of Margrét?" came that same voice again, and this time he did see whom it belonged to. No surprise either, the long muggish face, his chin jutting beneath that smug little mouth.

But how did he even know about her? Who was Margrét to Uri Ovechkin? Or any of them, for that matter, yet more voices were chiming in now, men and women alike. "What of Margrét?" "Where is Margrét, the shepherd girl?" Olybrius glanced over at Zitri, who hardly seemed surprised – never surprised by anything a mob came up with. His fingers wiggled restlessly.

"Release Margrét!" the people cried. They were on the verge of an almost chant-like rhythm, but Olybrius was focused back on Ovechkin the ringleader, his face serene in feature, but red with rage and something else teasing at the corners of his little mouth: tremendous satisfaction.

And at that moment, as the two were looking directly at each other, a kind of stillness descended, as if time itself had slowed, or stopped. It was only a moment, just long enough for Olybrius to realize what was about to happen. He glanced beyond the sea of faces, out onto the bridge and the caskets and the guards all parked around them.

The unseen thrust came first, an invisible concussion shoving all the people surrounding him *at* him; then a deafeningly loud explosion and a shudder as Olybrius himself was slammed against Ymir's bench. His head struck the stone and for a moment he lost consciousness. He wasn't sure how long, but when he opened his eyes again, Zitri was kneeling over him in the fountain.

The air was all dust, thick but not so thick that he could not see: the near-side remains of the bridge were gone, as were the dozen soldiers who had been guarding it, as were the caskets, which had never been caskets at all clearly, but bombs.

Already there was gunfire in the street. The demonstrators all were scrambling, some with gleeful smiles on their faces.

"Do you know where you are?" asked Zitri urgently.

Olybrius nodded.

"Then declare."

Olybrius shook his head, still groggy. What?

"Declare!" he said again.

Olybrius understood this time. Zitri wanted command. He wanted Martial Law. More gunfire sounded in the streets and Olybrius nodded yes. Zitri turned directly to his first lieutenant, Vilnius. "You heard him. Go!"

Ironically, Zitri had far more resources at his disposal than anyone might have expected, owing to the fact that that very morning three fresh battalions and a squadron of planes had arrived to participate in the parade, the one the Provost had cancelled last night. The Sylkan battalions all were waiting just outside the city. As soon as they received the order, they swarmed in and took the streets with due brutality. Sirens sounded for the next three hours. Anyone who ran or resisted was arrested or beaten, or worse. By nightfall, the university and the Cathedral had both been closed. All exits to and from the city were blockaded. Curfew was set at 5 PM, and the manhunt for Uri Ovechkin was under way.

His Majesty's ship was ordered out of the harbor. All remaining guests were deported, divided, and taken to the city jail, the Block. Some were let go. Others were kept under suspicion, including Margrét, whose boat arrived at the pier within minutes of the explosions. She and the Starets were met at the Long Pier by six members of the Royal Guard and taken directly to the pens beneath the jailhouse

.

XXX

The Flood

Margrét had no idea how long she'd been kept waiting because the men never removed the blindfold, and they had stuffed something like mud in her ears. She didn't know where exactly they had taken her either, only that there had been several tremendous explosions while she and the Seidre were out on the rowboat, all coming from the direction of the bridge.

He told her not to be frightened, and she wasn't. The sounds were the same as the night before, the popping of the guns and the shouting voices, the sirens wailing in the streets. They seemed more distant this time, yet she heard them more clearly. They sounded like toys to her, like a battle waged between children. It could not hurt her. It could not touch her. She was not there. The Seidre had said so.

By the time the two of them reached the pier, the men were there waiting – soldiers or police. They took hold of them both, smuggled them into a wagon of some kind and drove them to a building made of marble. By her elbows she was carried and pushed and shoved down into a small room underground. The Seidre was still there, still telling her not to fear. They sat her on a chair. They bound her arms behind her. This is where they stuffed her ears.

Then they made her wait. Hours? Days? She could not say. A long time, but he waited with her, not saying a word out loud. *Go where you like*, he said. Silently.

She went to the pastures. It wasn't hard. She could smell the wool; the sheep were there, Nella and Yosi and all the rest. She could smell the heather and the clover, the wet stone. But there was something else in the air as well. Something briny almost. The birds could sense it, too; already they were taking flight. The snakes were fleeing through the grass. And now she could see the water seeping up through the ground, sponging her feet when the guard began to strike her.

(Did she think they would spare her because she was a woman?)

She had never been struck before. Once when she was six she had fallen from a fence and hit her head. Here the force was so blunt and so unexpected, it did not hurt so much as it stunned, and only drove her further back, and further away.

(Did she think he cared that she was fair? The man's face was inches from hers, but he might have been wailing at the bottom of a well.)

She looked to the high ridge. She could not see it yet, but she could tell, the water wasn't only here below. There was a great sea teeming and churning just behind those mountains, waiting to enter the valley.

But where was Inger? And Torvald? She should find them and tell them not to worry.

(Not worth one drop of their own men's blood, they said, or something like that.)

They were like barking dogs, weren't they? With chains around their necks, but they were clearly frightened. At least they understood that much: The Gods would be sated on the blood of fated men. No one would know mercy. But what was the use of trying to explain that this was as it should be? For herself she was not worried. She had no fate. She was not she (as the Seidre said), no longer bound by the thought of Him, or the picture of Him, since He had never been, so neither had she.

She must have smiled at this, because they struck her again, and the water spilt over the ridge.

(Who was with her? Who did she know? Where had she come from?)

Such questions, she barely heard. The water was tumbling down the ridge, gushing, finding the steepest paths first. She climbed up into the oak tree, she lay in its limbs. The only voice she really heard was the Seidre's.

"It won't do you any good," he was telling them. "You cannot harm her now."

They asked him who he was. He said he was the one telling them: "You're only making her stronger with all this," which they of course took as a challenge. She felt their hands again, on her hair, tearing and yanking. She felt their fists. She tasted blood. Oh, how they despised her, silly gnashing dogs, barking names at her that she did not know, telling lies about Inger. Inger was not there. Inger was here, singing in the hut.

> *Then I began to bloom,*
> *To be wise, to grow and to thrive...*

They raked her. They said they would keep raking her until no one recognized her, but she howled back at them, she did not care. She was the Wolf Fenrir. They had no rope to bind her with, "...Not without the tread of a cat's paw," she said, "not without the woman's beard and mountain root –"

Quiet!

"– and the bear gut and fish breath and bird spittle –"

Quiet! They would rip her tongue, they said, if she kept that up. She snapped at them. She would leave them with one hand, she said. They hooded her. They stuffed the hood into her mouth and bound it. What did it matter, it was far too late for them. The water was all across the valley now, and rising. It was halfway up the limbs. Inger had stopped singing. The sheep were swept away, poor lambs. Don't be afraid, she said. And she was not afraid. She was a wolf, a fish, a blade of grass. She felt the water rise. She felt her head slide underneath. No fear rose up, nor panic. She welcomed it, each involuntary shudder only pulled her further down and away. She was a fish. She was a snake, a mermaid, curled up in his limbs, while he nuzzled down among the coral. She reached into the pocket of her tunic and took out the little conch. She heard their voices. She held it to her ear, but she wanted to see. She looked in through the hole:

ASMODEUS

The room was like a little doll's house there, or the dungeon of a little dollhouse, with torches on the walls keeping them warm and dry. The men were standing in a circle around her, and she was in her hood, lying on a board – her body was – tilted back into a kind of coffin filled with water. She was not moving. Her hands were limp at her sides. One of the men was stalking, heavyset, with startled eyes, wild hair, and a bulldog face. The barker, he must be. He snorted and slobbered, while the Seidre stood impassively behind her. The other two were looking down at her, nervous.

One asked, *Is she dead?* (or something like that; it was hard to hear up here).

The other reached down into the water and tugged the hood from her face, and then the blindfold. They all leaned in. Her eyes were open, but blank like fish.

Pull her out, said the bulldog barker.

As they levered the board back out of the water, the torches all flared, and they continued flashing and hissing as the men unclasped her hands and feet.

"Do you see?" the Seidre was saying.

Proves nothing. They shoved her back into a chair and pried her eyelids as wide as they would go.

"No," said the Seidre. "There. Do you see?" He pointed at the torches. The flames were still dancing, veering, leaning toward the wall as if the room were whirling.

The others didn't understand, so the Seidre showed them. He took one of the torches from its sconce and brought it back to where she was sitting, the shadows wheeling around them like a mad sundial. He held the flame up to her face –

(she blew into the shell)

– but they still didn't see. The Seidre held the torch closer to her cheek –

(she blew again)

– the flame veered away, afraid. It gathered on the opposite side of the torch, as if it were averse to her flesh

168

The barking bulldog grabbed the torch to see for himself, but just then another set of bustling, thunking, echoing steps sounded outside, and there was a flash of lantern light as three more officers swept in like little tin soldiers. The Provost was one, looking very dashing today, in black boots and his red coat draped over his shoulder. They were speaking about another prisoner, freshly caught. Had he said anything useful?

Only if you counted speeches and lectures, the Provost replied. *What about her?*

(She was still having trouble hearing. She had to choose either to put the shell to her ear or her eye.)

The bulldog shook his head.

I thought you said you had ways. (Or something like that.)

Only if she's right in the mind. He pointed with the flame. *Not like this.*

She laughed. She covered her mouth, but she could see what he was saying. There she was, drenched and dripping, gazing up at the corner as if an angel were hovering there; looking up at herself looking in. Shshshsh, she whispered.

What was wrong with her, the Provost wanted to know. He asked the Seidre. *What do you say? Is she worth our while like this?*

"What is it you want from her?"

I want to stop all this! the Provost shouted; he stomped his feet. *I want to know what she knows! Aren't you the one who said she was with them?*

"Not that she was with them, no," the Seidre said calmly: "I said she was the cause."

Stop playing games! The Provost kicked an empty chair. He stalked the room, gesticulating wildly, telling the Seidre he was on thinner ice that he knew. *Tell me what are they talking about? How far gone is she?*

The Seidre only turned his hands – how could he explain what others meant?

Here, however, the bulldog brought the torch up to Margrét's face to show the Provost. He moved it from side to side, and the effect was the same as before. The fire scrambled away, it wanted no part of her. The only difference was that this time, as the dog brought the torch around behind her, her hair began to rise like snakes or tendrils. All the men stood back, except for the Seidre.

And she won't drown either, said one of the guards.

The Provost looked at the Seidre. Was that true? Was this another trick?

The Seidre raised his hands in innocence while the bulldog continued to tease and test the flame, sweeping it back and forth in front of her, her hair rising and falling. He grinned nervously. *Like a puppet,* he was saying, when suddenly the flame leapt down his arm. He started flailing to get it off, panicked, but the fire attacked him more ferociously, climbing up and over his shoulder and devouring his head and his body, all while the maiden's eyes kept drifting about the ceiling.

The others were slow to react. The bulldog staggered for the tub, accidentally kicking it over with his boot. The water spilt across the floor. He flung himself down and began rolling in it, still engulfed in flame. At last the other guards fell on him, smothering him with their coats. The Provost offered his as well, but watched with a queer impassiveness, more concerned than horrified, his attention evenly divided between the guard, the girl, and the Seidre.

The flame finally tired and withdrew, having made its point. The victim lay before them in a state of shock, blistered and blue, trembling, his mouth agape.

"To Hospital," said the Provost. "You, and you."

The guard and the second officer took the bulldog away, carrying him out into the hall where they were met by the shadow of two other guards, come to see what all the shrieking was about.

The rest remained – standing in the smoke of burnt hair and flesh and wool. They all were looking at the Provost, who was looking at the young maiden with a very grim but deliberate expression, as if he was deciding his next move. The flames licked harmlessly, tauntingly, patiently in their globes, awaiting his verdict, though they seemed to know already. Finally, but firmly, he decided:

Hang her, he said. *And him.* He indicated the Seidre. *Tomorrow, with Ovechkin.*

The others traded glances. The Seidre? Was he sure?

He was. *Unless he can provide a single person who knows who he is or where he came from.*

All eyes turned to the Seidre now to see if he would protest or defend himself.

He only smiled and held out his two hands, touching them gently at the wrist.

XXXI

Failure

Orabas did not slow for so much as a stride on his way back to the Trading Post. He rode the Academy's horse until it broke down. He hitched a ride with one of the quarrymen as far as the river. He walked to the Trinko's farm and borrowed a second horse. He didn't sleep. He didn't eat. A five day trek he managed in three, but the closer he came to the Trading Post, the stronger he could sense that he was not, in fact, closing in on the discovery of his worst fear.

In the first place, if Modo had come this way, there'd have been stories, sightings. The animals would have known, and they clearly didn't. But more than that, he could feel it in his bones, the same way he knew if a trap out ahead was empty or not: Modo was not here, had not been here. The tether that joined them, that pulled them toward each other, had stretched and stretched and now for whatever reason it had gone slack.

And that was good news, of course – if it turned out to be true, if the beast had spared his family. That was the best news possible, because if Modo had not come for them by now, then perhaps he did not need to. That would mean that they were safe, and what more could Orabas ask for?

He finally arrived in the middle of the night. A new snow had fallen, but lightly. As he trudged up, Noli was already standing at the door, roused by the sound, but he knew his master's scent and tread. He trotted up as Orabas dismounted, and was there to lick his hand as soon as he touched ground.

Per-Malfi was up as well. Per-Malfi fixed him a bowl of porridge. They sat in the main room while Orabas ate; it was his first warm food since he had left the Bend, but for whatever reason, the porridge held no savor.

They spoke as quietly as they could, and sparingly, just the two of them and the grandfather clock.

"No sign of the wolf?"

Per Malfi shook his head.

"Or the falcon?"

Per-Malfi shook his head again. "Maybe he got what he wanted, eh?"

Orabas shrugged, maybe. He forced down another spoonful while the clock tut-tutted.

". . .Worse things," Per-Malfi said, coaxing the bowl of his pipe with another long match.

Orabas agreed, much worse. They could hear Anna's gentle snore, more like a purr, in the next room.

"I should still go to the Bend," he said.

Per-Malfi tilted back on his chair and nodded, probably so.

The splintered croak of floorboards announced that Maren was up as well now. Even before she appeared in her nightgown, Per-Malfi pushed himself up and shuffled away to his room to let them be alone.

They embraced. Orabas had yet to bathe, but she held him long and close. She drank him in, but not desperately. He could tell she had not been so frightened in his absence. Not for a moment had she entertained the thought that he would not be back. She only wanted him back sooner.

She took his hand and a lantern and led him to the little room where she and Anna had been sleeping. There was just the one bed. They stood a moment and looked at Anna, tangled in her blanket. Orabas pulled it from between her legs and lay it back on top of her again. She didn't rouse.

"How is she?"

Maren was slow to answer. "Better."

"And you?" The question was directed at her womb as well, which was showing more clearly now.

She nodded, fine.

The clock outside the door pondered for them both. They looked at Anna again, then finally Maren spoke: "It isn't dead, then?"

No, Orabas shook his head.

"She says you killed it. She says that's why you left."

Anna turned over, but didn't awaken. Her face looked especially peaceful in the pale moonlight.

"I shouldn't be here," he said. "I should go back to the Bend."

Maren only gripped his hand.

"He knows my scent. I may have led it here."

She looked at him; they both knew that wasn't so. What Modo wanted was not here, or at the Bend. And Orabas reminded himself, this was the best possible news. This was all he could have hoped for.

"Are you tired?" she asked.

He wasn't, but he knew she wanted him to hold them both, and for them to sleep, and so although his heart was thumping in his chest uncomfortably, he lay down between them and waited. He closed his eyes and pretended, but as soon as he heard their breathing slow, he got back up. Quietly he went out to the front door, stepping over Noli, who only lifted her eye to watch. Alone he walked out through the moonlight and the shadows of the hitching posts to the edge of the woods, where he knelt down and was sick on the ground.

XXXII

The Long Pier

By dawn the gallows were in place, built according to instructions that had had to be found in the Ministry archives. There had been no executions in Kreisenig since the rebellions of 1824 and '35. Those had taken place out on the Long Pier as well, so the people could all come and see together the price of defiance, and that their then-overlords, the Sud, were not going to be cowed by fanatics, heathens, and sorcerers. Construction of the Cathedral started the very next year.

The Ministry sent out no official proclamation this time. As was custom, they preferred to let the city awaken to the sight. Let the street-sweepers see, and the boatman, and let word spread from there: Someone was getting their comeuppance. The piper was being paid today. If the people wanted to know who, they could come and see. They were expected to.

Margrét had been given a tea of opium, ostensibly to soothe the pain of her injuries. A whopping amount for her petite frame, it put her into a deep and helpless, harmless sleep. She didn't really awaken when the guards came for her at dawn. She had to be dragged from bed, but on orders from Zitri they gave her another dose of the tea right there, just to be safe. They bound her hands and carried her out to the wagon, one of three that would make their way from the Block to the Long Pier. That, too, fetched notice.

By then the day was breaking, apparently unapprised of its agenda. The air was clear and crisp, with tight clouds like ribbons, a set of orange ridges giving way to pink, rolling east to west for painterly purpose.

No one was distracted. The sweepers and the boatmen had played their part well. By the time the sun had crested the eastern ridge at Monpel, the crowd was thick all up and down the riverfront.

That was as close as the public was allowed – security around the Long Pier and the Ministry and all government buildings was immense – but the people were dozens deep along the boardwalk, the front rows whispering back to the others what they could see.

The stage was ten feet high, and another ten feet up was the single crossbeam from which three nooses hung. Three lessons, then, but the only one the people seemed aware of was Ovechkin, who (rumor had it) had been captured. No one had seen him for days.

To avoid the crush of spectators, the prisoners arrived by boat, launched further up the river beyond the lighthouse. The top brass did the same, and were given front row seats not thirty feet from the gallows. There was the Provost, of course, and Zitri and Markus and a half-dozen others, all of whom had breakfasted together at the Ministry to go over the day's schedule, which included the processing of more cases; more reviews of detained prisoners; more troops due to come.

Olybrius had suffered no second thoughts, not a moment of remorse or misgiving, even now as the guards escorted the prisoners up the wooden stairs. Margrét was wearing a grey smock, not unlike the one she had been wearing when he first saw her out on the heath. Her face could barely be seen behind the wild, frenzied veil of auburn. Clearly she had been drugged. The guards had to carry her up the twelve steps to the stage. Even there her arms and legs were ropes. Her eyes drifted and wandered and she had to be helped to her chair, the one set before her noose.

The others, Ovechkin and the impostor, required no assistance. Both ascended the stairs calmly, with their arms behind their backs. Ovechkin seemed to welcome his fate; he was dying for a cause. The Starets, whoever he was, was more difficult to read, but Olybrius saw no distinction between the three. Not anymore. He even felt a certain unaccountable sense of vindication that Margrét, like these other two, had been rousted out and exposed, and that she would be exterminated. Signals must be sent, after all.

The hangings would be performed in succession: Ovechkin, best known of the seditionists, would die last, to keep the crowd. The "holy" imposter would hang before him. Before him – departing first – would be Margrét.

The Minister read the blessing quietly and as a matter of form, that Almighty God should have mercy on this maiden "and all who bear us evil." As he made the sign of the cross upon her, three pigeons came and alighted on the crossbeam, and across the way a falcon landed to watch along with all the rest. The hangman knelt before her and tied two weights to Margrét's ankles – two stones taken from the riverbed, fastened by coarse rope. He then placed the hood over the maiden's head and helped her stand. He led her to the trap door, four steps, but she shuffled unsteadily with her hands behind her back. He took the noose and slid it over her head, which was already set at a queer and lifeless angle. She's gone already, thought Olybrius, or he hoped so – preferring that to the thought of what she might be thinking of, dreaming of, what image she bore in mind as the hangman tightened the rope around her neck, and her last moments on earth drew nigh.

What happened next, all saw. None would quite remember how it started, though – at least in every detail. In fact, in the days and weeks to come, none would recall there ever having been such a man aboard the *Minarik*. There simply was no Starets. Theodosius had sent no emissary. Goulu had healed himself. Margrét endured her interrogation alone. The third noose? What third noose? There were three *pigeons*, not nooses

All they would remember – and tell their friends and neighbors and rivals and anyone who would listen – was that the beast had returned, the one from the night of the reception, the one they said had been a tarp, a bat, a flock. None of these things remotely, it had swept down from the Cathedral again, they said. Or no, from out of the river it came, or others still (and theirs became the most accepted version) said that it had come from *underneath* the pier, where it had obviously been hiding, sleeping, lurking, since its first appearance, now that its proper home beneath the bridge had been destroyed by His Majesty's dynamite.

By the account of no one present had the creature actually been sitting up on the gallows stage, there beside the others, in a chair, in a black tunic tied at the waist by a golden rope. Not even Olybrius would countenance that, though in fact he had been looking directly at the Starets when the change occurred. They all were waiting for the hangman to release the trap door – it was the moment just before. The Provost had briefly turned away – perhaps demurring from the image, perhaps distracted by the movement – but he had seen the Starets lift his head slightly. Even underneath the hood the opening of the jaw had been perceptible, wider than one would have thought possible. At first a kind of mist had issued, or a smoke, then a blackened oval where the mouth had been, then suddenly a glowing orange rope. A jet of fire came spewing out, aimed directly at the other rope, the one tied around the sleepy maiden's neck. The flame enveloped it, blackened and burnt it in two, just as the trap door opened and Margrét fell through, landing with a harmless thud and crumpling beneath the stage of the gallows.

That sight, of her vanishing from the crowd's eyes, no doubt distracted some from what was taking place behind – though not Olybrius, who saw the Starets wrestle loose from his ties and begin sweeping his arms round and round in such a way that the billows of his black robe had seemed to grow. Or they did not *seem*. They did. Many gasped at what they saw (and would soon forget), which was that this man somehow expanded and changed. The same as happened to his sleeves now happened to his face. It expanded, too, while never really losing its resemblance to the man. The features darkened, lengthened, grew plates and barbs and horns while the neck elongated, and the tail fanned its infamous thorns. The wings released from its back, and there, in the time it takes a dog to shake dry, a fully fledged and furious dragon stood before them.

It reared, twisted its head, flaring its wings, not just to preen its rage, but to summon up its strength and powers, which it for a second time expressed as a blast of flame from its gaping maw, spreading wide its jaws and sending down another plume of fire at the three standing guards. It roiled around them, engulfing and swallowing them like a hellfire. A column of officers on the far side took aim and fired, but the sting of bullets, though new to the beast and impressive, only fueled its fury. With a sweep of its tail the dragon flung them from the pier. It smashed the rail and then set about destroying the gallows, but not before it found the maiden. It snatched her from beneath the stage, thrashing and spewing fire while the remaining guards scrambled, dove and covered.

Olybrius, who had found no cover at all behind his chair, was looking out through the crook of his elbow. He saw all this, and therefore also saw the beast pause briefly in the midst of its own mayhem to find his little, blinking eye. They looked directly at each other – the disbeliever and the disbelieved – just long enough for the beast to convey that if he chose, he could do the same to him right now as he had done to Zitri's men – finish him with a sniff – but that he preferred to let him live in the knowledge of what he had seen. The dragon offered a final snort, then lifted its wings and, with the maiden still limp in its clutches, leapt from the pier. It dipped out over the water, touching it lightly with his hind legs, then with two quick strums achieving full speed and flight.

It turned and made for the city again, not for the main way this time, but the avenue one over. The people watched. They craned and screamed as he swept over their heads and on into the concrete ravine. Shopkeepers setting up shop, street vendors setting up their stands and those guards specifically assigned to protect the Ministry saw it come, saw the right front claw holding fast to the maiden, saw it open its mouth and drive another blast of fire at the second story balcony, softening it before landing there decisively, smashing through the burning French doors with its horns, then sticking just its head and neck inside. The people below would later say it was like watching a hound go after a mole.

But they could not see inside, where Vassago was, where he had merely been copying the Provost's letters, opting out of the morning spectacle in order to catch up on some paperwork; re-dipping his pen when the mad rush of fire whorled and roiled against the window-panes, and the balcony caught the beast and the whole building shook and shuddered and then the great head burst in and found him, precisely the one he was looking for.

Too horrified to grasp the clarity of the monster's purpose, the Steward staggered back from the writing desk. He dashed for the bureau for no good reason – to climb inside, he supposed. It made no difference to the beast, who merely took the whole thing in its jaws and crushed it. The letter and shirts and cufflinks scattered and splayed, the gem nowhere among them. It was still pressed against the Steward's chest, there for safekeeping under his shirt. The beast was well aware. He shook the little man from the box, clamped him, gnashed him and shook him again until the stone fell free, then he tossed him aside like gristle.

With his tongue he swept up the gem. He took it safely in his mouth, withdrew his head and in full view of the crowd below, spread his wings once more and lunged from the balcony, still with the maiden clutched in his front claw. He beat upwards and upwards, over the Cathedral tower and once around to gain his bearings. Then he headed north again, cutting over toward the river and following its line past Old Yinny. He flew for another half mile before disappearing behind the high ridge of Monpel, leaving behind two billowing trails of smoke, one from the Ministry, one from the Long Pier, where the Royal Guard and guests were only just now emerging from the blood and the cinders.

PART THREE:

The Northern Castle

XXXIII

Flowers

Inger was mercifully spared all that: spared the sight of Margrét being brought out in public, bound, hooded, and fixed with the hangman's rope; spared having to watch the terrible beast seem to appear from nowhere, demolish the pier, then snatch poor Margrét, her dear sweet Margrét, in its taloned claws and swoop away with her – again, no one knew why or where to, but none of the possibilities seemed comforting.

Ingrid had seen none of this, and was not told about any of it until well after, and after certain other apparitions and appearances had served to reassure her that there was still, despite everything that had happened, hope.

Following the explosion at the bridge, she had been swept up briefly in the street riot, but Antonia Pecca – her little almond-eyed, oval-faced, bow-lipped guardian angel – had found her and brought her to a kind of safe house near the University, a gutted three-story brownstone in which Antonia and what seemed to be at least two dozen other people, all students, had taken nest. That night the house had been more full than usual. Ingrid shared a couch with a factory girl from Tuvin, but did not sleep a wink. She was just beginning to drift, in fact, when the police burst in at dawn with guns and clubs, looking for Ovechkin. They couldn't find him, but as Inger had no papers she was given the choice either to come with them to jail or be taken to the city limit, which was by then under strictest blockade.

She chose the latter – not just because that's what Antonia Pecca had urged as she was being dragged away ("Tell them! Tell the people what you have seen here!"). Inger frankly wasn't sure what she had seen, but in hopes that Margrét had found a way out of the city as well, she accepted the escort to the limit, and actually walked

183

halfway to Armen. That was where her cousin Jeppe lived, the one with the suitable horse and carriage. Halfway there a lorry picked her up and took her directly to Jeppe's door.

Margrét was not there, as she had slimly hoped, and Inger was in great despair, not knowing what she should do or where she should go. She could not make either Jeppe or his wife Vita understand the things she had seen, but Vita had finally given her some milk and brandy to calm her nerves. That, combined with the exhaustion built up over the last several days, finally managed to bring sleep, and sleep brought a dream which contained a kind of premonition. Inger did not know exactly what it all meant, but she did awaken with a much firmer sense of where she should be now.

The dream had been of Five Homes. Margrét was not there either, but Torvald and all the families were. They were cleaning up what seemed like an endless number of stones from the floor of the hut, rubble. But when she looked out the window, there were sunflowers everywhere. They were surrounded by them, thousands upon thousands of yellow sunflowers, all eye-high and gaping back at her.

The following morning, she asked Jeppe if he would take her up north as soon as possible.

XXXIV

The Northern Castle

Margrét awoke to the image of a shifting, shadowy figure looming directly over her, like a giant head on the tip of a high tree limb. It shifted and glazed, and in the time it took her eyes to tear and to clear themselves, she saw it was only the Seidre offering water, and she was much relieved.

"Welcome."

She drank. The water was intensely cold, so cold her head throbbed, but it was good, and was served in a golden goblet.

They were in a large dim room, some sort of sleeping chamber to judge by the size of the bed she was on – a four poster, above which was high, vaulted ceiling, covered with paintings. Clouds? Children? Cherubim or flowers? Something like that; the space was half-lit. She could see chests across the way, bureaus, bowls and dried flowers, all shimmering and flickering in the light of a great stone hearth

"How do you feel?" he asked.

"Very well," she said, and this was true. She must have slept deeply. She sat up and couldn't remember feeling quite so well, refreshed. "Hungry."

He wasn't surprised.

A pair of soft catskin slippers were waiting at the foot of the bed.

He led her to another grand room, a dining room, warmed by a hearth of its own and further lit by wall sconces all the way around, as well as a great wooden chandelier, like a rack of antlers, suspended above a grand ashwood table.

Her plate was waiting for her – pears, bread, and cheese. The Seidre did not eat, but sat across from her and watched as she shamelessly gobbled. They were the best pears she had ever tasted.

"You don't want any?"

He shook his head. "I've eaten."

She tried to remember. There was the ship. This was not the ship. She hadn't liked the ship. The ship was fraught, but this was bigger and more solid. Even from the inside she could feel.

But it was hard to keep track of what was real and what had been a dream, though she supposed that was the point. The whole thing had been a dream in a way.

She finished her plate and asked for another, and when she was done with that, she asked to see more.

"Of course," he said.

He led her up a steep dark flight of steps, down another corridor and a dark, chilly hall. The light of his swinging lantern lashed at the moldings and the wood inlay and the painting that covered the walls – portraits and landscapes – and as they went, she thought she could hear others, the pitter patter of feet and the murmur of voices but she couldn't tell where from.

"What is this place?" she asked. "Is it yours?"

He didn't answer; they had come to a balcony. The light was so sudden and bright it blasted her eyes. All she saw at first was white – the snow and ice and the sky. A frozen cape draped the cataract that fell directly beside where they were standing.

They were in the high tower of a castle that seemed to have been carved directly into the side of a cliff, or to have grown right out of it, the rounded tower walls emerging directly from the russet limestone, then sprouting spires and cupolas, dark slate shingled roofs and widow's walks and turrets.

Across the way was a cliff as well, or the same cliff, as she could see now – just beyond the cataract the wall abruptly turned to face itself perhaps a quarter of a mile across, with nothing between them but water, high water, extending all the way down the jagged ravine and most likely out to sea.

Now she understood; now she remembered: the flood. The waters had come. They'd arisen and broken through just before she'd fallen asleep, and here was the world they'd left behind, the world they'd spared. The dry peaks of the old one.

"There's no one else?"

He shook his head without a glint of regret.

She looked up into the grey-white sky, and that confirmed it. The stars had all been vanquished, just as the books had said. Skoll the wolf had eaten the sun. His brother Hati had eaten the moon, all while she'd been away, slumbering in the shadows. Loki slain by Heimdall; Heimdall slain by Loki. Odin, devoured and avenged (Torvald had never liked that, except for the avenging part). The poisoned seas had risen and swallowed the world. The world was sleeping underneath – Torvald too, no doubt, and all of this while she'd been gone; swept up to the castle here, higher than the waters had reached, where there was just the two of them, just as the books had said: Lif, who must have been the Seidre; and Lifthrasir, who must have been herself. She was quite eager, after all.

"There are fish, though."

"Lots of fish," he said.

"And birds."

"Lots of birds."

She turned and led him back inside

Of course she might have thought that she'd be upset by this, or overwhelmed at least, but she wasn't. She'd been reading about this her whole life. This was how she'd *learned* to read, and so she knew. Just as the flood was bound to be, it was bound to be that the waters would eventually recede, come spring, come sun. Life had not been ended entirely, after all, for here they were. The only news, really, was that she was the one who would have to pass it on. And he. And that wasn't really so surprising either.

Down another several shallow-stepped corridors they passed through a kind of theater with a stage, and then a room full of pools, six or seven, but all connected and all of different shapes and depths, and all fed by the same slow stream running through and further down.

"You can bathe here if you like," he said. "No one will bother you."

Of course, she thought. Who else would?

Another, shorter hallway led to what appeared to be a dressing room, filled with clothes and mirrors, although some of the clothes were more like costumes – with headdresses, feathered crowns and helmets with plumes. Clearly they were all for her, or hers to try if she liked. She would come back, she thought. Already her heart was lifting, filling with the idea of all she'd do.

"These are my favorite," she said, remarking the flowers tucked in the brim of one of the hats. "Larkspur." She touched them. Silk.

The next room was for jewels, but a countless supply, it seemed: rubies and agate, lapis, pearls and gems she didn't know the names of, but dozens and dozens of each, hundreds, some set in crown and rings and necklaces, some just laying about like pebbles, like piles of grain, pearls like rice, and diamonds like brookstones.

"How did you get all these?" she asked, trying not to seem impressed. "Are you a thief? Or a King?"

He smiled at the distinction. "A collector," he said, which wasn't really an answer, but it certainly seemed to be true. And not only of jewels and gems, but plates as well, and bowls and bureaus, chairs, paintings, lamps and chandeliers. Each room was like a picture from a book, from the rugs across the floor to the fixtures on the wall. The lamps were all like statues. It must have taken lifetimes to collect all this, she thought.

"What else?" she said.

He showed her. He brought her to a kind of a library like the one on the King's ship, except this one was bigger. The ceiling was three times as high, and there were no windows, just row after row of books, and galleries so high there were ladders on wheels for reaching them. She wouldn't have been surprised if this was every book there was. It certainty seemed to be, or close. Pray the sun doesn't return too soon, she thought. Again, she thought to herself, I want to read them all.

"And what's through there?" she asked. Down at the far end of the room there was another door – an enormous oaken door with iron hinges –

"We keep that one locked," he said. She didn't press. She understood, some things must be locked away, always. And there was that sound again, of voices – singing.

"I thought it was just us."

"And the wind," he said. She listened again. She supposed he was right, but if it was just the wind, then the castle was like one great pipe organ. Such a beautiful, comforting sound it made.

She felt herself grow very sleepy all of a sudden. Her limbs felt heavy. Her eyelids too. She yawned.

"Would you like me to take you back now?"

She nodded, so he did. She could barely walk she was so tired, and she could never have found her way alone, but finally they did come to the chamber where she had awakened.

Where the lilies had been there were now blue larkspur. And real.

"That's nice," she said. She yawned again and lay back down in the canopied bed. (But had there been a canopy before? She couldn't remember.) He asked if she was warm enough. She said yes, but the fire replied by swelling slightly, as if another door had opened.

"Why am I so tired?" she asked. She could barely get the sentence out before her lids descended and she was asleep.

§

She was tired because he was tired, because it is one thing to transform oneself in the eye of the beholder, quite another to transform everything the beholder sees.

But he could not let her see this. He waited beside her until her breathing deepened and lengthened, then he released all he had been keeping. The walls of inlaid wood and marble turned back into stone; the bed into pile of sedge grass. The rugs on the floor to moss, to pelts.

189

ASMODEUS

And finally the man as well – the hands, the lips, the hair, the brow, the feet, all lay down within him and slept, while he himself resumed the plates and thorns that he was born to, and that he'd been wearing when he first had glimpsed her, and she him, through the skylight window of the *Minarik*. Here again, his natural figure crouched beside her in the dank darkness of the cave, watching her in silence as she slept, struggling with cravings which were new to him, both tender and violent, and which he could only really compare to hunger.

XXXV

Hope

O rabas was still at the Trading Post when word arrived of what had taken place down in the capitol. He had been preparing to leave for the Bend the following day. In fact, he had laid out everything he would need, most of it borrowed from Per-Malfi, when the traders started appearing mid-morning.

It was the usual crew – the Trinko brothers, the quarrymen, Koos and Gaino and Yusted, and Andjes, of course, as ever the leeriest of the bunch. As usual, they gathered round the front room with their pipes and skins to trade the latest stories, though on this day there was just the one, even if the versions they'd heard were all slightly different.

"No, no, no," said Sami Trinko, who seemed to be the best informed; he and Olly had a cousin who worked in the city. "The hanging was separate from the ball. The hanging was two days later."

"But so then this thing shows up twice?"

"Twice," Sami confirmed, using his fingers. "Night of the reception, there's the shooting on the pier. Then there's a riot in the city. Then the hanging, two days later."

"That sounds like three."

"Right, but the thing – the monster – doesn't show up for the riot."

"Who were they hanging?" asked Koos.

Sami shrugged. "Troublemakers."

"And what did the thing look like again?" asked Gaino. "The monster?"

Koos shrugged again.

"Troll?" offered Koos. "I'd imagine. If it come from under the bridge."

"Could have been a bat."

"And they said it flew, no?"

"Ya, from the Cathedral."

"Come, come, it's no bat," said Andjes, exasperatedly. "And it's no troll, either. Am I the only one who'll say it?" He looked around the room, but there were no takers. "...It's Modo, no?"

Little bursts of pipesmoke answered, but Andjes was convinced. "And didn't Yuli say they seen him out along the fences?"

"Modo," Gaino scoffed. "In the first place, he'd have to be eight hundred, nine hundred..."

"More than that, but then it's his son," said Andjes. "And what's a thousand years to a wyrm like that. Of course it's him. Who else?" He turned. "Bazja? Am I wrong?"

Orabas merely shrugged, as if he had no real opinion on the matter. "Could be Modo, I suppose. Could be mead."

The room chuckled; that was true, too. It wasn't long after that, though, that Yoonas the postman came with actual copies of the *Lür*, the latest edition of which had actual photographs of what had happened at the pier. Not very good photographs. There were three, taken at five-second intervals from the top of a stepladder set all the way back on the boardwalk, which distance the Royal Guard had apparently deemed sufficient to furnish the desired image: of three hooded seditionists hanging in a row.

The distance did less well to capture the attack of the mysterious creature, who was only barely visible in the first of the photographs – all black, and provided very little relief against the backdrop of the wooded shore across the river. A neck and the edge of a wing perhaps, which Orabas only recognized because he'd seen it. Ridden on it, in fact.

The second photograph made it slightly more clear. Again, the beast was a black silhouette and blurred, but the length could be seen well enough to make out its resemblance to a great serpent.

The men were all gathered around a single copy. "That's the head?

"Tail. That's the head there." Eyes squinted to make sense.

The third photograph was obscured by the glare of the fire engulfing the gallows – a white glow from the photographer's vantage. The panic of the guards could be seen, but the monster's outline was difficult to decipher, swallowed as it was in the light. There was what might have been a wing rising up from its back, or it could just as well have been its spine or a tree on the far shoreline. The men at the Trading Post took turns holding it to the light.

"…No troll, that's for sure."

"No, that's him all right," said Andjes. "And look at the article. Read it, Koos."

Koos read that, according to eyewitnesses, the creature "bore a clear resemblance to the legendary beast mentioned in King Ulrik's history, Moder."

"There, see?"

The article furthermore claimed that there had been nine fatalities, who went unnamed, but that thankfully these had not included Bazja's brother the Provost, who was mentioned as having briefly imposed, and then lifted, martial law.

"Talk to your brother lately?" asked Andjes; he wasn't provoking this time.

"Not since this," said Orabas.

They all looked back at the photographs.

"And what do you think roused him?"

"Didn't it say? The bridge."

Other weren't so sure.

"Well, whatever it was," said Andjes, "I warrant they deserved it."

On this the room agreed, with all respect to Bazja's brother. Indeed, as mad and as horrifying as it all sounded, a myth somehow re-emerging to destroy the Long Pier at Kreisenig – and part of the Ministry, don't forget – the mood in the room seemed to have lifted with the appearance of the photographs. Every heart, while thumping a bit quicker and more nervously, was slightly swelled as well.

Business concluded early nonetheless, as the traders all settled their accounts, bought their own copies of the *Lür* and hustled back home to be nearer their dogs, their children, their guns. After all, who knew?

Per-Malfi didn't seem concerned. After the last had gone, he and Orabas shared a smoke in the back room while Per-Malfi measured out some parcels of poppy seed that Sami Trinko had brought.

"There it is, then," Per-Malfi puffed. "Got what he was looking for."

Orabas replied with a distant nod.

"Which is good news, no?" Per-Malfi tapped the scale and squinted. "Means the Bend is safe."

Again, Orabas nodded, more than likely. The dragon had obviously come back for the jewel and taken it. That's the only reason Olybrius would still be alive. That was the only reason any of them were. He'd got what he wanted.

Per-Malfi took up his mortar and pestle. "Ever ask yourself why, though?" He dumped a handful of seeds in the bowl and started grinding. "Why a big fella like that should be so interested in a little jewel?"

It was a good question. Stranger yet was the fact that Orabas had never really considered it. The shamir was the shamir. He supposed he had always taken its attraction for granted, as he took for granted the moon and tides, bees and flowers. Why was the dragon susceptible? He could have asked the same question of himself – or his grandfather, or his grandfather's grandfather – and he'd have had no better an answer.

The subject was not mentioned at dinner. Neither Maren nor Anna had seen the paper, and Orabas chose not to show them. Anna used her father's lap as a high chair, as she had been doing since his return, but he sat cold beneath her, not saying a word the whole meal, other than to scold her twice for the way she held her fork.

Following dinner, she had gone off to read with her grandfather. Orabas and Maren had separated as well. He remained at the table, alone, while she went to her father's pantry to continue preparing his satchels for tomorrow's journey. Preserves and biscuits. Dried fruit. He knew. He could have guessed everything inside the little pouch that she now carried past him and into the room where they'd been sleeping.

He could see her through the door jamb, kneeling down, finding a pocket in his rucksack to tuck it in. The image sparked an unaccountable fury in him. He bolted up from the table, stalked in and swiped the sack away from her. He kicked the pile. "You leave it to me!" he growled. "I'll see to it."

The house went suddenly silent. Per-Malfi and Anna included. Orabas stood above Maren, heaving, flushed, not even looking at her he was so surprised by his anger. Finally, she simply stood and let him be. She left him there in the dark.

With nowhere else to go, he lay down on the bed, though he was not tired. Per-Malfi took Anna outside to look at the stars, and Orabas felt as if the whole world and the sky were falling down on him, or in on him. He felt like the drain beneath a fetid, brackish puddle.

True, he should be thankful. His family was safe. Modo had in all likelihood returned to his lair up north. They could go back to the Bend and resume, but he did not feel this. All he felt was his own failure. He had been given one simple task in life – after all the things he had seen and done – he had been asked to guard a stone, and he had lost it. Worse, he had not even fought to protect it. From the moment the wyrm had appeared he had been its minion, like a servant whose only purpose was to keep the silver safe while his master was away. The dragon had only had to look at him, and Orabas had yielded like a reed. He had turned on his own brother.

And of course he knew why. In his entire life he had never encountered anything so overwhelming, so vast and enfeebling as Modo's mind, the swarming, enveloping, invading intelligence of it. Even now, the idea that he might go and challenge it, steal back the jewel and redeem himself – for that is what Barbatos would have done, no? Or Naberius? – it was unthinkable. How? There was no trap, no gambit, no weapon in the world that could threaten that fortress.

And so he was left with this, this crushing sense of failure and defeat. It weighed down on him like a leaden blanket, the knowledge that his name would forever be remembered with the likes of Colais and Hamad, the scoundrels. The idea that he should have to carry this burden back to the Bend – even if it was safe – the idea of living there, of fathering a son in that house without the shamir in place, seized up in him like a poison. He could not imagine it. He did not believe it.

There was a shadow at the door. Maren. She had given him his time alone, and now she'd come to be heard.

"You raise your voice all you like," she said, a dark silhouette standing the frame. "You raise your hand, I'm not afraid, but you will look at me."

If he had spoken, it would only have been to say yes, I mean to. He would have given anything to be able to look Maren in the eye again, but he could not. That was why he was so angry, because he was so weak –

"Come out!" called Per-Malfi, from the front side of the house. "Come out!" His voice was filled with joy. And Anna's too.

"Come see! Mama! Papa!"

Orabas sat up and followed Maren out, though he was still weary.

Anna and her grandfather were standing among the hitching posts and looking straight up at the sky. Per-Malfi had a sense for these things. Anna ran to take her father's hand; she bore no grudges. He lifted her up in his arms and they both looked up.

The surrounding trees made a kind of dial out of the sky, small enough that on clear nights you could almost see the stars moving, all rotating on their spindle. This night they were a field, across which much faster, nearer lights were streaking from one side to the other, like fireflies.

Anna laughed and pointed. "Look, another!"

"And another!" said her grandfather

Orabas looked at their faces, divided by sixty-some years, lit by the very same wonder, and who knows how such things occur – whether it was that, or Maren's hand, or the stars overhead, teasing his brain with flashes of light – but that was when it came to him: that the question he had been asking all along and the question Per-Malfi had asked just now might have the same answer. Why did Modo want the shamir so much? Because it was the only thing on earth he feared. It was the only stone sharp enough, hard enough, pure enough to slice him through, and that is why he guarded it so jealously – because as long as he possessed the blade, the blade could not be used against him.

"What?" asked Maren, looking over at him now. She could sense the change in his mood. He was smiling, and not about the shooting stars. He only had to turn and look at her, the same spark in his eye.

There was hope, in fact.

She took his hand and looked back up at the shower, her own heart sinking.

XXXVI

Goats

Back in the capitol, an eerie stillness had descended. What the newspapers said was true. Zitri had lifted martial law after a week, but for some reason the people remained in their homes. They hadn't come to work on Monday. Or Tuesday. It wasn't clear why, if they were on some kind of strike, or merely frightened – plotting, or praying. And if they were praying, then praying to whom?

Here it was Wednesday and the streets were lifeless again. Olybrius was just returning from a meeting out at Old Yinny with the designers of the new bridge. He had taken the car, he and his new driver, a Sylkan officer named Drozny. Drozny drove very slowly, the better to take in the ghostliness of the streets, and all the new graffiti, which seemed to be everywhere now. Under dark of night the street artists had been coming out with chalk and paint, defacing the walls with their crude renderings of "Modo the Monster," most of them extrapolated from the pictures in the newspaper, but from old shields as well, and flags.

Olybrius didn't actually mind them so much. They were so crude and silly, they functioned more as a way to forget what had taken place than to remember. They abstracted an incident that hadn't been abstract at all; rendered it a kind of art, and therefore artificial.

Much more disturbing to him were the stray encounters that brought the moment back to him – the passing of a steam vent; the smell of burning garbage; the neck of a lamppost. That would summon the image of the great tail whipping, or of the blood splattered on all four walls of his (now former) office (poor poor Vassago. Why hadn't he simply come to the pier? More flowers for him tomorrow). The light of the lamp might summon the dragon's eye as it had looked at him so pointedly – letting him live, so that he could see and understand and never forget: Bazja was right. Bazja was right all along. Olybrius thought of his brother constantly now. He wanted to go to him, or to write him at least, if only to make sure he was well. But how would he even begin?

Perhaps "You were right..."

Around the next corner they came upon one of the few signs of life in the streets. Outside the Cathedral Bakery, a small crowd was gathered, mostly of police and soldiers, there to lunch on the famous potato dumplings. Olybrius sent Drozny in to pick up a bag. While waiting in the car, he noticed another scrawl on the wall across the way – eyes and fangs and fire, this time adorning the rectory of the Cathedral itself. That was too bad. He also noticed there was a wagon parked in front of the Cathedral steps, filled with bales of hay. Strange.

"So what was the prognosis?" The car slump beneath the weight of Zitri's boot. Apparently the General had developed a taste for the dumplings as well; he had a grease-stained paper bag in hand. "What is the future of our Yinny?"

"The same as it was," said Olybrius. "Their inclination is to proceed as planned. Just rebuild the eastern side."

"That'll cost."

"Well, the men need to get to the factories."

The General plopped a dumpling in his mouth and began chewing vigorously, with the same overly aggressive swagger that had been animating him ever since the attack at the pier – that obnoxious air of vindication peculiar to all military lifers, stemming from the clear and entirely unwarranted conviction that if only everyone else had listened to them, if they had simply been allowed to act *more* quickly, *more* forcefully, if they'd been given the proper resources to display the fullness of their might, then all the current bother could have been avoided. Olybrius found it intensely grating, if only because it was such an act. Zitri was as embarrassed as anyone. The posters and papers and stories were all flowing down river, down to the rest of the warmer world, telling of how the all-powerful Sylka had ventured north to brandish their arms, only to meet with an ancient beast who'd caught them off guard and cut them to ribbons.

Olybrius salted the wound.

"What about Ovechkin?" he asked.

Ovechkin was still at large, but around the barstools and breakfast tables he'd become something of a folk-hero, and the New Welanders were his band of merry men – who'd thumbed their noses at the new regime, got pushed, shoved back, and somehow harnessed that same legendary beast to their cause. Modo had saved their leader from the gallows, set him free, and all the new regime could do was bribe, offer a reward for information leading to his capture. Clearly no one had yet come forward, as testified by the irritated whistle coming from Zitri's nostrils.

They both looked over at the Cathedral. Someone had just emerged from the doors with a shovel and two heavy buckets – a farmer, it looked like. He set them in the wagon there, hoisted a hay bale onto his shoulder and started up the steps again.

"You shouldn't allow that," said Zitri, helping himself to another dumpling.

"What are they doing?"

"You don't know?" He glanced up at the steeple tower. "They've got sheep up there. And goats. A whole barnyard."

"In the bell tower?" Olybrius craned and shielded his eyes. The tower was too high to see from here, but the bleating of goats could be heard. "What the devil for?"

"The devil," answered Zitri, still chewing. "Offerings. In case that thing returns." He licked his thumb. "This is what I said to you. A little scare and they fall back five thousand years." He shook his head wryly. "If I knew where that thing was hiding, believe you me…"

This was not the first time Olybrius had heard Zitri grumble something to this effect: if he only knew where he could find it, the beast, the thing, the snake; he never used the name. For the first time Olybrius replied, "Then what? What, if you knew?"

Zitri looked back at him, eyes beaming, as if he'd been waiting for the question: "I'd bring it back on a chain," he said — was there any doubt? "I'd cart its carcass through the streets. Show them who is master. Who gets the goat."

"What, you and a cross bow?"

"Me and whatever it took." His mustache spread like wings.

It was the very next day the letter from Maren arrived on Olybrius's desk, informing him that Bazja was headed north, alone, with nothing but his sled and hunting knife.

XXXVII

Seven Rooms

There was no thaw in sight. A bitter, frozen cold had them locked inside the Castle. The waters surrounding them were still high, but Margrét did not feel remotely trapped. There was too much to do.

She had counted seven chambers when the Seidre first toured her through, but that wasn't nearly right. There were many more than that, running much deeper inside the castle than even she dared go, and filled with more things than she could ever imagine.

She used to have a dream back at Five Homes. She and the sheep would come over the eastern ridge and suddenly find whole meadows she hadn't seen before, or that she had forgotten about; or in the village itself, beneath their hut were holes and trap doors leading down to caverns that she had likewise completely forgotten. But how? For here they were, and whole other wings neglected under dust, unlit, awaiting her.

Here it was like that, as if a whole world of treasures and memories and secret histories was hiding within the cliffside: galleries and ballrooms, herbariums, bestiaries, and apothecaries. Anything one could imagine seemed to be there. All you had to do was look. Look for one thing, find another, something he had found instead and put there for her. There was no end. The castle was like his mind in that way, but exactly: dark and magnificent, fathomless. To be there was like living inside of his mind.

And yet the Seidre didn't seem at all proud of it. As vast as his keep may have been, he did not seem to care for it one way or the other, or to need it. He could just as well have lived inside a cave. That's where she pictured him, in fact. That's how she imagined his room, the one beyond the library: a simple cave, for praying, or sleeping, or whatever he needed his solitude to do, while all around him the castle glittered and grew. It was always changing, changing because he made it change, changing because it was alive, and living things change.

That went for the water – its currents, its tides and temperatures. The colors changed, the light was never twice the same, finding its way in through various skylights and crannies, painting the walls all different purples one moment, golds and oranges the next. But the little things, too: how the quilts would mysteriously shift pattern, but subtly. The chairs would turn, or there would be two, a new one over there, new rugs, a vase she had not seen before, or at least it had not been there, with such pretty flowers painted on. Lilies today. Jasmine tomorrow. Sometimes when she went to the library, instead of books there would be jars along the shelves, with scrolls inside, or sometimes the jars didn't even have scrolls. Sometimes the words were inscribed on the clay, in letters and pictures that Margrét couldn't read.

Nothing was ever quite the way she had left it. Sometimes she felt as if all she had to do was step outside a room and step back in, and something would be different – the placement of a painting, or the smile within a portrait. And she knew that he was the one who made it that way – who'd set the glove there on the bench, or the hat. He was the one who'd warmed the water, cooled the light, or closed a distant door like the valve of a giant flute, so that the music would sound different today, darker or more light. Whether she could see him or not, she could feel he was there, always, so every change – from the largest to the small, from the shift of a hearth to the ripening of each berry on the vine – she attributed to him and to his attention. It was his way of treating her.

She knew this because it was the same as he treated her in the dining room. He never served her quite the same plate twice. There would always be something from prior meals – the custards, the berry pies, the venison all were favorites – but there was always something new as well, something she hadn't tried before, like oysters or cockles, or roasted sea bass. (She had never had *that* before, what was that? "Lobster," he said. "You would like it again?" Again she nodded and on the list it would go.)

"Did you know that in Solomon's palace, the animals lined up to be served?" she asked. She had been reading about Solomon.

"Is that so?"

"That's what the book said. It said that his wives would cook for him every night. Seven hundred he had, and three hundred concubines as well – what is a concubine?"

"What did they serve?"

"Oh, everything, and they didn't even know if he would come. That was the point. They'd create whole feasts in hopes that he would, which is why even the animals agreed. It was such an honor, just the idea that they *might* be eaten by him, they entered the kitchen themselves. The chickens and geese marched right into the pots and ovens."

He nodded nostalgically. "I don't remember geese," he said, and she laughed.

She never thanked him for any of these things. They were not given as gifts, or as bribes, but more as tests and experiments. So she never mentioned it or did anything other than to avail herself of whatever was new, whatever was different, whatever change had been made. If there was a dress, then wear it; a fruit, then eat it. That was the way to thank him. To explore, to wear, to taste, explore again. Or read. Read, read, read above all. The jars as well as the books.

Because she had come to realize, that was the reason she was here: so that someone would know, someone would remember. She was here so that when the sun returned, when the water and the ice receded and life resumed, the memory of everything that had gone before would be preserved, through her. She would *be* the memory, and the link, and she accepted this. This made perfect sense.

So that was how the days divided. Not by light, or by time, or meal, but by expedition. Every morning after waking she would go out onto the balcony to see that the ice was still there; there was no life – except for the falcon. The falcon would return from her survey to let her know: not from her height either. Not yet. There was still time.

So in she'd go and spend the whole day filling her bowl – that was how she thought of it, and of herself. Whatever there was to taste, she would; whatever there was to touch, she would. Or smell, or hear or understand. Again, she spent most of her time in the library, going from book to book, or jar to jar. She discovered that if she took the jars into the music room and simply put them to her ear, she could hear stories as clearly as if she were reading them to herself. She heard them all, and often if she was so inspired she'd go straight to the dressing room and find whatever she needed – the gown, the tunic, the turban or the suits of armor. She would take up the bows and swords and stand before the mirrors, and the mirrors would reply with villains and muses and nemeses, courtiers, paramours, challengers and fiends. And it wasn't long before she realized the mirrors were not mirrors at all, but frames and thresholds leading into deeper tunnels, dungeons and catacombs. All she had to do was step through and she could slay knaves, dance Orientales, escape dark dungeons. She could be all things: a queen, a maiden, she could be king, scientist, alchemist. Each garment set off another world, another past and future, filled with her in its guise. She could conclude the war; dress the wound; finish out the sentence; remove the head or have her head removed; she could starve or gorge, fly (as she already knew how to do); but swim the deepest oceans too; command, obey, chisel, play, pray, betray; everything a human could, or any beast had ever done, she could do.

Or almost everything.

No wonder, then, that every day should end with sheer exhaustion. Finally she would be so tired she'd lose all track of where she was. How could she know, with all these doors and halls and little corridors she followed? She'd try retracing her steps back on through the picture frames or mirror frames and jars, but sometimes she would simply lie down where she was, right there on the rug or in the nearest chair, and that was fine. That worked too, because no matter where she fell asleep, she always woke up back in her bed again, and in her room, where there would be a new light coming in, a new blanket, and new flowers on the bureau, waiting to greet her.

And he'd have done that too.

XXXVIII

Fruits

The plan had been for all the families of Five Homes to start north as soon as Inger and Margrét got back. That was before they'd left, of course, but deep down no one was assuming that Margrét would even be back. Whoever had sent the invitation might well lay claim to her, or she to him, and no one at Five Homes had ever thought that Margrét would be with them forever.

Still, they hoped. Every night after supper Torvald took out the book, the one that Margrét read to him before bed, and thumbed through all the pages. The words meant nothing to him, of course, but he looked at the engravings, and he could hear her voice.

Jeppe's's carriage appeared late in the day, the fifth day after Inger and Margrét had left. Torvald was first to see it trundling up the southern road. He herded the sheep down from the pasture to meet them, and the other families came out as well and squinted to see if Margrét was aboard. They removed their hats. Tasha ran out as well, but slowed. Her tail descended. There was only Inger and her cousin. The other families put their hats back on.

Inger had also been harboring hope. As the carriage ascended the last long rise, her eyes had searched the hills and meadows. When she saw Torvald out with the sheep, she knew. Then she saw the faces of the other families. The mouths all smiled to welcome her. The eyes were grieving.

She smiled back, but as soon as she and Torvald were alone, she wept in his arms, saying she didn't know where Margrét was. The King's men had kept her on the boat, she didn't know why. Nothing she said made much sense, and Torvald meant to consol her, but he thought it best to let her cry. He waited until her cheeks were dry and her nose was blown.

"The Völla was here," he said.

She looked up at him. "What?" She blew her nose again.

"Out by the oak," he said.

"When? Did you see her?"

"No. She left a blessing – Onni-miika says."

"What kind of blessing?"

Torvald shook his head, he didn't know. "Sheep won't go past the first meadow."

The following morning, Inger took the sheep out herself. She tried to walk them all the way out to the tree, but Torvald was right. The flock refused to go north of the vale, as if they too were determined to wait for the girl. Inger had to climb the knoll alone, but when she reached the oak, she saw what Oni-miika had. Hanging from the second branch was the forelock of a horse.

She looked around as if the Völla might still be there, though Inger knew she was long gone by now. She did see something strange, though. Coming up the Southern road was a wagon drawn by two oxen, with what looked like at least a dozen people in it.

By the time she got the flock back to Five Homes, the wagon had moved on, but the dozen strangers were standing in the Common. She did not know the faces, but she recognized they were students from the scarves they wore and the thin coats with the collars.

"Is this Antayak?" asked young man with a red beard and white teeth. "The home of Margrét?"

"Have you seen her?" asked Inger. "Do you know where she is?"

They shook their heads.

Down the lane she saw there was a second wagon coming.

"What's your business?"

They didn't seem to know exactly, but they'd brought cherries as a gift, and bread. A little girl, no older than six, had a garland of blossoms that she had made.

"You will be cold."

Inger offered the pit of their outdoor fire. And charcoal. She went to the paddock to get them blankets. That first night three of them slept in the fold.

"You needn't worry," she told Torvald, who refused to sleep. Strangers made him nervous. "They mean no harm."

He wasn't convinced, but the following morning, a dozen more visitors appeared along the road. They also were from the city, and Antonia Pecca was among them. Inger took her in, and a friend of hers who also lived in the brownstone. That was the first Inger learned of what had taken place at the pier. Antonia was not sparing in her description – the hoods, the nooses, and then Modo. Inger could barely listen, and yet the presence of the strangers seemed somehow to leaven the horror. In fact, the students didn't seem so fearful of Modo. They seemed to take heart in his appearance.

By the end of that day, the second day, hundreds more had arrived, all by way of the southern road. They were like a little town camped out along the creek. Inger's eye continued to search among them, in hopes that Margrét might be hidden in their midst, or might be coming along the road with the stragglers. But they were just more students, more pilgrims, coming and coming, and covering the meadow like wildflower. Or sunflower.

The other families of the Five Homes might have objected. They did, in fact, until they saw the gifts the people were bringing – sheaves of grain, fruit, ale and wine. They brought stews made of heart and brains of boars and horses, and bloodbowls, pelts and hide, cereal, flowers and herbs, lambswool. Even a he-goat. They gathered the first berries and cresses, and they shared whatever they found.

By the third day there were enough of them that word was spreading among the neighboring villages. Jurgen the charcoal burner came down to see for himself. His wife Til stayed up on the ridge with her hand on her hip, dismayed and steaming. Jurgen found Torvald helping a new group with their tent. Inger was there as well, bringing them kindling, but Jurgen didn't speak to her.

"Where are they all from?"

"City," said Torvald.

Jurgen looked around. But there must have hundreds of them. Thousands maybe. And the city was fifty miles away.

"What are they doing?"

Torvald shrugged. "Waiting."

They were dancing, sharing books and bowls of milk. "Waiting for what?"

"Margrét."

XXXIX

The Door

One might have thought that more time she spent inside his Castle, the more Margrét would have tired of the Seidre, but the opposite was true. She ached for him when he was not there, or when she did not know where he was. She felt an actual pang inside, as if his not being there somehow made *her* hollow. The only thing that made the loneliness worthwhile was how she thrilled when she did see him again, entering the room, or revealing that he'd been there all along.

Often, she would go and sit outside his door, the one at the far end of the library. She would take a book with her, but instead of reading she'd put her ear to the keyhole and listen. There wasn't much to hear usually, but how her heart would quicken at the merest shift or tread.

"Let me in!" she wanted to call. "I'm right here." She wanted to tell him everything she had been thinking. The strangest, wildest thoughts she had been having of him – mostly in dreams, which she realized now had been about him all along. The limbs of the oak tree were his, and even though she was sure he knew, she wanted to tell him. "I know you think I am not ready. You think I am the same, but I have changed. You of all people should know." She wanted to tell him she was glad she was here, glad it was just the two of them, glad it was him she was with. "There is no one else I would want to be with. No one else I could even imagine."

But she could never bring herself to say such things, because he had changed as well.

Back on the ship he had been more open, more bold. He had looked her more square in the eye. He had touched her. In the Map Room. He had purposely touched her back, and the memory of that moment, of his hand upon her, was more alive to her now than when it first had happened. It was like a coal inside her, the mere thought of which was like air, was a breeze stoking it, causing it to glow and spread its warmth throughout her body, from the middle out to her skin.

Here, they never touched. Their eyes barely. If she reached out to take his hand – for him to come hear the music, say ("You must come now!" she would plead) – he'd snatch it away as if she were a flame. They both would notice, but nothing would be said, except that when she returned to her room, she would find a new gift waiting for her – an anklet or a plum – and so these feelings only grew in her, without vent. They fed upon their own hunger and they got bigger and stronger and more restless.

"And do you know what else they said of him?"

"Of whom?"

"Of Solomon. The King," she said (she liked to tease him about King Solomon). She took another spoonful of persimmon, which he had frozen for her. It scooped like ice cream. "They said he's the one who trapped all the demons and the tempters."

"Do they?"

"Yes. They said he knew how to control them. He knew their names and all the spells. 'Keys', he called them. You should read more of your books."

"I should."

"But they also said he knew that they were trouble, more trouble than most men could bear."

"Wise King Solomon."

"They said when he knew his days were numbered, he locked the demons in a coffer made of brass. And that he hid the coffer underneath his temple. Had you not heard this?"

"Versions." He neither shook his head nor nodded. He looked at her.

"And there it remained," she continued. "But what do you think that means? Do you think that means there was a time with no demons tempting anyone? How dull."

"Imagine what was happening inside the coffer."

"True."

"So what happened?"

"What do you think?" she said. "Another King. Nebu–... Nebu–... Nebucha–"

"Nebuchadnezzar."

"That's the one. They said he came and sacked the city and the Temple, and that he found the coffer where it was hidden. He didn't think twice. He took it back to Babel."

"Babylon."

"That's where they opened it, thinking there were jewels inside, which one can understand. He was going to give them to his Queen, but when they opened the lid, all the demons flew out instead. They say there were seventy-two. There was Eligos, who knows the future, and Bael, who rules the skies, and Shax, who steals away your senses –"

"Did you want more?" he asked, about the persimmon.

"No." She licked the spoon. "So that was that. They all flew off into the air, and that is where they've been ever since, according to the book, 'preying on the righteous and the pure of heart'."

"So we're safe."

§

What else was he to say to that? What else could he do but take refuge in his room again, his cavern, and find some way to calm the storm of urges she set off in him. Swim. Find the coldest water he could and soak. Or go hunt and kill. There were elk up here all year round, and adder and bear. Whale. Out through secret passages he would go, set sail with his wings and search, and though the purpose was to put his mind on something else, still he would think of her.

From the moment she had awakened, her presence had been a kind of exquisite torture to him, and it was only growing worse. He did not know how to be with her, how to treat her now that she'd discovered the power of her spells and how to cast them – letting glances linger, turning away in order to be seen, coming nearer to him and staying longer, hovering so close he could feel her warmth. She was a temptation upon which he could not act, and as such an unstinting reminder of just how base his native instincts were. Compared to theirs. Her presence made it all too clear, there were things that he did not know, yearnings he would never satisfy, but that they in their genius – their filthy, rotten, lying, petty, all-too-human genius – had somehow managed to capture; fleetingly yes, but also exclusively.

And there must have been a kind of magic in it. How else could they bear it? This concentration of being, this impossibly impacted self was tumorous; like being a knotted tree, bound by wire, but stripped as well. He felt naked with her, always – exposed and vulnerable – so that his mind could never rest. It was like a swarm of gnats, searching the dark, but for what?

Out here, he knew. There below: an elk, nuzzling through the snow for moss. Modo snorted – just for fun, just to see the little ears flick, the head rise and go still. The deer understood (far better than she), and off it would go, bounding through the snow as fast as it could run, but much too late. Down the dragon swooped, he and the deer and his blue shadow in a three-way race. He'd glide a while above it, just to watch it run, then snatch it up like a hawk on a rabbit. Alive one moment, dead the next, in a single flex. Soon to be food, then scat.

Yes, he should definitely take her away – to the coast, he knew. He had been thinking this: take her while she was sleeping, some-where safe. There were places across the sea, thrones he could set her on, or beds – real ones. He could make all of this a dream. That would be the better thing. And not just because of him, but the men too. They would be coming for her, or for the stone. (He'd even started looking to the southern ridge for signs of them. He had the falcon checking as well.)

Then he'd returned to the lair with his kill, and usually sneak back in one of the lower entrances, though even from there he could smell her. That was the best part of the hunt, in fact – returning. Her scent was everywhere. She permeated the air, so that just to climb back in the cliffside was to seem to enter her.

By hidden passage, he would bring the kill back into his cavern, the one he had forbidden her to enter. There he'd settle in, roused again, and begin dismembering the body. And he knew when she was there – crouched outside the "door" and listening, unaware that even there, with her tiny body folded up like a wing, she was his master. He'd wait for her to grow bored, or lose her nerve, get up and leave in hopes he'd follow – to go read, to raid, to ape. Then he'd continue with his meal alone, even though he wasn't hungry anymore, in that way. He would finish what he'd brought, then lie there at the center of his lair, sated and unsated, while the elk bones softened in his belly, or the blubber turned to jelly.

That would be the noble thing, he thought – the human thing – to take her away from here. It would be the safe and the wise thing, too, to be rid of this hunger once and for all. He just didn't know if he could, if he even had the strength to let her go. A funny thought.

He listened again. He heard the quiet. He knew that sound, too. She had fallen asleep. And he would think, I should go and check on her, just to see that she is safe. And maybe this will be the time I will take her away as I should. He'd follow the scent to where she was, thinking of all the distant beds where he might leave her. On the Emerald Isle? Or the volcanic one? The men had towns there as well. They'd be happy to have her – the beautiful one who fell from the heavens. That was their favorite story, no?

He'd find her lying on the stone, or on a broken chair, her foot dangling over the rest, one hand high, and he would gaze at her, her cheek that deep deep pink, that rose-colored blush that only seemed to come when she was sleeping; how her flesh seemed to drink from her dreams as if they were milk. He'd watch her eyes turn beneath their lids, and the faint swell of her breast every time she breathed, and he would think to himself, not this time, no. Not now. Not ever.

XL

Crows

The bullfinch and the warblers were returning already. And the birds who'd never left – tree sparrows – were awakening, sticking out their heads and calling to each other. They called down to Orabas as well, who would look up from his slanted blue shadow and think to himself:

"Sing it all you like. I don't understand you now, but when I return I will. I will sit out on the porch with Anna and with her brother, and I will tell them the secrets you tell me."

He had brought three maps with him. The first was of the whole Northern Territory including the fjords, and he had drawn it himself, years ago, as he had been thinking of this journey since he was a boy, dragon or no dragon. He and Bizja had spoken of it – just to go and see what once had been, to see if the lair was even still there. He had charted several routes, depending upon the season – all leading to the tip of that particular fjord he had in mind, the one he considered to be both "northernmost" and a fjord, which was a subject of dispute. He and Bizja disagreed, in fact, not that that had mattered. Bizja was never quite as interested.

The second map, copied directly from the Squire's book, was more for when he got there. It detailed the layout of lair itself, all the tunnels and chambers and entrances as best the Squire could remember, based upon his and his liege's three month stakeout, plus the three-quarters of an hour they actually spent inside. This map would be crucial for when Orabas got there, of course, as the assumption of this whole journey was that the weapon he needed was already waiting for him, in a special cavern that the Squire referred to as the "Sanctum."

The third map was probably the most useful right now at the outset of the journey. That was the one that Per-Malfi had given him

216

just before he'd left, identifying all the active and abandoned home-steads he might find along the way. Orabas kept to his route as best he could, but let Per-Malfi's map nudge him this way and that, each next stead serving as another pin along which he could string his slow but steady progress.

And at least at the outset, he did find people – Laps and Uplanders, lone hunters and hermits. All received him warmly and let him share in their fires, their food. But he never stayed more than a night. He listened to what they said about given passes, where the snows had fallen recently, where the thaw gave way to mudslides, things like that, but he never told any of them where he was headed or why. True, there was the chance they might know something useful; might have seen the beast, and known legends or secret routes, but it was by that very token – the likelihood that their information would have been handed down or hearsay – he didn't want to be swayed or tempted astray. He trusted his own line.

When time came to sleep, he'd find a separate space from theirs, as he liked to end each day the same, by opening his maps and studying them again – where he would go from here, how many days, how many miles. And he would study the map of the lair as well – which tunnels went where, what was the swiftest route to the Sanctum from this entrance, or that – all so that he would know when he arrived. And this was in keeping with his overall approach. Plan nothing, but be ready. Be patient, like Naberius. Find a safe blind. See if the ledge behind the cataract was still there. Cover his scent and observe a while. When did Modo awake? When did he emerge? And by which exit?

These were his last thoughts before he went to sleep. They were often what he dreamt of, and were usually his first thoughts upon waking. Then he'd gather his things, which weren't many: his rope, knife, flint, coat, the hat, charcloth, charcoal, birch bark, skins for water, fishing line – altogether not more than a dozen pounds. He would accept the breakfast of his host, if he had a host, then the last thing before he left, he'd open up his journal. Per-Malfi had given it to him so that he might record the things he saw. "Draw," he had said. Or write. But all Orabas ever did was tear out a page, scrawl his name, the date, and his next intended destination. Then he'd find a little crack somewhere in the cabin or the cave. He'd fold the note and tuck it in, just so that if anyone should decide to look for him, some son or grandson or great great grandson, he could follow the trail. They'd know his route, they'd know his pace.

As experienced a frontiersman as Orabas was, the journey was not nearly as arduous for him as it would have been for most others. He knew which trails to follow, when to stray and how to recover, which to avoid, how to ration, how to think, which meant focusing on each next step. Not to let in doubt. He was not the first to come this way, after all. Many had tried. Few had returned. He knew their names, but he kept the thought of them at bay, or if he let it in at all, it was to proclaim his intention: to do better; not to make the same mistakes.

The skies were working in his favor, as was the calendar. The days were growing longer. Eight hours of sun now, which did well to balance the increasing ruggedness of the terrain, for he wasn't only going north. He was climbing higher as well, day by day, into increasing wind and thinner air. His progress marked a stalemate between the sun and the altitude. Some days he felt as if he were being borne into the winter, step by step. Others he felt as if he were actually bringing the spring along with him, when it seemed the runners of his sled and the souls of his two boots were themselves melting the snow, yielding up the crocuses in his wake. They were practically sprouting under heel.

Another ascent and he entered the frozen snow line again – the "Shelves" – up where the woods left off entirely; the weather was too harsh for trees. He seemed to have passed beyond the realm of men as well. Per-Malfi's map said so. So did his eyes. The Shelves were barely habitable for much of the year, and even during the warmer season, they were for nomads and hermits. He saw none of either, only the occasional dug-out cave or lean-to. It felt as if there was just him and Modo now. One couldn't even be sure if the rest of the world existed, and with the air growing thinner, finally all those doubts he'd done so well to keep away, they all came down and landed right beside him.

He'd come to a high ridge. The white-blanketed tundra rolled down to the east, giving way to a great valley, while to the north a flat plateau ran ten miles or so before running up against another ridge of mountains, the last shelf, if the map was right. It was up over those that the northernmost fjord would finally come in view.

Five days? Maybe three if he picked his pass right. But the window of light was closing fast on this one. Also there was an abutment of shale that would serve him well for a night, and what looked like a stream not far away. He might load up some trout, maybe even some salmon if he got lucky.

He gathered bramble and dried sedge for fire. As the ground was frozen, he couldn't dig, so he made the base with stones. He was building a wall to protect it, when two ravens flew down, the first he had seen since leaving Per Malfi's.

They certainly weren't here to court. This was not the time or place, though they might have been mates. They stood a while observing him, tilting their heads and wondering aloud, cawing and mocking him.

He replied as he'd replied to all the other birds. "You make no sense to me." He set another stone in place. "You make no sense."

And yet they did. Already.

"*Not another,*" they were saying (for birds in flocks share what they know. Orabas knew that at least.)

"*How many does that make?*"

The mate shrugged, who knew? "*But look at what he brings.*"

"*Are these gifts?*"

"*I hope these are not gifts.*"

"*But are they his weapons then?*"

"*I hope they're not weapons.*"

"Shoo!" Orabas threw a stone at them, but they merely stepped aside, watched it thunk into the snow behind them, then took another hop or two closer to the fire to get a better look at the camp and at him.

"*Do you think that you're the first?*" cawed one.

"*We've seen your like.*"

"*We've nibbled them for supper —*"

Orabas groaned. "Off with you! Let me build my wall."

But they stayed and watched: "*Oh, but he's the one who doesn't think he needs the weapon. He's the one who thinks it's there.*"

"*Clever.*"

"*Fool.*"

They circled around him. "*It will be a noble death, though.*"

"*To a squandered life.*"

They shook their heads. "*Poor thing,*" the first one cawed.

"*Tut-tut,*" the second agreed.

"*Oh, but not you,*" they said together, leaning down to catch his eye. "*We are only thinking of the son, poor thing. Hasn't drawn a breath and already his name is fouled.*"

"I said *away!*" Orabas shouted, flinging another, larger stone in their direction. With that they left, flapping their creaky black wings and laughing, but they were right. This was a mission of pure self-interest, designed to fail, but lend his life one final note of heroism, through martyrdom. "He tried," they'd say, and imagine his fall, his crash, his fiery death. "We cannot say he didn't try."

"Or pay."

He had escaped, that was all. He had fled...

Now just how long the sound had been there it was difficult to say, what with the ravens mocking him, but while he knelt there in the snow, not finishing the wall, a distant buzzing did finally manage to penetrate his gloom. It was a sound he was actually quite familiar with, yet all the way up here, so far removed from the world of man and man-made things, he did not recognize it at first. He had to turn to see.

Far in the distance, and down below his line of sight, a small squadron of airplanes – SPADS and triplanes – was hovering above the low horizon, so far away they looked almost like fireflies, or tethered kites, except that they were growing larger – ever so slowly – which meant that they were coming this way.

He got out his journal. Without even waiting to see their colors or their make, he wrote three words.

Bizja is here.

§

He was right. But Bizja was not alone. In his search, he had come with a small convoy of military personnel, eighteen strong, under the command of General Zitri, whom Orabas had never personally met, but whom he had heard of certainly. (Zitri had heard of Orabas as well – the Provost's bolder, blunter brother – and of the infamous slaughtering he was said to have delivered the Sud at Denben.)

They set up a proper bivouac right beside Orabas' hollow. That evening they dined on a meat-and-cabbage goulash familiar to Orabas from his tours against the Sud. Hardtack bread. Beans. And while the officers ate, they quizzed Orabas about his maps. He showed them which fjord he believed the dragon lived in, and how best to get there. They didn't question him.

"Where did these come from?"

"The first is from my father-in-law," he said, indicating the trail of active homesteads.

"The others are from a book," Olybrius put in. He did not mention the book's name, however, or the fact that these were the very same maps that he and Bazja used to play their imaginary games with when they were boys. Zitri and Zitri's men all accepted them, confirming Bazja's estimation that from here they were still a good five days away – by foot, that is.

It was agreed they would set off the following morning, not on foot.

After dinner, flasks in hand, Zitri and Olybrius escorted him back to the trucks to see the arsenal. There was enough to take over a sizeable village. In addition to the eighteen active-service infantry-men and the four pilots for the four planes (the other two having been left behind with engine trouble), there were: three tractor tanks outfitted with howitzers, two armored cargo trucks, twelve Vickers Machine guns, six submachine guns; eighteen bolt actions rifles;

seventy hand grenades; three flamethrowers; over a hundred Stokes mortars; two dozen gas masks –

"What are those for?" asked Orabas. They hung on the side of the canopied truckbed like a rack of ghouls, waiting to be freed. Zitri answered by pulling back another canvas, covering a raft of thirty canisters, and then twelve more already encased in artillery shells.

"Is that chlorine?"

"And mustard."

Orabas half-whistled. "You're taking him seriously."

"If you'd seen what he did to the pier, you would too."

Through all of this the brothers hadn't had much chance to speak to each other – to offer much in the way of explanations or apology. By the time they did, the need seemed to have passed. They were given a tent of their own, two cots and an oil lamp. They lay side by side, just as they had done at Denben, and Kroylia before that, and before that in the onion-domed cupola of Iso-aitti's dacha at Debrovo, four eyes staring at the ceiling. This one here waffled in the night winds as the brothers calmly passed a hand-rolled cigarette between them. Their words came slowly and easily, and might not have been spoken aloud at all but for the pleasure of watching them mingle and swirl in the hovering smoke.

"So why do they think I'm here?" asked Orabas. He assumed Olybrius hadn't mentioned the shamir to Zitri; that would have been too far-fetched. "What did you tell them?"

Olybrius took a long drag to contemplate. "Well, that you're mad in the first place." The answer drifted, milky blue, from his mouth. "...And you like a good hunt."

"They believe that?"

"Believe it? Zitri agrees. And he's mad too, by the way." He extended the cigarette.

"He wants the head for his wall?"

"As soon as the parade's over."

Orabas smoked. "...Big wall."

He kept his next thought to himself, which was that Zitri was a dead man. As awesome and insidious as their arsenal may have been,

Orabas was still convinced that there was only one weapon capable of killing Modo. If all this firepower and poison had any use at all, it would be to distract him – perhaps – kick up enough dust that maybe he, Orabas, could slip inside the lair, make a dash for the shamir, then see what he could do. (*I am indeed mad*, he thought.)

"And why do they think you're here?" he finally asked, handing back the stub. "For the girl?"

"The girl?" Olybrius scoffed; he was done with her. "For my brother," he said, as if that would be convincing enough, and also as if it were true.

XLI

The Key

One night, Margrét returned to her room to find a gift awaiting, a pomegranate (because she had tasted one a while back; because she had said, "Mmmmm, what's this?").

"I will eat it by the baths," she said aloud. She took the pomegranate. She took a carving knife. She brought them to the baths. On the white bench beside the water she sliced the fruit in half; its deep red juice burst from all the seeds inside and stained the marble with purple flecks – nicely. She ate a tart-sweet handful and the stain was on her fingers and her wrist, which she licked clean. She left the rest on a plate.

"If you like," she said.

She removed her robe. It fell, a gentle satin heap at her feet, and she slid into the water. It was warm, just as she preferred, so near the temperature of her own skin she might not have felt it at all but for that one cooler degree of difference. It swept around her, enveloped and caressed her as she pushed through, ducked under. She felt her hair fill and drift about her, weightless. She swam as she did every night, surrounded by shadows, blotted by lamplight.

She knew he was among them, somewhere. She could always feel when he entered – not the water. He would never do that, but there would be a kind of thickening of the air when he was near. She could sense it now – him – there to protect, to be sure, to be silent company, and to observe.

At least she thought so; she could never be absolutely sure, could she? Since he never showed himself in here, since the castle was his mind really, he was always there. She was always inside him. She felt. She swam. She turned onto her back and drifted, languid.

"Hello…?" Her voice bounced off the ceiling, the tiles dappled by the water light. "Did you want me to sing? …I'll sing…."

Again, only the ceiling replied, but something moved, she thought. A flame had flicked. Something. So she sang, to torture him as much as anything. He liked to pretend her singing pained him, but he quite liked it. She knew. She sang the lullaby.

> ' *Bide, bide, 'tis eventide,*
> *Till Háki comes home*
> *from greenwood wide...'*

The room was silent, all but for the intermittent drip of water.

> …*Right willing, I ween, was he to bide;*
> *The harp he set by the warm fireside.*

Only that. That was as much as he deserved if he was going to be that way, so silent and shadowy. She turned again. She ducked down under the surface. She pulled herself deeper under to where he could not see her – even he – she spun and kicked. She stuck out her tongue, then pushed herself back and cleared the surface for breath. The water shimmered and danced around her, to its echo-ey droplet song. She paddled to the side again, to where the shelf came up. She found it with her knee, and climbed back out.

She stood there a moment, dripping, looking all around. Still nothing but black. She looked to the bench. The plate was there; the pomegranate as well, just as she'd left it.

"Hmph," she sniffed. She turned. Another drip, another drop, plinking into the water and off the surrounding walls. Only now did she notice, over by the fire there was a divan. Had that been there? She didn't remember it.

"Perhaps I will." She adored the divan, after all. Divine divan. Dark purple velvet, so dark you almost couldn't tell it was purple; but it was, like an eggplant. She went and lay down on it. Set her head against the golden, tassled pillow. She lifted her legs, scissored her ankles and let them down again to rest, while the dry heat of the fire drank the water from her skin.

She waited. She sighed. She lifted her arm above her head. The other she let stay, it was so comfortable there, her fingertips stroking the velvet of the cushion, then sliding up to her hip. Softer still.

She cleared her throat, but there was no reply.

They had played this game before, of her pretending she did not know that he was there. A tricky game, a dangerous game, because you had to *believe* he was there, even if there was no reason. You had to imagine it. You had to believe the silence was his, that he was keeping it, and then it was easy. Then it was fun. Her heart began to thump, and she sighed again, without quite meaning to. She tried calling out to him, but without using her voice this time. She called out from the hollow in her, and from the heat. She thought of him there, not answering, just standing, and her heart beat even faster. Her breathing grew quicker, shallower. She could feel the flush in her cheeks, and how he must see this too.

But of course she did not know, and that was the dangerous part. Not thinking he was there – that was fun – but supposing he wasn't, because if that idea so much as flitted into her mind (as it did now, on a breeze, on a cool draft curling in, because he would not have let that happen, not if he were here; he would not have let the outside in with her this way), then she would stop.

"Hello?"

Because if he was *not* there, then there was this instead – this cool shiver of shame, and thinking how she had let herself be seen... by nothing?

She hissed at him. She often hissed at him, because it wasn't fair the way the castle worked – that he should have a place where he could go and hide, whereas she ...well, he saw everything, and she let him. And he wasn't even here.

"You are a demon, you know."

And she meant this too. She had seen his name in that book, the book of keys, and the moment she saw it, she knew it was him. He had lived with Solomon. He had done King Solomon's bidding, and he had been locked away, but he had escaped, and he had been preying on her. And not just here, but before, on the *Minarik*, and before that even, making her feel this way, the very way she felt right now, making her yearn and feel empty, and cold and warm, which is why it didn't make sense that he should be so distant, so reluctant. What was he afraid of? That's why she was here, wasn't it? To be with him.

"Why else?" she cried out loud. She was tired of all this... pretend. She was angry now. She stood, not bothering to cover herself, but still there was no answer, other than the wind again, whistling through the castle flute. He was not here.

"I have the key, you know," she said, "which means you cannot stop me. I know the way. If you want to stop me, you will have to come out and show yourself."

She waited, but there was only the aimless flute.

"If you do not stop me, that means you want me to come..."

And now she was hoping he *didn't* reply, and even if he did, she wouldn't have heard, her heart was thumping so loud; the blood was rushing to her ears. She was going to do this now. She had decided. This was what he wanted too. Every step he let her was consent – down the long hall, turning right and further down, she entered the library. She had been thinking of this moment, after all, the one where she would finally just go. He knew that. He knew it was coming, too.

She did not even look at the books. She crossed directly to the door, the souls of her feet not quite dry yet, leaving behind the unwavering paisley trail of her determination. She knelt beside the door and listened.

Nothing but the hiss of silence.

She looked through the hole, but as usual she could not see.

"Are you there?" she whispered. "It's me."

And how absurd, she thought. It's me. But now she leaned in closer. She set her lips to the hole and whispered the name:

"Asmodeus..."

Silence. Silence and blackness. She couldn't really sense him either, the way she usually did. So again she set her mouth up to the hole, but whispered more slowly and clearly.

"…Asmodeus…"

Again she waited, but not as long. This time the silence yielded to the clear and gentle sound of tumblers turning, stopping, clicking. A moment later the great door swung inward on its wrought iron hinges.

XLII

The Sanctum

Had she not pictured the room just this way? It was not a room, even with all the things he might have had – the grandest bed, an ornate bureau or wardrobe, a mosaic bath – but no, none of that. This was more a cavern or a cave – and dark, as always. In fact there was only one source of light (or two, the second being a reflection of the first), but the first was a hole in the ceiling, a long column leading up to a skylight. It must have been a hundred feet up at least, to a small circle of lavender. It was dusk, then – outside – but the light it cast down was enough to show there was water here, more a canal than a pool. She could see it, and hear it, leading round to several more entrances on the far side – or exits, she supposed – which led further inside the castle, inside the cliff, and further down into the black.

But there at the middle of the room, and the most direct object of the skylight's waning attention, was what appeared to be a kind of nest, only it wasn't made of sticks and thistle. It was made of jewels – diamonds and sapphires, some loose, some still on their necklaces and bracelets, crowns and tiaras, and there were pearls, countless strings of pearls all tangled, and agate and lapis lazuli, and at the center of them all was one more little jewel – the other most prominent light in the cave.

Margrét took a step closer, and though she hadn't been expecting it, in another way it was no surprise at all: she saw it was that necklace, the one the Provost had tried to give her back on the ship; the one the Seidre had been so curious about the first time he'd spoken to her.

But what was it doing *here*?

She took it in hand. As before, she felt its extra weight, and as before there was something in its presence that disturbed her for some reason. It only took a moment to see why. Back on the ship, it had been the gem that let her know her father was not there, that she had been lying to herself. Here again it was the gem that burnt through the veil she had been looking through. Holding it in her hand, she turned around and saw there was no door there, and no iron latch, no keyhole. There was barely a threshold at all. A boulder.

There was no "library" on the other side: Two standing shelves. Two dozen books, if that, frayed and splayed by water damage. She saw the corridor beyond was nothing but a narrow dug-out passage. There was a filthy, tattered runner on the floor, but otherwise no rugs or carpets, only mold and stone, and moss and fungus. The walls were all a jagged limestone. There were no moldings or lamps, no paintings of fruit or landscapes. There were no tapestries. A few pillars, yes, but no fluting, no marble, no vaulted ceiling or parquet floors.

The only thing that was the same was the water. The sound was everywhere surrounding her, quiet, dripping, roaring, running through in pools and streams.

And now she felt the presence behind her, entering the space just now. For a moment she took heart, assuming it was him. Who else could it be?

"Where am I?" she asked, but when she turned, she saw instead something mountainous emerging from the shadows on the far side of the space, something monstrous and horned.

What are you doing here?

At first she could not answer, she was so terrified. Were those scales on its body? And were those wings? But it was so large, and black and barbed.

You should not have come here.

Were those two lanterns flashing in its eyes? And why did they seem so familiar. She found her voice. "I wanted to see him. I wanted to see where he goes."

She continued searching his figure, trying to see the length of it, the shape, but she could only make out that there was something at its feet, limp and lifeless. A carcass of some kind.

"What have you done with him?" she asked

He isn't here. You have to go.

But she could feel him near. Again she tried to see the body the beast had dragged in.

You have to GO!

The great head dipped and lunged, and as it glanced through the pillar of light, Margrét realized: she had seen him before.

"You were on the ship."

Why have you done this? his voice returned, and that too was familiar to her now.

Was there something that you lacked?
Something he did not give you?
Did he not give you back your life?
And he asked only one thing in return —

"Where is he?" she said again, but louder, and again his eyes flared like two glowering torches.

Why must you be told again?
Did you not see around you?
You might as well ask where is the Castle?
Where is the door?
Where is the library and all books and jars?
He is with them, and now you know —

ASMODEUS

"That isn't true."

You have seen what you wanted.
The man was no different. A figment—

"That isn't true!" she shouted, though even she could hear the uncertainty in her voice. How could she deny it? This was not the place she had thought. The air was dank and fetid, but then why did he feel so near?

"How do I know *you're* not the dream?" she said.

The dragon replied with a contemptuous sniff that briefly lit the room.

Then wake up.
You will see what I am telling you:
He never was. He never breathed.
He never tasted...

And here she suddenly calmed again. Her heart even seemed to lift in her chest when he said this. He'd meant to frighten her, but he had said too much. He had just lost the game. She smiled.

"Did you think you can fool me?" She tilted her head. "He is too here. I know because I hear him – because those were his words exactly." She took a step toward him and he reared back like a frightened cat, the great gargantuan beast. He hissed.

"But you don't frighten me," she said. "Did you think I wouldn't know? Your eyes are his. Your voice is his."

Then listen to what he says!
You are in danger here.
He is not what you think.

But Margrét only shook her head. "Why do you have this?" She held up the necklace, and the beast drew back again.

the northern castle

Put it DOWN!

The voice boomed, but she could hear the fear in it. She took another step toward him, and held it up higher. "Why?"

But as he didn't answer – other than to command her once again to put the thing away, she lifted the chain up over her head and let it fall around her neck.

The great wyrm tried to look away, but couldn't. His eyes were glowing, their glow reflected off the jewel, and she could see his shape more clearly now. He was the most beautiful, the most hideous and magnificent creature she had ever seen.

And he saw her just as clearly now, standing before him in the nest of gems, her small white frame naked but for the tattered smock they'd tried to hang her in – that and the jewel against her breast.

Just then, a call sounded from on high, outside. The falcon. He knew why.

We have to go.

But no. Her eyes wide open, fixed on his, she knelt down on the treasure bed.

We have to go. Now.

No. She lay back instead, supine. She raised her slender arms above her head, and he was flooded by every craving he had ever known. All he had needed was her assent, and she was nodding.

The falcon called a second time, but he did not even hear. He had succumbed already. He leaned down and took Margrét in his mouth. He held her by the hip and lifted her up. She offered no resistance. He turned his great long head up to the skylight and let her slide down his throat into the warmth of his long black gullet.

His brain thrilled and burned with a maddening combination of ecstasy and self-loathing. She was within him. He tasted her as she entered into the warm pitch of his stomach, and he was rapturous and furious, triumphant and ashamed. He lifted up his head again. He tilted it skyward in his inexpressible agony and bliss. He had never been so alive, or wanted more to be dead.

The falcon cried again, and now in fact he heard them, too – the grunting, belching, buzzing sound of the mechanical birds he'd seen in Kreisenig, sweeping directly over the lair like a bug past his ear.

He leapt straight up. He did not use the passage, but bounded up through the high skylight, a tunnel a hundred yards long. He scrambled up and up and up like a lizard, clutching and clawing at the sides, his wings tucked, his long tail snapping at the stone.

XLIII

Finale

"**There.**" Zitri was first to see him from the far side the fjord. He and four other soldiers in his troop – including Vilnius, his second – were crouched behind a shelf of stone, but he was speaking on the field phone. "Up on top."

In another blind, one counterclockwise tick to Zitri's right, Olybrius lowered his glasses to see with his own eyes as the black creature scrambled out into the sun, like a beetle from his hole.

Zitri's voice returned: "...Ugly bugger, isn't he?"

Orabas, who was also on the line, commanding yet the third unit of marksmen, had been thinking quite the opposite, how elegant it appeared in the distance, how its wings glinted like tar in the sun.

"...Hold your fire," said Zitri.

None of them had been certain until now that this actually was the place, though Orabas had pointed out how precisely it matched the Squire's descriptions: the inner tip was shaped like a spearhead; the cataract was a milk-white gash sliding down the cliff, dissolving into a mist before it hit bottom. His preference would still have been to lay low for a while, to stake out and observe Modo's habits, but they'd come upon the fjord much sooner than they had anticipated, and with the number of men they'd brought, it would have been impossible to hide their scent for long. As it was, they'd barely had time to take their positions, which Zitri had laid out.

It was his plan was to conduct a kind of aerial buffalo hunt: Use the planes to lure the beast out to the middle of the fjord, then pummel him from all sides. To that end they'd stationed themselves in three separate blinds around the ledge of the fjord, dividing the men and the weapons more or less equally. If the cataract that marked the high entrance of the lair was twelve o'clock, Orabas and his company were positioned at three; Olybrius and his were at four-thirty, while Zitri was at six, farthest from the lair but having the most direct view. Each battery had a complement of four men armed with sniper rifles, submachine guns, grenades and mortar shells, some already outfitted with mustard gas and chlorine gas. Zitri had reserved for himself the use of the howitzer. If the dragon managed somehow to escape all that and flee down the western length of the fjord, two more planes were waiting to intercept him, both outfitted with machine guns.

Of course, Zitri, Olybrius and Orabas had all been in enough combat situations to know that such plans were a kind of fiction, a best-case scenario conjured up to sustain officers' spirits until the battle was actually joined, at which point all bets were off and the winner was either the one who reacted best or had the most resources.

This proved to be especially true in the present instance, in the first place because no one had expected the beast emerge quite so quickly, and also because they could never have imagined him to be quite so primed for a fight. Clearly the second of the SPADs had no idea. Only moments after the dragon's appearance, the plane came swinging down much too close to the opening.

"What's he doing?" Zitri barked into his phone.

"I don't think he sees," Olybrius replied, and he was right.

Like a tiger, the beast leapt, beat the air just once and grabbed hold of the little plane by the tail. For a strangely suspended moment he wrestled it in the air – he seemed almost to take pleasure in the gyroscopic power of the propellers – but they were no match for the strength of his thrashing wings. Zitri hadn't wanted to give away his position so early, but he had no choice. He signaled his gunmen to fire. The air burst with the *chuggachug*, as from every battery the charges zipped out across the fjord like a fishing line.

The dragon felt the first flicks and flecks, turning just in time to see the larger blast of Zitri's howitzer come wizzing by to his left and crack a good chunk from the cliff wall. Unfazed, he replied by crushing the wing of the plane, splintering its propellers and flinging it away like a toy; it tumbled and spiraled, spewing a black ribbon of smoke, then crumpling like paper at the bottom of the fjord. A moment later it burst into flame.

Modo didn't bother to look. His eyes were dancing about, finding the enemy in their little roosts, and identifying them, scent by scent, pulse by pulse: the brother, the weakling leader who'd tried to hang her – he was there, as was his dullard twin, the noble father. Further along was the brush-faced bully, all of them working together now, united in purpose, and impressively armed. The weapons they'd brought were of an entirely different order than the glowing swords and anointed daggers of the past. These weapons aped *him*, in fact. They gnashed at the air, the same as these flying machines, so corrosive and menacing and pathetic, how they barked and ground and pounded the sky. Here came another cannon blast, curling by and exploding on impact with the cliff, knocking down a stone sheet the size of a cathedral tower.

He looked back at them all with pity and contempt. What did it matter? What did they? Margrét was within him now, and she had found the man…

§

…She had emerged from the black water, whole and intact, to find the ridges high again; the sea receding. The moon had returned, round as a plate, to fling sharp shadows all across the heath. The sound of the guns was a distant thunder, nearly lost in the shush of the grass and the leaves.

But what tree was this in front of her? The oak? The flood-waters had been good to it. They'd revived it, its limbs were full and thick with leaves again, but more like willow leaves. They were a dark drape hanging down, and she knew that he would be inside.

She stepped on through into the shade, but she could see by the light of the jewel. He lay on a stone slab beside the roots, deathly still. She leaned down close to look at him. His face was so unlike the dragon's, and yet the same – a faithful map, every crease and scar accounted for; every whisker growing from his chin, an analogue. She touched the thin fold above his eyelid, his brow and the line of his jaw. The jewel danced against his clavicle. She set her ear beside his nose and mouth; the jewel lay flat. She felt his breath.

"Wake up," she said, but gently. "It's me."

He had not expected to hear. He had believed the wyrm – the Seidre was nothing but a shattered spell – but breath by breath, touch by touch, Margrét re-conjured him in human skin. From his own black depths he emerged beneath her, even as the thunder rumbled out beyond the hills and the hunters took their aim and fired, he felt her hands, and she felt his. And they did not restrain themselves.

§

The story is told of how God became man to know men's suffering, so that he might forgive them. What, then, of the God who became man to know men's most exquisite pleasure? He slew them. He took out all his fury on them. He welcomed their guns. He sought the bullets. He drank their fire. He chased their wavering teetering aeroplanes. He felt the heat of their engines, the barrels of their guns. He gloried in their hideous, guttural din.

Like a hawk on a stoop, chasing down a pigeon, he snatched them from the sky; he toyed with them; they could not fly with him, these tilting, sputtering, stuttering machines. They could not dent him with their exploding stones and pebbles. They pinged off his hide. The shells he easily dodged. He danced away. Let the cannon cleave into the cliffside, send cracks up and down its face. Let the walls fall down in sheets and shelves. Awakened by the thunder, a black cloud of bats swarmed from the high mouth, joining the fray much sooner than they figured; they swirled and swallowed the third of the planes, splattering in its propellers, downing it as well.

The dragon gave chase, for fun. He smacked the spiraling invader with his tail. He dashed it against the stone. He swooped round to the batteries they'd set up, all tucked away behind their ledges and stumps. He harrowed them from their perches. The soldiers fired away. They poured water on the guns to keep them cool. For what? To fling more bullets, to throw more sand? Each hunter saw his eyes, the smoldering golden orbs, like crystal balls containing within them that glint of mad abandon. The beast was burning, seething, churning with life. His every sense was filled twice over. He smelled the musk of fear and of desire. He heard each beating heart distinctly: the staccato panic within the chest of every infantryman and pilot; the marching drum of Zitri's; the racing throbbing red thrum of Olybrius and Orabas; the brothers were the same, though separated – the one up in his roost, the other...where was the other exactly? And did he care? Did it matter? For he heard hers as well, felt hers inside him, above and astride him, guiding him, commanding him to thrash, to rake, to thrust and plunge and fire. He routed the first battery, the one at the very end of the fjord. He caught another of the planes and drove it into them like a battering ram. He flamed them and tore away at their roost. He snatched the tank by its cannon and hurled it clear across the canyon. A bird it was not. It clanged against the far cliff-side. It tumbled and plummeted, catching ledges and shoulders before spiking the ground and snapping its gun.

That was all for now. He spread his wings and made one more circuit of the space – out in the open air, then curling around the cliff face, like a manta ray across a tilted ocean floor, but all the way round and past the batteries again. He picked them off with the hard horns of his spine and whipping tail – two more men from Zitri's team, severed and gone, just like that – then on he went, further down the fjord. He drifted away like that same manta ray, or a shark after its initial round. He left them casually almost, the silence of his departure disrupted here and there by more falling stalks, and the stray, pathetic fire of the guns.

Zitri looked back at the other two batteries and grabbed the field phone. "Are you there? Do you still have him?"

"...Yes." It was the Provost, in the second battery.

"Still?"

"Yes...yes...and no, just lost him."

"Which way did he go?"

"South southwest."

So down the fjord and off to the left. He was diving, gathering his strength. They had weathered the first storm but barely. They'd lost at least a half dozen, and a tank, and two planes.

Vilnius looked to Zitri. "He could be coming around behind."

"How's our view?"

Vilnius clambered up and scanned the plateau behind them. It was a long sloping field, but there could easily be hidden tributaries tucked away behind rolls. Their maps were nothing but drawings really.

Vilnius turned. "We could send in the gas now." The canisters were all there and ready. "While the coast is clear."

Zitri pondered. He took up the phone. "Team one? How quickly do you think you can get inside the lair?"

The line crackled out its silence. He turned his field glasses to the first battery.

"...Korda?"

"Here." It was Olybrius.

"Where is your brother? Did you see him?"

"...No."

"Team one? Come in."

Again the silence hissed.

Zitri scanned down to the bottom of the fjord. He hadn't seen anyone fall. Had he fled? Did the dragon have him?

The same thought occurred to Olybrius – he could picture his brother, undaunted, flailing away at the monster's claw, gnashing at it with his teeth. He peered down the ravine, but there was nothing to see. A seagull drifted. The water lapped in slow motion.

He didn't believe it, though. Bazja wasn't with the beast, or dead, or fallen, because he could feel him. He was still close by, but hiding.

§

ASMODEUS

Quite close, in fact. He was standing on the narrow ledge behind the cataract, the same one that Naberius and the Squire had spent three days and nights on, scouting Modo from behind the rushing veil of white. It was also the quickest way to the high entrance of the lair, for which Orabas had started the moment he saw the dragon take down the first plane. No one out here was surviving, he could see that. Modo would kill what needed killing. His only hope, their only hope, was getting inside the lair, where wings made no difference and he might find the shamir. He still preferred his chances with that.

The question was whether he should make a dash for it right now. He could see a fair ways up the fjord from where he was. He saw the same lazy gull, and his conclusion was much the same as his brother's, and Zitri's. Modo might be coming back this way right now. He might be coming up from the south, or the north. He might have found another, safer lair; he might be headed out to sea.

He could be anywhere, that is.

(Only not here, with Margrét – no one was thinking that, other than the beast himself, who knew it to be true. He was with her even now, in the leaf shade of the tree – beneath her, above her, beside her, feeling for the first time the million touches of unarmored flesh; the scent of hers combined with his; the taste of that same scent. This was the secret that Life had been keeping from him: surrender, but eagerly; relinquish, but greedily, and as one. Abandon self into the body, and the body into another body, and let the body be hers. He was a swimmer in her ocean. She was the smashing white wave on his rock. They were clouds colliding, the thunder and the lightning that he had failed to hear while he was dreaming, but the dream had been of this, of being lost in her, and found in her, and all and everywhere within her. And the bliss of this began to rise up in him now, and seek release.

She felt it, too, though for Margrét there was no surrender; she had done all that already. She was here to drink and to devour, to receive him and everything that he encompassed. And this bliss she likewise felt arising from his body and from hers, and from the sun and from the shade and the air in her lungs, from the dancing jewel around her neck. It was no gift. It was a key. It was a window on another world, and the world was here with him in the land of light and living, and all the rest, all the rest, all the rest, was Death.)

"I have something," said Vilnius. "South. There he is."

"I see."

The dragon had indeed veered to the South, a half mile at least. He'd swooped up onto the bluff and was now coming back around at them from behind, increasing his speed with each stroke of his enormous black wings.

"All right then. Turn," ordered Zitri. "Turn and fire. Now."

They were trying, but none of the larger guns were outfitted to swivel that far, and the embankment was blocking them as well. The tanks tried turning their muzzles and turrets, but they jammed just short. Modo appeared to be aiming for Zitri's battery, giving the gunmen in the other two blinds a better angle, but they couldn't keep pace, and now the beast was upon them, swooping right over them a lunge away, sending down a blast of flame and acid, and swiping at them with his tail.

Zitri ducked down, but even through his clamped lids he could still see the orangey-red of the flame surrounding them. He could hear it too, roaring, and he thought of hell – of this little pocket as an endless and eternal place for those who had succumbed. He gave thanks that he was saved. He heard Vilnius now.

"Masks on!"

He opened his eyes. There were just the two of them left. The gunmen had either been smashed or swept off. He looked to the canisters. He didn't see that any had been discharged, but better safe. While he strapped on his gas mask, the first and second batteries kept firing at the dragon, who was out in the middle of the fjord again and turning, arcing down toward the water below, seeming to dance with their tracers and bullets as if they were pilot fish or hummingbirds. Down into the ravine he swooped. The guns did their best to tilt, but either they were blocked or jammed.

The dragon took note – his flock, his little shooting stars seemed to have trailed off. He looked back up and set his sights on the second battery this time, the Provost's. He circled back around, gaining speed, then made straight up the side of the cliff, like a dark shadow rising.

"He's down below you!" Zitri cried into his phone, but the line was dead. "He's down below!" he yelled. They couldn't see, but he was coming so fast that Zitri assumed the beast would sweep right past like a missile.

Instead, it pulled up at the last moment. It extended its claws and talons and landed directly in front of the battery, face to face. What followed was by far the grizzliest of its attacks. Zitri couldn't see so well, in part because of the goggles, in part because the dragon's wings were thrashing so violently as it clawed at the cliff and lunged with its great neck, battering with its horns and head, gnashing with its teeth, incinerating with its breath, one cloud after another of churning, flaming acid.

Zitri and Vilnius refrained from shooting. They hadn't wanted to hit their own men, but they could hear the cries, and they wondered who and what was that? What were those shreddings that flew from the monster's mouth?

There was one who managed to escape and scramble free. It looked like the Provost. He was reaching into his belt for his pistol. *But he might as well spit,* thought Zitri, until he saw that he had more than a gun. He had two hand grenades.

Oh, good boy.

And Olybrius knew. He knew he was going to die. They all were. Bazja was right. Bazja was right. The sentence was still like a bell in his head. This was his end right here, and he did not mind it. He had been in battle. He had faced this moment several times before – in prospect, at least – but never had he tasted it quite like this, the certainty of it. The only question was how exactly, and whether there was anything he could do now to help his brother, who was in the lair. He knew that too. All of this was very clear in his mind as he clambered up and over the top of the ridge and sprinted away, firing back to try to get the dragon's attention, his legs practically numb with flight.

He simply had to time it right, make sure that Modo was near enough when the charge went off. As soon as he was clear and he had managed a good separation he turned. He pulled the pins, the one and then the other. Zitri saw him do it. He understood. *Good boy,* he thought again, but then on second thought, *why such a mess.*

The dragon lunged up and over the cliff's edge – a single strum was all it took. He tackled the little man, and that, in all likelihood, was the last Olybrius ever saw. No one could have survived that blow. The beast loomed over him a moment –

That's right, thought Zitri, *make sure –*

And *b-booOOM!* Off went the two grenades, one after another. Powerful ones, too, enough to take out a trenchful of Sud; that had been proven. So, Olybrius Korda, Provost of Ileya, Governor of Kreisenig, son of Sigemund Korda, great great great great grandson of Barbatos, greater grandson still of the legendary Questor Naberius, was one moment a terrified but reconciled man; the next, a spray of flesh and bone. Even the great beast with all its armor was blown back, its body flung all the way to the edge of the cliff. Stunned, it actually clung there a moment, bleery but not entirely out, just thirty yards away from Zitri, its great head facing him directly, one eye closed, the other drifting.

Zitri didn't waste his chance. From his battery he grabbed hold of a submachine gun and fired, peppering the ground leading up to the fallen beast, who, with his open eye, saw the little turf geysers headed his way and simply rolled once over, off the cliff, tumbling down until he was clear of the ledge.

A lesser creature might simply have fallen to its death, but with the last of his strength, the dragon opened his wings and they carried him out across the open fjord, the air reviving him as he glided back to the lair-side. He landed low and hard against the cliff face, thudding against the rock, a third of the way up, maybe a hundred yards above the beach and the water.

From Zitri's angle it was difficult to tell how bad off the beast was. He took up his field glasses to get a closer view, but in that moment, and looking through the goggles of his mask, he lost him.

"Where did he go?"

"Inside," said Vilnius.

"How?"

"There's a hole. Down there."

Zitri put down the glasses. "Hit it."

Vilnius hesitated.

"Now!" barked Zitri. "Give me that!"

He jammed a mortar shell in the cannon and sent one off, just to judge the range. Up it went, over the water, then down and down, landing at the little strand of beach at the foot of the far side. The sand flew up like flour, and several stalks of icicles fell down and shattered, playfully.

Before they even hit ground, however, Zitri had sent off another shell, aimed higher this time. He didn't wait for it to land before sending up another, and another. The explosions slowly climbed the wall, up to where the beast had disappeared.

"More!" cried Zitri. "Again!" They struck higher up, and they knew that they were nearing the mark, as now the jewels appeared. The cliffside coughed them up like innards, bursting forth with diamonds, goblets and golden coins, a spray of glittering blood. The guns kept firing. The cracks kept fracturing. Fissures splintered off into smaller ones. The ravine resounded with a growl and a crack as now an entire sheet of the cliff-face fell down, majestically crumpling at the foot of the fjord, crunching and shoving its way into the water.

Zitri held fire and all was silent throughout the ravine, as a grey-orange cloud of dust rose up from the pile.

He peered, but he still had his mask on; the goggles were fogged and dirty.

"See anything?"

"I can't," said Vilnius.

Zitri pulled off the mask and reached for his field glasses again. Vilnius did the same. It was possible the beast was somewhere in the rubble. He scanned over and back, and up and down, only pausing a moment on the higher reaches, the image was so remarkable:

The barrage had exposed a whole complex of tunnels, like a rabbit's warren or the hidden maze of an ant farm, the difference being that even from this distance he could see the jewels again and the treasures, whole string of them drooling down from the high runnels.

How very strange, thought Zitri. *What a strange, strange sight that is.*

And near to the last he would ever know. A moment later he felt the burning in his lungs, as if a fire had caught in his chest. He couldn't breathe. He looked at Vilnius, who was coming to the same realization, his eyes bulging, writhing in their sockets, skin blistering like the surface of a boiling cream soup.

Lord help us, thought Zitri, *the gas.*

For one more moment, the two officers looked at each other, apt reflections of their own horror, drowning in invisible fire, choking as the dark and frothy blood came gurgling up from foam-corrupted lungs.

Then all went mercifully from red to black.

§

Orabas had heard the barrage. Fortunately he was by now far enough inside the catacomb to have escaped the damage. And he knew where he was. That was the amazing part, how accurate all the descriptions had been, including the hand-drawn map; how little seemed to have changed in the several centuries since his ancestor's last visit. He had entered by the same opening as the Squire had instructed, the one nearest the fall of the cataract. He followed a long, rather broad tunnel leading down and in. By the light of his electric torch, several more had offered themselves, but he kept to his charted course. He passed the so-called "pool room," confirming his position, bore left and then right again, passed several chambers of gems and treasures, but not just jewels. Modo had a taste for fine furnishings as well, presumably plundered from cargo boats and palace towers. Perhaps the inlay attracted him, perhaps he took the ornaments for gems, or gem settings, but there were bureaus, torn couches and cobwebbed chairs. A bookshelf. Books even. And who was to say he hadn't found some family heirlooms hidden inside cubbies and hollowed reams?

Orabas had nearly reached the central-most cavern – the "sanctum" as the Squire had called it – when the shells started hitting outside. His first thought was that Modo had come back for another round. They'd fired, missed, and the stray shots were landing here. However, as the bombardment continued, he realized these were not stray shots. This was an intentional strike upon the enemy's home, which meant either that Modo was still circling and that Zitri had decided to deny him haven upon his return – or that Modo was himself back inside the lair somewhere and under direct attack.

And a severe one. The entire cliffside was shaking now. The tunnels were like writhing snakes, crumbling and shattering. Orabas held his position in a little archway while the mortars kept coming, and he could feel the limestone giving way. When he heard the massive, cliff-wide crack that signaled the collapse of the face, he was prepared to drop with it, but luckily the fault line was a good ten feet from where he was. The chamber shuddered as the great sheet fell, and a sudden gust of air sucked past him, drawing bats with it, screeching and flitting and flailing like black kerchiefs and blown umbrellas. Some resettled, some flapped down the tunnel and out, while the floors and walls continued to shudder from the impact below and all the fallen rock collapsing into itself and slumping out into the fjord.

Finally, though, all was silent again. The attack seemed to have passed. The sanctum was still there in front of him. He could see it better now, in fact, though the air was a sea of whirling dust and spores. The light was brighter, having fewer walls and corners to bounce off of on the way in. There were stones and boulders all over the floor, and several columns had split, but the hole in the ceiling was there, just as the Squire had described, its light spilling down onto a great nest of jewels.

If the shamir was in the lair, it would be there.

As Orabas approached, however, he was suddenly aware of another presence. Not here, not yet, but over on the far side of the sanctum there was another passage, presumed by the Squire to lead further down and back out to the fjord by another, lower exit. Modo was deep inside the shadow there and coming this way. Orabas could feel the force of his mind like gravity.

He looked down at the jewels. Where was it? He swiped his hand through. It had to be here, but there were so many, and now he could actually hear the great wyrm slumping this way, his breathing labored. Orabas grabbed a handful of jewels and stuffed them in his pocket just as the gargantuan black figure emerged from the tunnel.

He appeared to have come for refuge. One wing was bent, and the right hind leg seemed to hang loose from its inverted knee. He was dragging it. He stopped wearily, white mucus stringing from his mouth, but maybe the most telling sign of his injury was that he did not seem to be aware until this moment that anyone else was here.

He turned up his eye, just one – the other was mangled and nearly closed – but the pupil of the good one narrowed.

... You

Orabas might have run – any other man surely would have – but it did not even enter his mind. Modo was hobbled. What better chance would he ever have? If he could only put his hand on the stone. He swiped again at the pile. He shoved another fistful of jewels into his pockets – not to steal, but in hopes that it might be in there among the rest, and he would have it if he needed.

The dragon saw this, of course, and understood. His reaction was mixed: a note of amusement, but fury, too, at the impertinence. His good eye flared, as the great tail lifted up behind him and then came down, smashing against the floor, and causing the remaining hangings to fall. More bats as well – maybe hundreds – flew down at the shuddering, just in time to catch the blast of fire from Modo's throat. And now they were alight, flitting like cinders in a windstorm, swirling and diving at their shadows, spastic with pain, screeching and scuffing against the walls, clipped by falling stones. Orabas ducked down, but he could see Modo coming at him through the swarm. Another large stalactite fell from the ceiling, and for a moment Orabas thought he might be saved, that the great stone spear might cleave the beast and pin him, and it did hit him square on the back, but splintered off his armor like a dry twig.

And now Modo was upon him, jaws wide, extended by that enormous neck, as powerful as a cedar, as lissome as a snake. Orabas felt the sudden chill of death, but he was not afraid. What struck him most about the moment was its unlikeliness: to have come this far, to have reached the very place he had been meaning to, only to find the thing he had been looking for *not there*. Could it really be that he was about to die? Here? For having *failed* to find the shamir? Because he was more certain than ever that if he could just have put his hand on it, he'd have had a chance.

But much the same as the first time he had come face to face with his own death – and that had been the incident at Denben, sur-rounded by ten Sud – some force rose up in him and rejected it, said simply, *no, I will not die, not if my will should count for anything in life*, though this time there was more than just his will at play. There was the intimation of his unborn son, and the determination that he, his son, whoever he should turn out to be, should not have to bear the burden of his father's failure, or the need to come and finish his father's business. That was the last of Orabas' humane thoughts, on the heel of which came that familiar flood of adrenal fury, the very same as had come to his rescue once before.

He reached down and pulled the hunting knife from the holster on his leg, raised it high and charged. Again that same admixture of bemusement ringed by rage flashed in the dragon's good eye. He braced himself for the attack, turning slightly so as not to leave himself exposed. The two wings flared as he inhaled, then came a blast of flame.

Orabas dove straight in, treating the fire as his veil. He pivoted to the right, burst through and leapt up onto the dragon's back, using its haunch as a step. Modo craned but couldn't reach around entirely, leaving Orabas free to strike.

Of course, the plates were impervious. Orabas hadn't expected doing any damage there, but he did manage to clamber up and drive his blade down into the base of the injured wing, right where it met the trunk. He thrashed at it, plunging the knife deeper and deeper until he felt the tendon snap.

As if by reflex, there came a stunning blow from the right, knocking Orabas straight off of Modo's back. The good wing had whisked him off somehow and in the same motion the giant, barbed tail came whipping at him, hitting him square and sending him a good thirty feet through the air, landing him in the deep slow stream that ran around the edge of the chamber.

A fortunate thing. It softened the landing, and it braced him, awakened him from the blow. He was up again quickly, and in the dragon's blind spot. Another chunk of ceiling fell down to the left. A giant splash went up. Modo turned his head and Orabas charged again, this time leaping straight at the neck, driving the blade into the flesh like a piton.

The wound was a scratch, but again the dragon took note of his opponent's pluck. Most animals knew enough to concede once superiority was established, but this one kept slashing, hacking at the underside of his neck as if he might actually kill him. And indeed the eerie determination of this man, in combination with the fact that the dragon's entire purview of the battle was – because of the other, much more appealing call upon his attention – as through a kind of dirty lens, made the moment slightly more urgent than it might otherwise have been.

The man was high up now, in a position that Modo could not easily reach with his fore claws. He swiped at his own throat, inadvertently delivering the deepest wound yet, but missing the man, who scrambled to his snout, and was hacking at the horns and tendrils there, as if, like Sampson's hair, they possessed the dragon's power. He was too close to snort away, too close even to see, except for the flash of his diving, dashing, slashing blade. The great wyrm had to lower his head to take another swipe, but again only clipped himself; the man had swung down again by one of the tendrils and was clamped upon his throat.

With no other choice, Modo lifted his neck up high and, as though it were a fifth limb, slammed the man down against the stone ground of the cave. The force would have crushed most other creatures, and it did shake Orabas loose. He lay on the floor, dazed, and without his weapon now. The hunting knife was still lodged in Modo's neck, though the dragon didn't seem to notice. His purpose was to finish the man before he roused again. He lowered his great head to where their eyes were level, drew in a lungful of air, and opened his jaws. Orabas looked into the black maw and thought of Maren. He thought of Anna, and of his son again. He wanted them in mind.

But no flame came.

Instead, the dragon gagged, jerking violently as a smoldering ooze gurgled from the side of his neck. One of the stab wounds must have punctured the canal of his breath weapon. He staggered in pain, but remained clear in his intention. He reared up, raising his right claw, and once again the face of death appeared before Orabas, but once again he marveled: how could he have come so close and failed? Was this not the very position he had always dreamed of? Modo's heart was right there in front of him, thumping away. He could practically see it glowing. If he had only had a spear, a knife, his fist and the shamir, but where was it? Where else could it possibly be...?

(In front of him. Inside the beast; hanging from Margrét's neck; pressed between them and their two pounding hearts, like a flame inside a drum they both were beating. She could not help herself. She tried holding it tighter inside, but the deeper she drew him in, the more he seemed to grow, and the light between them. It was as though the very act of holding only caused the radiance to bloom; but more than bloom, it exploded like a star. It was too large for her to keep. Like the earth, she tremored. She convulsed, but again her grip only quickened its expanse until she could not hold herself any longer; her boundary dissolved into paroxysm, and she released him out onto the blackest edge of heaven…)

Orabas was quite sure now: the Great Wyrm's heart was glowing, or something in there was. A golden orange light was growing and flaring inside him, gleaming through the softer, paler flesh of his underside. Like a flame within smoked glass it flared again, and his eye rolled. He reared higher now, and shuddered as the light inside him grew; it grew so intense it seemed to pierce the flesh, to slice him open from within. Like an angel, his wings spread out. His head stayed high, tilted upward at the ceiling, the great jaws parted slightly, and the room was filled with a pure and blinding white, so bright that Orabas had to cover his eyes. He could only hear the slump and thud of the beast's collapse, and then the sound of something spilling out. What it was he could not see until the light withdrew, hue by hue, back down upon a frail body lying there beside the open gut. Was it a deer? A fawn? The innards spilt away and now Orabas saw it was a woman covered in the bile and blood. And she was whole, and moving. She was breathing.

He pulled her clear of the slithery muck. He saw the necklace and the gem, but he did not take it from her. He lifted her at once and carried her through the rubble to the water.

The stream was running faster now. He lowered her down, and there in the presence of all the swiftlets who'd fluttered in to watch, and the spiders and the snakes and surviving bats, he let the water wash over her body and revive her. Her head turned. She moved her arms and legs. Finally her eyes opened. New and knowing, they took in the space around her. They took in the man attending to her, and she stood under her own strength. She finished bathing herself. She washed all the blood from her hair, then she climbed up to the dry stone again. Orabas followed. She did not glance at the carcass, or search among the entrails. She led him and all the other creatures out through one of the back passages, up a narrow tunnel to the high plateau.

The peregrine was waiting for them. She landed beside Margrét as if to tell her, look now. The snow is melting. Halfway down the plain the ground is showing through, and further down there's grass and wildflower. The trees are in leaf. Spring is here. The way back will be clear.

Glossary of Names, Terms, and Places

Andjes, Koos, Sami Trinko, Olly Trinko, Gaino, Yoonas Sloot – frequent traders at Per-Malfi's trading post.

Anna – Orabas's three-year-old daughter.

Antayak – The province of the Uplands in which Five Homes is located.

Antonia Pecca – a member of the New Welanders; Ovechkin's lieutenant and, presumably, lover.

Barbatos – distant ancestor of Olybrius and Orabas, credited with having stolen the shamir from Modo.

The Bend – Orabas's home.

Brazhny, Lieutenant – Officer in charge of the investigation into the poisoning of Goulu.

Cassandra, Nella, Yosi, Bjul, Marta, Lina – sheep and lambs.

Debrovo – Country Home of Olybrius' and Orabas's paternal grandmother, Iso-aitti.

Five Homes – a small village in Antayak; winter home of Margrét, Inger and Torvald.

Goulu, Monsieur – Event Coordinator on the Minarik.

Great Wyrm – the classification of the largest, oldest, and most powerful dragons; usually at least 1500 years old.

Henryk –King of the Sylka, the new imperial power in Ileya.

Ileya – the setting of the story, a northerly vassal state in the empire of the Sylka.

Inger – Margrét's nursemaid.

Irena – Margrét's mother, an aspirant to the convent of the sister of Hamar, mistress to Theodosius.

Iso-aitti – Olybrius's and Orabas's paternal grandmother.

Jurgen – the charcoal burner of Tami. Til's husband.

Koenig, Lieutenant – Zitri's second.

Kostitsin, Admiral – commander of *the Minarik.*

Kreisenig – capitol of Ileya.

Maren – Orabas's wife.

Margrét – shepherdess; illegitimate daughter of the Bishop Theodosius and his mistress, Irina.

The Minarik – King Henryk's ship.

Markus, Captain – Chief of Police in Kreisenig.

Modo – the last of the Great Wyrms (a.k.a. 'Asmodeus').

Naberius – a distant ancestor of Olybrius and Orabas, also credited with having stolen the shamir from Modo.

New Welans – a student group, dedicated to the preservation of the Old Ways and native tongue of Ileya.

Olybrius ('Bizja') Korda – Provost of Ileya; also twin brother of Orabas ('Bazja').

Oni-miiko – neighbor at Five Homes.

Orabas ('Bazja') Korda– Keeper of the shamir; younger twin brother of Olybrius ('Bizja').

Ovechkin, Uri – leader of the New Welan movement, a student movement dedicated to the preservation of the Old Tongue and Traditions of Ileya.

Per-Malfi – Orabas's father-in-law, father of Maren.

'Seidre' (AKA the 'Starets')– a male shaman.

The Shamir – ancient legendary gemstone mentioned in the *Midrashim* and the histories of Solomon, and over which Modo and man (including the ancestral line of Olybrius and Orabas) have been vying for some ten centuries.

The Squire – Naberius's squire, credited with having authored, *Tales of the Questor Naberius.*

'Starets' (AKA the 'Seidre') – a holy man and spiritual counselor.

The Sud – Western neighbor and former sovereign state of Ileya.

The Sylka – Eastern neighbor and newly sovereign state over Ileya.

Tasha – Margrét's ermine.

Til – wife of Jurgen.

Torvald – Inger's brother, Margrét's "uncle."

Theodocius – Highest ranking bishop in the Sylkan empire and father of Margrét.

The Trading Post – Per-Malfi's home and place of business.

The Uplands – Northern Territory of Ileya, located north of the Southern Ridge.

Vassago – steward of Olybrius.

Villiers-Lornyay, Madame de – Margrét's Lady-in-Waiting on *The Minarik.*.

The Völla – a wandering female shaman, seer, and soothsayer.

Welan – a native of Ileya. Also, the name of their language.

Zitri, General – head of the Royal Guard to His Majesty King Henryk.